S0-AYX-706

Elegy
For
Paula

A Novel

M. A. Dennison

M. A. Dennison

Trap Dock Press
Chatham, Massachusetts

TRAP DOCK PRESS
3 Champlain Road
Chatham, Massachusetts 02633

This book is a work of fiction. Names, characters, places and incidents either are products of the author's imagination or are used fictitiously. Any resemblance to actual events or locales or persons, living or dead, is entirely coincidental.

Copyright © 2013 by M. A. Dennison

All rights reserved, including the right of reproduction in whole or in part in any form.

Designed by Shareen Davis
Text set in Adobe Garamond Pro
Cover Photo by Shareen Davis

Manufactured in the United States of America

ISBN 978-0-578-11726-3

For Christian and Karin

ACKNOWLEDGMENTS

Deepest gratitude to Petronelle M. Cook for inspiration,
to wordsmith Rose Connors for meticulous editing,
and to cherished friends near and far for essential support.

Although it's been years since I found her grave, I still sleep with the lights on. I still dream about Paula, the Scotsman, and their short lives together in England. In the dream, a shovel leans against a moss-covered tombstone, then my name shimmers beneath hers. I'm wakened by the sounds of metal scraping dirt. An owl screeches from the thicket outside my window and I whisper the 23rd Psalm.

Drenched in sweat and half-awake, I escape the tangled sheets and steel myself against the memory of his hands around my neck. Feeling like a stranger in my own house, I cross the living room where he once courted my friends, then pad into the kitchen for a cup of cocoa. Checking the alarm system's panel mounted on the wall near his empty wicker chair, I hear an echo. "Fancy a cuppa, darling?"

The drink scalds my mouth. It's too sweet. Sweet as he seemed before I suspected he'd killed her. I add more milk and swallow my rage, the same rage that drove me to prove he had.

Perhaps in time, the nightmares will fade. But now, questions persist. Why did he publicly mourn her after he came to the States? Why did he press on once he learned my closest friend had lived in the very same English village he left behind? The six degrees of separation between us should have sent him running for cover.

And yet, he considered himself a religious man. He struck deals with God and curried favors from patron saints. Even now, I can't imagine what deal he cut that morning when I returned to church after a long absence. Had it been raining, I would have ignored the pealing bells, stayed home and spent the day reading by the fire. Or I might have bundled up in foul weather gear and taken my yellow lab, Rumpus, for a beach walk. Either way, I probably never would have met him.

And I never would have heard her name.

Chapter 1

It was a rare morning of hot sun, promising a day seldom seen before the onset of tourist season in mid-June. And I lay in bed, nursing a guilty conscience for boycotting our minister's politically-charged sermons.

Chatham's town clock struck eight times as I weighed the pros and cons of living in a resort town, closed up tighter than a clamshell for six months of the year. I stared at the silver-framed faces of my late husband, Sam, and our two children, both long gone from Cape Cod. My son, James, settled in Annapolis, Maryland near his wife's family. And my daughter, Sally, followed her love of the great outdoors to Boulder, Colorado after her divorce, where she spends her free time hiking and skiing with her ten-year-old daughter.

The responsibility of maintaining our old carriage house with its leaky roof and peeling clapboards had challenged me for years. Handymen had become hard to find since Chatham's town fathers, keeping a relaxed watch over our sleepy fishing village, found themselves blindsided by commercial schemes. Overnight, it seemed, mega-mansions and chain stores appeared on lots once deemed too fragile to develop. Land values spiked, taxes tripled and locals who once worked for reasonable rates had little choice: overcharge to make ends meet or throw in the towel and abandon the Cape.

Wary of outliving Sam's dwindling trust fund, I felt disillusioned, frightened by the prospects of running out of money and aging alone. It would have been sensible to sell my house and move closer to one of my children. But I stayed on, patching and painting after each nor'easter. Sensible or not, I knew I'd never leave. My roots were too deep.

Like most wash-ashores, my heart started beating to the rhythms of the tides the moment Sam and I arrived. Despite bleak winters and vexing changes over twenty years, I still believed Chatham was my safe harbor, though a lonely one at times. I'd flirted with the idea of finding another husband, or at least a compatible gent with a tool box, and wondered if I dyed my hair to snag one or to stave off the ravages of time. Probably a little of both, I thought, daring myself to finish the "winsome grandmother" personal ad I'd started weeks before.

The frenzied clanging from the Methodist Church belfry, more like a man overboard alarm than a call to worship, pulled me back to the present. Assuming salty air had corroded the bells' timer, I dismissed the notion of danger and turned my thoughts to Memorial Day and the rapidly approaching tourist season. The boat and croquet set needed sanding and a coat of paint. It was time to renew my clamming license, fertilize the garden, and bury my grudge against our well-meaning minister.

Pastor Gil relied on me to host a few cadets from West Point's glee club each summer. The unflappable "Mrs. T" and her team expected me to show up with brownies and bus tables at our weekly chowder suppers. But most of all, I missed my old friends. I pictured the tender faces of our faithful congregation and longed to worship with them again. Mind made up, I grabbed a towel and raced through the kitchen door to take the season's first outdoor shower, a Cape tradition that baffles most visitors until they try it.

Sheltered behind a hedge of boxwoods in a corner of the brick patio, I stood beneath the hot water humming along with the chimes from the Congregational Church's carillon. Startled to hear *I Would Be True*, a hymn I'd selected for Sam's funeral, I searched the clouds for his face and marveled yet again that a New England blue blood had married a simple country girl half his age all those years ago. Painfully shy and socially insecure, I'd needed valium and a stiff drink to face his country club friends. To this day, I cringe when I think he probably heard me rehearsing tipsy *hellos* in front of the bathroom mirror.

Slipping on a terrycloth bathrobe, I fended off a sudden reluctance to leave the bags of fertilizer and Sunday papers. Overhead, a chevron of honking Canada geese flew toward Gull Pond as I made my way back to the kitchen.

Upstairs, I dug through the cedar closet to find a beige suit that had seen better days and pinned a gold starfish over a stain on its lapel. I slashed a streak of coral across my lips and plopped a wide-brimmed straw hat on my head to hide hair that looked like trampled marsh grass after a frost. From the full-length mirror, a slim, much younger woman looked back. I laughed at the transformation, remembered the many times I'd created illusions to impress Sam's crowd and thanked God for giving me the sense to stop drinking after he died.

Then I flew out the door, expecting to encounter a few raised eyebrows. I'd missed too many Sundays to count.

Chapter 2

Robed choir members milled about in the vestibule, including the invincible Mrs. T. Her eyes said, *I knew you'd be back.*

"Missed you all so much," I told them, grateful for their warm embraces, then stepped into the candlelit sanctuary.

Instantly soothed by the organ's prelude, by the familiar scents of flowers, musty hymnals and burnt wax, I surveyed the sea of white heads. A tanned, dark-haired man sat alone in the front pew, a spot normally reserved for visiting clergy. He exuded an undeniable air of authority, but he didn't look like any Methodist minister I'd ever seen. Flickers of apprehension ran up and down my spine.

His broad shoulders, rigid posture and fixed gaze upon the altar set him apart from the people pecking cheeks and shaking hands behind him. I wondered if he was a guest soloist, or maybe a missionary reviewing his appeal for foreign relief.

The usher led me down the aisle to a seat several rows behind our silver-haired resident saint, Mrs. Macrae. I craned to see more of the visitor, then paged through the bulletin hoping to find his name. Nothing. Bowing my head, I prayed for Sam and my children, recited the Serenity Prayer and resumed my watch.

At some point between the Scripture lesson and the choir's anthem, when I was certain all latecomers had been seated, I discreetly dropped my glasses. Reaching down for them, I slid to the end of the pew, improving my view of the mystery man facing the pulpit. Handsome, I thought, wondering where he'd gotten such an even tan. A prominent nose, deep-set eyes, and a high forehead gave him that European look I'd always found irresistible.

As we listened to Pastor Gil promise salvation to those who repent, the stranger's beatific expression mirrored those of the Apostles trapped in the stained glass windows. Humbled to witness his rapture, I vowed to open my heart and pay more attention to my spiritual life. Later, after scribbling out a check for the offering, I watched him toss a tightly folded bill into the collection plate and wondered if he was a modest man of wealth or one with a miserly heart.

The congregation rose as the organ sounded the beginning notes of *Heavenly Father, Bless Me Now*. Last to stand, the guest opened the hymnal, rested it easily in the palm of his huge right hand, but didn't sing. He stared into space, then pressed a folded white handkerchief to his eyes. Moved to see him weep, I felt a powerful desire to meet him, to know why he suffered.

After the benediction, he could have joined the congregation's prayer circle to sing *God Be With You 'Til We Meet Again*. Instead, he skirted around the circle to Mrs. Macrae's side and carefully positioned her walker. His gentle courtliness was reminiscent of my late husband's natural ease. I understood her pleased expression as he shepherded her down the aisle, his head lowered in deference, or perhaps controlled impatience, until they reached my pew. When our eyes met, his face turned the color of cranberries.

He reminded me of Tom Conti, who starred in *Shirley Valentine*. I wondered if he was a summer actor with Monomoy Theatre.

Just then, Mrs. Macrae's granddaughter sailed in toting a cranky toddler, muttering a stream of apologies as she collected her grandmother.

I felt him approach, grateful for the wide-brimmed straw hat that hid my flushed face.

"Hello, Miss," he said, bending over to retrieve the child's lost painting. "Perhaps you'd best tuck the wee boy's picture into your basket for safekeeping. Do they still make them on Nantucket Island?"

Unable to speak, I nodded.

"I worked for an heiress who had a basket like yours but I haven't seen one since I left Philadelphia."

I was bewitched by his sweet, gentle lilt. "You're Scottish," I said quietly. "That's how you know Mrs. Macrae."

"Aye, but she's from Aberdeen and I'm from Edinburgh."

I told him my grandfather was born in a town north of Edinburgh. "He was a miner from Penicuik."

"Haven't heard that name in donkey years," he mused, calculating the distance from Penicuik to his family's hotel in Musselburgh.

"I've loved your country ever since I was a child and first saw Grandfather in his kilt. My friend, Morgan, married a

Scotsman, a BBC golf commentator. After he retired, they sold their flat in Sunninghill, a small town near Ascot, and moved back to the west coast of Scotland, a mile from the Royal Troon Golf Club."

He seemed lost in his own thoughts, or worse, bored by my chatter. Hoping he wouldn't rush off to the basement to join the congregation for cake and coffee, I asked, "What brought you to our little village?"

"It's a long, sad story," he answered, then noted the time on his gold wristwatch just as the organist's postlude reached an ear-splitting crescendo. I waved him into my pew. "The short version is," he said, heaving a weary sigh, "I immigrated to your grand country several years ago after I lost my wife, Paula, in a skiing accident."

"You're widowed?" I whispered, breathing in his musky lime aftershave. I longed to pat his arm, but instead absently fingered my gold wedding band, a reminder that I had once belonged. On his left hand, he wore a surprisingly feminine platinum band studded with pave diamonds that I assumed matched Paula's.

Nodding the way people do to express sympathy, I offered condolences and told him I'd also been widowed. "Years ago, but it still hurts."

"Paula's death crushed the verra life out of me," he said hoarsely. He lowered his eyes against the memory, or perhaps against the noon sun streaming through the side window. "Everyone told me time would dull the nightmares, but it wasn't until I heard your vicar's stirring sermons that I started to believe she's at peace. And that I might someday be forgiven for sending her off to ski alone."

He frowned, knitting his dark bushy eyebrows. "Incidentally, we lived in the same English village as your friends."

I gasped. "Did you know Ian and Morgan Mackenzie?"

"I've heard of Ian." He recalled Sunninghill's pub gossip and the pints he'd raised after rounds at the nearby Wentworth Golf Club. "Well-thought-of chap it seemed," he said, perking up. "Say, you could ask him if he covered Wentworth's Pro-Am Tournament in '89. He might remember me, the hacker from his village who…"

"Hacker indeed." I laughed. "Did you win?"

"No, but a lucky putt on the fifth tied me with Seve Ballesteros for the Captain's Cup."

"Amazing. But what's even more amazing is that you and the Mackenzies lived in the same place at the same time."

"Quite a coincidence," he agreed, and then listened patiently as I listed the places Morgan had lived since she'd married Ian.

"They were in Sunninghill in 1989, the year I went back to college. By the time I had a chance to visit, they'd moved up to Troon. But could our paths have crossed in 1979 when Morgan and I visited Ian's cousin in Edinburgh? We stayed at his lovely Georgian house on Brighton Place for a weekend. Do you know the Village Café near the Royal Mile?"

He smiled mysteriously. "When you were at Brighton Place, I lived a kilometer away on the Firth of Forth with my first wife and children. The Village Café is 'round the corner from the pub I once owned."

"I'm stunned."

He glanced up at the Good Samaritan's sunlit figure in the stained glass window and asked, "Do you believe in destiny?"

"Since spending a semester in Greece, I do. What do you think?"

"Fate's been both kind and cruel," he said, then labored through a grim account of his first wife trading him in for a professional soccer player, losing his pub in the divorce and leasing his ancestral home to Edinburgh University before moving south to Sunninghill. "Where my luck changed," he said, "when I bought the Highclere Hotel, a handsome house next door, and met Paula."

Warmed by his trusting face, I remembered the old gypsy woman on Crete who told me I had a gift for holy listening. "Where did you meet?"

"In the London Clinic's car park, where she was fussing over a puncture. I changed the tire and invited her to tea. What she saw in a mug like me, I'll never know; she was a cancer surgeon who looked like Grace Kelly, but with flashing green eyes."

I wished I'd taken more time with my appearance that morning. "So your good deed was rewarded."

"Aye. It was love at first sight and the bonny doctor mended my broken heart." He beamed when he told me she was one of the youngest to receive the Order of the British Empire, and then went on to describe her research at Oxford, her renowned lectures at medical conferences, the philanthropic committees she chaired, and her commitment to orphans in third-world countries.

His account sounded more epical than credible, and I assumed she'd grown more saintly with each passing year since her death. "You mentioned a skiing accident."

He grimaced. "Talk about fate. We should've been in Tenerife, but at the last minute Paula insisted on joining the clinic's ski trip to Switzerland."

"Oh no," was all I could manage.

"Aye. I gave in, changed the tickets. She hit black ice and crashed into a tree on the morning of our third wedding anniversary, while I slept. The ski patrol roused me to tell me of her death."

He shuddered. "I nearly lost my mind. Leased our house to Johnson & Johnson Corporation and sold the Highclere. Took a position in Jordan, managing Queen Noor's summer palace."

I'd never heard a sadder story.

"Three years later, the prime minister ordered all foreign staff evacuated. Sent royal helicopters down to Aqaba just hours before the first bombs dropped on Baghdad and the Gulf War began. And that was me, finished. A lost soul again."

"I'm so very sorry."

His eyes watered and he nodded at the altar's gold cross as a single tear escaped. "Prayer helps a little, but Paula still haunts my dreams."

"A sensitive person never gets over grief. But don't be afraid of your wife's *hauntings*. Dreams are where our souls connect. They're gifts. My husband's spirit has never left me, either, and it's been years since he died of cancer." As naturally as I would brush a tear from a small child's cheek, I drew my fingers across his.

"Tell me about your children," I said gently, hoping to ease his sadness.

"Two from my first wife, both university-educated," he said proudly. "Drew has his own brokerage firm in Edinburgh, is married and financially set. Andrina struggled with London's high cost of living while climbing the corporate ladder, so when the Highclere sold I bought her a small house in Kensington. She now shares it with her accountant husband, Tom. They had a baby girl over a year ago, but I've yet to see the wee Fiona."

"It must be frustrating to live so far from them."

"Unfortunately, their mother persuaded them to estrange themselves from me when I married Paula. They manage to send a Christmas card each year," he added. "Maybe one day, things will be different."

My heart ached for this widower without a family or a country. He seemed like a lost boy in grown-up clothes. "Everything will sort itself out," I told him, though I had doubts about Andrina, who'd been given a house yet kept him from his granddaughter. "Write to them. Tell them your true feelings. Be real, like the Velveteen Rabbit."

He cocked his head, puzzled.

"You must know the story. About wearing yourself out for love."

With an amused grin, he agreed to look for it in the library.

"Every family has problems," I assured him. "For years, my children bristled at the thought of anyone taking their father's place. But since my son's married, he's more interested in his own life than mine. And my daughter is busy raising a precocious ten-year-old on her own. She gets a break once a year when my granddaughter spends her spring vacation with me in a rented cottage on Sanibel, an island off the west coast of Florida."

He covered my hand with his and I was struck by the magnetic energy that surrounded him, and by the reverent way he studied me.

The side door opened and our sexton hurried into the sanctuary. "Time to lock up, folks." Joe chuckled, jangling a ring of keys as he walked down the aisle toward us. "One of my favorite ladies. Where've you been off to this time, Mrs. Wells?"

"Sanibel for a month," I said. "Otherwise, home, waiting for spring like everyone else." To ward off further questions about my long absence, I listed the joys of hibernating by the fireplace with my lab, Rumpus, poring through stacks of seed catalogs and sorting old slides from Turkey and Greece.

"Mr. Macdade's been over that way. He could tell you about meeting Saddam Hussein at Queen Noor's palace. Be a nice conversation to have over brunch at the Wayside Inn," Joe suggested, his eyes merry.

Suspecting Joe's bright idea was instigated by his wife, the all-knowing Mrs. T, I fiddled with my basket's clasp and held my breath.

"It is short notice," said Mr. Macdade, "but you're the kindest woman I've ever met. Will you take our friend's advice and accompany me to brunch?"

Smiling, I pointed to the quarter board hanging on the wall: *Be Not Inhospitable to Strangers, Lest They Be Angels in Disguise.*

"Besides," I added, turning to Joe, "I'm dying to learn how Queen Noor's palace manager landed in our little seaside church."

Chapter 3

"Averra grand Sabbath it is, milady," he burred, ushering me through the vestibule's double doors. The quaint phrase sounded like it had been plucked from the pages of Jane Austen.

"Aye, that it is, milord," I lilted and dropped a curtsy.

His silent stare surprised me. I regretted teasing him, but when I rested my hand on his arm he rewarded me with a lopsided grin.

We bounded down the church steps, talking sporadically between fits of nervous laughter until we reached the crosswalk. "If you stand here for the July 4th parade," I said, "you'll see the kiltie marching bands at their best. The judges' grandstand is on the hill."

He doubled over, as if stricken by pain, and began hoisting an invisible load to his chest, droning the wail of skirling bagpipes.

"*Scotland the Brave*," I cried. Although flustered by his public performance, I was relieved to see he had a sense of humor. "You should be on stage," I cracked.

"I was," he said. "A one-hit wonder in 1965, the same year I married and sold my best guitar to buy a pram. You'd call it a baby carriage." He gave me a comical half-bow and took my hand in his as we strolled through the village.

Indifferent to rock-and-roll since high school, I gulped. "My friend Morgan's brother roomed with Peter Thorkleson, one of the Monkees, at prep school," was all I could say.

"Aye, and after the rascal rose to fame he shortened his name to Tork."

Encouraged, I recalled the Halloween weekend Peter visited Morgan's family. "You should've seen the withering look on our minister's face when he caught us in the church cemetery, wearing sheets, waiting to spook the senior choir after rehearsal."

"Not a proper girl like you," he chided, egging me on.

"Gene Pitney sang at our record hops until *A Town Without Pity* made him famous," I added. "How did you get to the top?"

"By the time I was twelve, I'd saved enough money from folding towels at the baths and catching crabs for the fishmonger to buy a guitar and form my own band, *The Athenians*. It was the '60s. Every kid in Porty dreamed of hitting it big."

"Porty?"

"Just outside Edinburgh's city limits. Portobello, a Victorian seaside resort about half the size of Chatham. Now it's poor, run-down, thanks to Maggie Thatcher closing the coal mines. It's easier to say I'm from Edinburgh than to explain where Porty is."

"Why didn't you work at your family's hotel instead of at the baths and the fishmonger's?"

"You're just like Paula, a little stickler for details," he quipped.

"Incurably curious," I admitted.

"It must be my lot in life to be surrounded by intelligent women." He then explained that during Scotland's lean post-war years, his mother sent him back and forth from the Ravelston Hotel to her father's farm, both in Musselburgh, just a few kilometers from Porty.

"Grandfather kept me well-fed and out of mischief. And although he was verra stern, he taught me all I know about vegetables and horses. His market garden and racetrack were famous. They attracted not only the Ravelston's guests, but old King George as well. When I was a lad, he traveled up from London each year on opening day, came 'round the stables before the first heat to take a cuppa with Grandfather."

"What an honor. Are there photographs?"

"All stored back in Porty, along with the king's chair and tin cup."

I made a mental note to brush up on my geography.

"On clear days, when Grandfather sent me out to pick raspberries, I could see Mum pegging the hotel's sheets in the distance."

"My father sent me out to pick gooseberries," I confided, thrilled to meet a man with a country heart.

"Aye, those were the worst," he said. "Think I still have a wee thorn in my wrist." He recalled the hardships his mother faced running the hotel during the war. "When Father was off fighting for Britain, she ran the Ravelston pretty much alone. Our pastry chef, Horst, helped when he could, but..."

"Wasn't it unusual for a German to live in Scotland at that time?"

"Doddering old soul was terrified of spending his last days in an internment camp. Mum hid him in the garden shed until the night he died in his sleep when the paraffin heater caught fire."

"Poor Horst. Your mother must have been devastated."

"Aye. She buried him in a field of yellow broom overlooking the sea. Kept him in her prayers 'til the day she died."

"What a soft-hearted lady."

"Father returned home a hero, but was never the same after seeing his men blown up on the beaches. Went glaiket," he said, tapping his temple. "The day I turned fifteen, he yanked me out of school. Waited in the corridor under the dismissal bell and thrust a waiter's jacket at me, blethering on about book learning being a waste of time."

My father's rampages had humiliated me, too. "But surely your father was proud of you," I said. "He groomed you to take over the Ravelston."

"Groomed me for a life of servitude, he did. The old coot nearly bankrupted the place. Wish he'd listened to my teachers, who told him to send me to university."

"The sins of our fathers are never forgotten," I murmured. "Mine was a miser. Pocketed every cent of my babysitting money from the time I was eleven and then refused to pay for college."

He pressed my shoulder sympathetically. "Must have been rough for you, being a girl and all. I'm surprised you didn't run when you heard my accent."

"Run? It was my grandfather who was born in Scotland, a gentle giant who sang Gaelic folksongs and took Morgan and me to see *Brigadoon*. She decided then and there she'd marry a Scotsman and live in Scotland. Years later, she did."

"Ah, *Brigadoon* caught the fancy of many a young lassie."

I changed the subject quickly. My imagination was spinning. "Tell me more about your hit song," I said.

"Shortly after my band broke up, I left the hotel, hitched a ride to London and landed a gofer job with one of the recording studios. A year later, they signed me on as a session guitarist. When the lead singer of *Unit 4 Plus 2* fell ill while recording *Concrete and Clay*, they gave me a shot. The rest is history."

He stopped in front of the tourist information booth to tie a frayed lace on his pointy-toed alligator shoe. Imagining him in topsiders and a preppie polo shirt like the local volunteer in the doorway, I resisted the urge to reach down and run my fingers through his luxurious dark hair.

"Maybe if you hummed a few bars, I'd recognize your song," I suggested.

He rose with an agility that belied his fifty-odd years. "You haven't seen the movie *Rushmore*?"

I shook my head.

"*Concrete and Clay* is on its soundtrack," he said. He seemed more charmed than offended that I hadn't heard of him.

"My parents always listened to classical," I explained. "And my husband, Sam, favored Dixieland. If I hadn't rushed into marriage and motherhood, I might have danced to your hit."

"You were wise to wed so young, spare yourself later regrets."

"It was a May-December marriage. I was barely twenty-one and Sam was over forty. He was my anchor to windward. Wherever I went, I could count on him watching my back."

"Good man," he said, nodding. "Say, I could bring the *Rushmore* CD 'round sometime," he offered, like an eager-to-please schoolboy.

I thanked him and asked if his parents had enjoyed his music.

"Father never thought anyone but Harry Lauder, Porty's own Knight of the Realm, had talent."

"What about your mother?"

"Aye, she was a fan. A mere slip of a woman with a kind heart and dark watchful eyes." He smiled. "Like yours."

My heart flip-flopped.

"When I was a bairn, Mum sent me to the public baths in winter with a shivery-bite, a slice of sugared bread to keep my teeth from chattering. Years later she fed my band – and Rod Stewart, before he was famous – with meat pies from the Ravelston's kitchen. I still see her covered in flour, pressing a ten-bob into my palm for petrol, waving us off with a smile like the noonday sun."

The tenderness in his voice, the image of the much-loved little boy running home through icy streets, teeth clenched on a shivery-bite, enchanted me. My mother's cold indifference had left a hole in my heart. I felt like the little match girl, wishing for a miracle, as I moved closer to him. "Is anyone left?" I whispered.

He shook his head sadly. "Everyone's gone. My father, grandfather, and Uncle Napie, named after Napoleon, all died of brittle lungs after breathing in a lifetime of Auld Reekie's soot. My older brother, Gordon, might as well be dead, but that's another story," he muttered, then went on to describe his mother's untimely death from stomach cancer. "She held on just long enough to see the photo of me accepting my gold record at the Royal Café."

"London's Café Royal? The one with gilded mirrors and red velvet swags, on Regent Street?"

He nodded. "The verra same."

"I have a picture of my mother's grandfather, Nazar Hadjii, in that café, wearing a fez and smoking a hookah. He was an Armenian rug merchant from Istanbul who escaped the Turks' massacre and set up shop in London. Do you ever wonder why some people survive the worst atrocities and others die so young?"

"Who knows? Losing parents, grandparents and uncles – it's all devastating. But losing a young wife was a fate worse than death. If it hadn't been for Pastor Gil's stirring sermons this year, I'd have given up completely."

"When I saw you alone in the front pew, I thought you might be a guest soloist or a missionary. Isn't it lonely up there? Do you have hearing problems?"

He chuckled. "No, I've keen ears. Sitting there is like receiving a pure injection of grace from God. If you pray long enough, all is revealed. And if you're lucky…But what is your name, dear lady?"

"Anna. My name is Anna Wells."

"Anna," he repeated, his voice as sensuous as a lover's caress. "Your humble servant, Andrew Macdade." He pressed his lips to the back of my hand.

I shivered. "Tell me about the English village you left behind."

"Sunninghill is verra picturesque. Cobblestone lanes, winding bridle paths and posh boutiques. About 30 minutes from London by train. Small like Chatham, but centuries older and steeped in tradition. Windsor Castle, Ascot Race Track and the Wentworth Golf Club form a big triangle. Those of us who lived and worked within the triangle were considered artisans, admitted to Ascot's Royal Enclosure and to the exclusive Wentworth by royal proclamation. I had entrée to it all."

"Like living in a glossy magazine. You must have met some impressive characters."

He shrugged, reminding me that everyone the world over has to shop and eat. "We all rubbed shoulders, at the chemist, florist, greengrocer and ironmonger. You'd call that a hardware store."

He then recalled queuing up behind Fergie at the butcher shop. "Full of high jinks and nice as they come. Nodded me forward once, she did, while talking to Linda McCartney, who lived just off London Road along with Eric Clapton, Elton John, and other '60s rockers."

"Did you and Paula get to know any of them?"

"Just a word or two in passing. Except during Ascot's race week, when we'd swap stories and tips over pints in the local pubs," he said, eyeing his wristwatch.

A heavy gold Rolex, outdated cracked leather shoes and frayed laces. Eccentric, I thought.

"Did you ever meet Princess Diana?"

"Saw her only once, at the polo grounds. All sunshine and silver moonbeams, poor wee lass. Though I met the Queen Mum's chef at the track regularly. I could tell you the secret of her longevity, if you're interested."

Of course I was interested.

"Brown bread, brown rice and poached white fish," he announced. "What's wrong?"

I giggled. "You sound like Sean Connery purring fairy tales. Are you sure all of this is true?"

"All true, I assure you." He grinned. "Y'see, m'dear, as owner of the Highclere, I was in the right place at the right time. Everyone – jockeys, golf pros and Ascot's aristocracy – needed lodging. They enjoyed the comforts of a small hotel, not to mention the generous measures of whiskey I poured. And thanks to Paula's affiliation with the local Heatherwood Hospital, it referred its long-term patients' families to me."

"She must have treated some well-known people."

"Aye, she did. I well remember the night Eric Clapton's mother rang, asking her to see an ailing auntie down from Perthshire. Paula never charged for that visit and she and Eric's mother became friends. They often rode the train together into London. Mrs. Clapton still visits my wife's grave regularly."

"She does?"

"Aye. Her grandson, Connor, is buried in the plot next to Paula's," he explained. "Eric's mum places flowers on both graves each week. Once a year, I post a check to cover the expense."

"How incredibly moving." I slipped my arm through his as he led me through the door of the Wayside Inn.

Chapter 4

The plump, salty-tongued hostess, who'd been crowned Miss Eelgrass years before, seated us in the near-empty Monomoy Room, its walls covered with hand-painted murals of Chatham Village. Andrew Macdade pointed at my Nantucket Lightship basket and confided, "I would've been too shy to speak to you if I hadn't recognized your basket at the kirk."

"My resourceful grandparents found it in a hospital thrift shop," I said, stroking the ivory sand dollar on its lid. "They gave it to me on my sixteenth birthday to remind me of the summers we spent together on Nantucket Island." I recalled the innocence of those summers, pedaling along the path to 'Sconset for saltwater taffy and Nancy Drew mysteries, flying home before dark to play Scrabble by the potbellied stove on damp, foggy nights. "Do you know the poem *John Anderson, My Jo*?" I asked. "It was a favorite of my grandmother's. She made me memorize it."

"You know Robbie Burns? What a braw and bonny lass you are." He rolled his r's, seeming amused by his own exaggerated brogue.

"Have you been to Nantucket?" I asked, thinking he'd make a charming character actor.

"Aye, briefly. I'd have taken a position at the Jared Coffin House last year if I didn't have obligations here."

I thanked God for small favors as he groused about caretaking the Chatham estate of Nathan Damato, a dot-com CEO married to a beautiful, but demanding, woman. "Hope she appreciates you," I said, and dismissed her as a nuisance.

Our waitress appeared and I ordered a seltzer with a lime twist. Andrew looked at me quizzically, then ordered a large bottle of San Pellegrino. "After Paula died," he said, clearing his throat, "I had some bad times with the drink. I took what we Scots call 'The Pledge' six years ago in Philadelphia. It's a rare gift these days to find a woman who doesn't drink."

"And it's a rare man who isn't muddled by the end of happy hour." My heart thumped at yet another connection between us and I confessed to drinking myself to sleep after Sam's death. "Took my own pledge years ago with the help of AA," I said.

He blinked back a tear and reached across the table for my hands. "We're so alike, Anna. So verra much alike."

I squeezed his strong, calloused hands and suspected it was no accident that Andrew Macdade and I had met. But rather than meet my gaze, he closed his eyes and lowered his head. To break the awkward silence, I reminded him he'd promised to tell me how Queen Noor's palace manager had landed in Chatham.

"More questions, eh?" He removed his hands from mine, fingered the knot of his tartan necktie and flatly explained that the Highclere Hotel was situated a few kilometers from King Hussein's English residence. "Buckhurst, as it's called, was managed by an American who knew Paula from a local fitness club. Walter enjoyed the racing at Ascot as much as we did, so we all became friends." He recalled the morning a frantic Walter rang, asking for help catering an impromptu picnic for Crown Prince Abdullah and his school chums.

"Later, after Paula died, Walter arranged an interview for me with the royal ministers in Amman. They liked me well enough to send me to the summer palace, where I passed muster with the king and queen. Sold the Highclere and stayed on at Aqaba for three years until, as I mentioned at the kirk, all foreign staff was evacuated just before the Gulf War broke out."

The look on his face made me apologize for dredging up painful memories.

"I've no secrets," he said, "but it's verra hard to speak of the past."

He paused, took a long swallow of Pellegrino and continued. "Jordan's royal references were a passport to your country's elite domestic agencies. I was placed in Michigan with *Mighty Al* Taubman, the head of Sotheby's, for a long year. Having proved myself, I was sent to Philadelphia to be the live-in manager of the Bayley estate. He's a semi-retired attorney who plays bridge with Ambassador Annenberg and she's the last heiress to a pharmaceutical fortune. Claudette Colbert and Marylou Whitney are two of her cherished friends." He smiled tenderly. "I well remember her delight when Oscar de la Renta arrived with his newest collection of evening attire and presented her with a basket just like yours."

I rolled my eyes. "Next you'll tell me that Imelda Marcos envied her shoe collection."

"Mrs. Bayley is one of the last grand ladies in America," he said quietly. "I was privileged to be in her service."

"Sorry to offend you, but I come from a long line of Yankee string savers. Afraid of running out of money, we're even more afraid of exhibiting excess, lest we appear vulgar. My husband provided generously for his family and community, but had his collars turned and his pockets replaced. So there it is."

He lit up like a Fourth of July sparkler. "So that's it. I never could fathom why Mr. Bayley demanded receipts for every household purchase or why he floated envelopes in his bathroom sink." He guffawed. "The old boy was recycling un-canceled stamps."

He nodded toward the buffet. "Shall we?"

Suddenly starved, I leaned into his warmth as we crossed the room. After I filled my plate with bacon, sausage and poached eggs, Andrew plopped a pecan sticky bun on top and winked. "Mum's favorite sweetie."

Seated again, I poked the egg yolks, creating the perfect bite. "Tell me more about the Bayleys," I said. "Why did you leave them?"

Tears glistened in his eyes as he explained that Mrs. Bayley had been crippled when her chauffeur, Radford Beasly, had a seizure and crashed into a tree. The Bayleys decided to retire to their Barbados villa for seven months of the year. "Scotland is a cold country and I can't take the tropical heat for long. Reluctantly, I saw them off in the care of a private nurse more than two years ago, just before Thanksgiving. I should've gone home then but I couldn't face life in Britain without Paula."

His face sagged as he set his knife and fork on his plate. "And then I made a terrible mistake, Anna," he whispered. "I pray to the good Lord that you'll stay and hear me out."

"Sounds serious." I laughed. "Did you join a circus, marry the fat lady?"

"No to the circus," he said. "Unfortunately, yes to the fat lady."

I couldn't speak.

"A yearning for family, a connection," he stammered. "I was alienated from my children, felt almost suicidal after the Bayleys left. I'm sorry to say I succumbed to the comforts of a woman."

"You're married?" Even as I spoke, the idea seemed ludicrous. "Are you crazy? How can you court me in public? Where is your wife? What's the poor woman's name?"

He inhaled deeply and exhaled slowly. "Sheila Peters. After we married, her mother sent us off to live in her Chatham house, a derelict place she'd abandoned thirteen years before. We moved up from Philadelphia and I've been working on it ever since. A week after we got here Sheila's sons moved in, two beer-drinking hooligans with Harleys."

He paused before adding, "It gets worse."

I sat in stunned silence, thinking that couldn't be possible.

"A month after the hooligans arrived, a Philadelphia health official called, telling us either we'd remove Sheila's mother from her condo or the authorities would. I drove down, collected her and brought her back to Chatham. It took her time to adjust, but now that the old dear thinks she's cruising on the Queen Mary and I'm her steward, she's settled down. She likes the sound of my voice and Sheila depends on me to read her to sleep. For two years now, I've been cleaning, cooking and waiting on all of them."

Feeling queasier by the minute, I stated the obvious. "That's insane. Why don't you leave?"

"I don't have the heart to abandon Sheila's mother," he said. "The poor woman is dying, so weak I have to lift her onto the commode."

"What does your wife do all day? Why doesn't she look after her mother and run the house?"

"Sheila's nerves are shot. After her mother arrived, she broke out in hives, gained fifty pounds and lost most of her hair. The doctor prescribed exercise, a low-fat diet and anti-depressants, but she lies in bed all day gobbling bags of sweeties from the Candy Manor and writing bodice-ripping rubbish in her diary. When her mother dies, she'll inherit the house along with an ample trust fund and my obligations to her will be over."

He hung his head. "It gets worse again."

And again, impossible.

"A year ago, I read Sheila's diary. She's been, um, fornicating with a young married man for years. He drives up from Philadelphia once a month while I'm at the Damato estate. In a way, I was relieved. Moved into the guest room without even confronting her. When her mother dies, I can leave."

His eyes pled for sympathy.

"Revolting," I hissed, shooting him daggers. "How did you meet such a woman?"

"Sheila was the chemist in the shop where I filled the Bayleys' prescriptions. After they left for Barbados, she invited me for Christmas dinner, made me laugh again. Three months later, I married her. Scottish men have loyal hearts and I was grateful for a home. Now, believe it or not, she doesn't trust me. Throws hissy-fits on Thursday nights when I go to the library, checks the books' due dates when I get home to make sure I was there. I've done everything in my power to help her. Why doesn't she trust me?"

"Maybe because you're courting another woman."

"Anna, I should have been up-front with you. But when I saw your wee face peeking out from under the brim of that big straw hat and heard your girlish laughter, something stirred in me for the first time since Paula died." Choking back a sob, he added, "Can you forgive me for desiring the kindest heart I've ever met?"

"Maybe," I whispered, close to tears, "considering the mess you're in."

The waitress cleared our coffee cups and handed Andrew the check.

As we left the inn, he asked, "May I walk you home before I have to face them again?"

It took every ounce of strength I had to pit common sense against the hopeful tenderness in his voice. "Perhaps another time," I said, patting his shoulder. "It's a small town."

"Your reputation is at stake, of course. But will you think kindly of me from time to time, Anna, while I disentangle myself from the most embarrassing chapter of my life?"

"We'll see, Andrew."

I sprinted off, determined to make myself scarce until his mother-in-law's obituary appeared in the *Cape Cod Times.*

Chapter 5

Visions of Andrew squiring me about Edinburgh's museums and tearooms danced in my head as I retraced our steps through the village. Morgan would be flabbergasted to learn I'd found a prince in a pew. Once past the church, I hopped over a crack in the sidewalk, then took the Knot Street footpath home.

Humming *Will Ye No Come Back Again*, I whirled through the kitchen door, caught Rumpus gnawing on the leg of a wicker chair and shooed him into the backyard. Serves me right for whiling away the afternoon with a married man, I thought. I searched the phone book for an address for Andrew Macdade or Sheila Peters. Not finding either, I called information and felt a flicker of unease when told the number was unlisted. Deadbeats, doctors and celebrities had unlisted numbers. Why gregarious Andrew?

And after running his own hotel and serving royalty, why was he caretaking the Damatos' estate instead of working at Chatham Bars Inn or the Beach and Tennis Club? Odd, but not all that different from other wash-ashores who'd left the mainstream for a simpler life on Cape Cod. I shrugged, told myself to stop borrowing trouble and punched in Morgan's number, but then hung up. Clouds were moving in and Rumpus was long overdue for a run.

A large black-and-white sign on Harding's Beach warned: *Positively No Dogs Allowed After April 15.* Year-rounders ignore the ban until late June, when hordes of birders arrive to guard nesting plovers and badger our beloved animal warden into enforcing it. Rumpus raced up and down the dunes with two beagles while their masters and I counted the days left.

Whistling for Rumpus, I braced against a gust of gritty sand, hooded my foul weather jacket and headed down the windswept path toward Hoyts' Lighthouse. A great blue heron lifted off from distant marsh grasses, soaring over a pack of scrawny coyotes. Out on Nantucket Sound, a lone fisherman bobbed like a cork in his dory. A wooden sloop with tanbark sails slipped silently through the channel toward Stage Harbor.

Memory pulled me back to a September sail to Cuttyhunk Island with Sam, just days after his oncologist told us that hope was the only weapon we had left. On our first night out we tied up next to a similar wooden boat, *Blind Faith*. We huddled on the bow, prayed for a reprieve and wept as the fiery sun set and the silver-gold Hunter moon rose over the stern.

Spellbound, I watched the sloop sweep by the channel's twelfth marker, where I long ago scattered Sam's ashes into the winter water. When Rumpus started barking, I looked up to see our hefty, ginger-bearded minister trudging toward us with his two shaggy dogs. "Gil," I called, waving both hands. "Did you see that sailboat?"

"Anna Wells. Glad you made it back to your pew this morning." He squinted at the empty channel. "What boat?"

"Guess it's gone." I wondered if she'd been a figment of my imagination.

"I was going to call you tonight," he said, petting Rumpus, "remind you about the West Point concert. Are you up to hosting the same cadets?"

"Certainly, they're great kids." I promised to get the piano tuned and stock the pantry with organic junk-food.

"Organic is okay," he said, "but make sure it's loaded with calories." He grinned and patted his paunch, then turned serious. "We've missed you, Anna. What's kept you away?"

I toed circles in the sand and stooped to scoop up a scallop shell. "It's awkward to explain, Gil. Those sermons, Sunday after Sunday, pleading with us to forgive that liar in the Oval Office. They made me mad."

"You weren't the only one who walked out," he said.

The despair in his voice left no doubt that the congregation's backlash had torn him apart. A sensitive man, he routinely tramped through dark icy woods with blankets and thermoses searching for Chatham's well-kept secrets, the homeless. Gil knew every one of them by name and made no bones about shaming the rich into opening their checkbooks to help.

"There was no good answer, Anna."

"There's nothing worse than a liar. You shouldn't have asked us to look the other way."

Gil gazed out across the expanse of sand and sea. "We can't right every wrong. There comes a time when all we can do is forgive."

He hesitated, staring at the Jacob's ladder fading from the sky, and then looked me in the eyes. "It's none of my business, but I saw the Scotsman, uh, discover you this morning."

"Indeed he did." I felt my face grow hot. "It's hard to believe but each time I've gone to see my friends in Britain, Andrew Macdade was living in the same village or nearby. The coincidences that connect us are staggering. What do you know about him, Gil?"

"He's so effusive that it's hard to see what's under the surface. But I sense he's fragile."

"Of course he's fragile. His wife, Paula, died in a skiing accident and he's now trapped in a miserable marriage with an unfaithful woman. Have you met her?"

"Once," he said dryly, "when she came to church with him."

"Well?"

"She's fragile, too. Her mother is dying and we've offered to help but every time we call at the house, her sons turn us away. No one's gotten through the door except Mrs. T."

He stopped abruptly. "I thought Paula died of cancer. Are you sure it was a skiing accident?"

"That's what Andrew told me. He should know."

"Look Anna," Gil said, groping for words. "He is not your intellectual equal."

"He's not formally educated, but he owned a hotel and managed a palace; he isn't stupid. And besides, he's touched my heart."

Gil arched his eyebrows.

"Maybe I'm wrong," I said, looking out at the horizon, "but I think I've found someone special to share all this wonder with."

He peered at me in disbelief. "And is Andrew contemplating divorce after one afternoon with you?"

"He's been biding his time all along. When his mother-in-law dies, Sheila will inherit the house and enough money to live on. Andrew will be free of his moral obligations. And yes, Gil, he's expressed more than a passing interest in me."

"He won't know what hit him. Do yourself a favor, Anna. Before you and Andrew make any more plans to save each other from loneliness, pay a visit to Joe and Mrs. T. They're two of your biggest fans." After a pause, he added, "Between them, they never miss a trick."

Chapter 6

Mrs. T answered after my first knock. "Just in time for supper," she said, pulling me into her warm, aromatic kitchen. She pointed to my jacket, then to a row of hooks behind the door.

"Joe, come in here. Anna and Rumpus are having dinner with us. Get a bowl for the dog."

Joe hurried in from the living room, winking at his unflappable wife. "Not enough food at the Wayside Inn this afternoon, Anna?"

I laughed. "More than enough. But now I need information about you-know-who."

"Joe likes him," Mrs. T said, facing the stove. "Don't you, Joe?"

"Seems solid," Joe replied. "More than I can say for his wife."

Mrs. T, tagged as such after years of turning town trouble right-side-up, pulled a pork roast from the oven and thumped the pan on the counter. "She's cold, Anna. Isn't she cold, Joe?"

He nodded. "Mean, too, just like her mother. I remember the day Edwina threw her husband's fishing gear out the window, boarded up the house and packed him off to Philadelphia. Don't know how Andrew got tangled up with that crew. The house is haunted, you know. Isn't that right, Mrs. T?"

"Haunted," she agreed. "None of the locals would go near it after they abandoned it. Edwina's attorney had to hire Hyannis people to service it."

Handing me a bowl of green beans, she pointed to the table and told us to sit. "Choir practice at seven, so eat fast, folks."

Pausing just long enough for Joe to say grace, she recalled asking Andrew to join the choir. "Strange. Said he's not allowed out at night. Then he volunteered to shingle the Habitat for Humanity house but erased his name from the roster a week later. Apparently, Sheila gets nervous if he's away on Saturdays."

"Mrs. T thinks he's a prisoner," Joe added. "Don't you, dear? Tell Anna what he was doing when you popped in with your tasty casserole."

"Wait," I interrupted. "First, tell me where he lives."

Joe slapped his knee. "I knew it the minute I saw your faces this morning," he said through a laugh. "Love at first sight. You're neighbors, almost. Andrew could walk from his garden to your clothesline in less than five minutes if he took the Knot Street footpath."

I gasped. "Not the house with broken asbestos shingles? The overgrown yard with the dahlias? Next to the listing green garage?"

"Yes," they said in unison.

48

"He's been fixing up the old place since they got here a couple of years ago," Joe added.

"And you can be sure he'll be keeping close tabs on you." Mrs. T grinned, gearing up for the rest of her story. "When I barged in, there he was alone in that drab kitchen, mashing vitamins into poor Edwina's bowl of shepherd's pie. Said he'd gone to the health food store for something to boost her immune system."

"Where was Sheila?" I asked.

"He didn't say and I didn't ask. Served me tea in one of his mother's Wedgwood cups. Said he had them shipped from Edinburgh. Touching for a man to be so sentimental, don't you think, Anna?"

"He's tenderhearted," I agreed. "Pays a friend in England to put flowers on his wife's grave every week. Has he ever mentioned Paula?"

"Oh yes," Mrs. T said. "And he told me Sheila resents Gil for suggesting they join a couples' bereavement group; that's why she never came back to church. She's jealous, wouldn't you say, Joe?"

"So jealous Andrew had to call Gil's secretary a week before Easter to cancel the altar lily he'd ordered in Paula's memory."

Mrs. T frowned as the clock struck six. "Sad situation. I followed him into the back parlor, where he had Edwina propped up in a hospital bed. She's gaga now, didn't recognize me, but when she saw Andrew she lit up. He spoon-fed every bite into her. It was a nice visit until he had to lift her onto the commode. That's when I left, with a promise to pray for all of them." She sighed. "He's a kind man."

"Seems to be," I agreed.

"Just between you and me," she said, rising to stack our dinner dishes, "Gil has been trying to draw him out for months."

"I saw Gil on the beach earlier today," I said. "He thinks Andrew is a bit shallow."

Mrs. T smiled. "No one will ever be good enough for you in Gil's eyes. Did anyone tell you about the sermon he preached a few weeks after Sam's funeral? It was about you, your courage and your love that lifted Sam's spirit right up to the angels. There wasn't a dry eye in the church."

"I never knew," I said quietly. "I wish he hadn't. It was a private time, a sacred time. When that orb of light hovered…"

"You've told me this story before, Anna, and each time I'm moved to tears. But if the good Lord has blessed you and Andrew with new beginnings, neither of you should waste more time living in the past."

A few minutes later, as I left with a slice of Mrs. T's famous apple pie, she called, "Don't worry. I'll keep an ear to the ground."

I'd been given the green light. By two pillars of the church.

Chapter 7

Chatham fog had rolled in sometime after dusk, shrouding the empty shops along Route 28 in silvery gray mist. Hunched over the steering wheel, I spotted Sam's favorite steakhouse, twinkling white lights strung over its entrance. I saluted him and crawled past, then squirmed, recalling the mortified look on his face years ago when I'd innocently aired his allegiance to Nixon over dinner with friends.

What would Andrew think if he knew I'd spent the afternoon airing his business? Why hadn't I kept my own counsel? Was I seeking Gil's approval? His disparaging remarks about Andrew seemed grossly unfair. Joe and Mrs. T certainly thought otherwise.

But removed from the warmth of their kitchen and Joe's infectious laughter, I felt confused. Andrew's bleak account of his wife's behavior, backed up by Joe and Mrs. T, made me wary of the hold Sheila had over him. She treated him like an indentured servant. Had the trauma of Paula's death reduced him to a milquetoast who crept about the house and obeyed orders?

Pity I couldn't pose as a census taker, knock on their front door and pump Sheila for information when he was off tending to Mrs. Damato, who had more money than manners according to Andrew. Odd that he'd managed to fall into the clutches of two difficult women. Then again, most year-rounders can tell a few horror stories about nouveau riche wives and their selfish demands.

What besides wishful thinking made me believe Andrew was stable, that he knew his own mind? He'd divorced, been widowed, and married Sheila on the rebound. Had he found me attractive because I nearly pounced on him the instant I heard his accent? I suddenly felt foolish.

How long would Andrew be content with a small-town girl who shunned bright lights? How long would he be satisfied with chamber concerts, library lectures and amateur productions at the Drama Guild? And how could I, an unemployed widow who felt guilty living on a trust fund I'd done nothing to earn, compete with the accomplished Dr. Paula?

Then again, maybe Andrew had had his fill of career-driven women. Could I bear another heartbreaking illness? Live through another loss? Even as I questioned, I knew each answer was *yes*. It would be crazy to refuse happiness. Andrew seemed to have Sam's gentle nature. And he looked healthy. With luck, we'd grow old together.

Did he say he left Sheila's bed and moved to the guest room a year ago? Or two? I wondered if Paula had really looked like an emerald-eyed Grace Kelly, if he sat in the dark mooning over her old films.

Would he settle for tenderness and comfy coupling? Or expect me to spa all day and glow at night in Victoria's skimpy secrets? Flushing with long dormant desire, I swept that scene aside and focused on the realities of feeding him twice a day.

Since Sam died, I'd gotten used to a steady diet of take-out. Soggy cartons of wonton soup won't impress a savvy hotelier for long. And he'll have fits when he sees my odd assortment of bent spoons and nicked knives.

I laughed, pushed my shoulder against the warped kitchen door and walked in, thrilled to see the answering machine's red light blinking.

"Bet it's him, Rumpus," I whispered, holding my breath as I pressed *play*.

"I'll ring another time, dear lady," he said softly. After a long pause, he sighed. "Cheerio, then."

Tingling, I listened again, grabbed a flashlight from the cupboard and rushed out the back door with Rumpus on what felt like a reconnaissance mission. Joe was right; Andrew and I lived within minutes of each other. Feeling like Broadway's mystery cat, Macavity, I stood under a street lamp, behind a tree trunk, staring at Sheila's dimly lit house and the shadows silhouetted on the front room shades.

Two motorcycles were parked in the driveway. I imagined Sheila's sons sprawled on the couch drinking beer while Andrew read to their grandmother. "Parasites, all of them," I muttered, and ached with regret over missing his phone call. Had he needed a kind word to ease him through another miserable night? Or some assurance that my feelings for him were as deep as he suspected?

Wondering why fate had brought us together that day, I reluctantly turned and padded back home. In all the years I'd walked past that house, I'd never seen anyone weed the garden or collect the mail, never caught a glimpse of any activity. I felt vaguely troubled, as though I'd lost something.

Freedom. My freedom would be lost. I'd grown used to coming and going as I pleased, eating cookies in bed and reading myself to sleep. Would Andrew grumble over a few crumbs? Resent the light? Maybe he was also a late-night reader. Would he cook his own breakfast, as Sam had, and leave me in peace with my morning coffee and e-mail?

Of course he would. Andrew's years of serving others had conditioned him. He'd be perceptive and respectful. And fun. I smiled, remembering the comical sight of him imitating a bagpiper. I headed for the woodpile and hauled a load of logs into the dining room, humming *Scotland the Brave*.

I pushed balled-up pages of the unread Sunday newspaper under Sam's prized owl andirons, laid logs in the open fireplace and struck a match. "One of these days, we're going to have company," I told Rumpus, tossing a handful of salty pinecones into the fire. Listening to them snap, crackle and pop, I flipped open my laptop.

Dear Morgan,

This morning I met the most handsome widower, right here in my own little Cape Cod church. Andrew Macdade is from Portobello, lived with his first wife and their two children near Brighton Place until they divorced in the '80s. Maybe Ian's cousin, Hamish, remembers them?

After the divorce, Andrew bought the Highclere Hotel and married a cancer surgeon, who died while skiing in Switzerland. Also, he tied for

Wentworth's Captain's Cup during the time you lived in Sunninghill. Please ask Ian, our favorite golf commentator, if he ever heard of him.

I went on to give her all the details, peppering a postscript with romantic clichés and exclamation points, extolling Andrew's real or imagined virtues to the one person who would understand how I fell in love with a stranger in less than twelve hours: my childhood friend with starry blue eyes and golden hair who once filled my head with stories from the mythical kingdom of *Brigadoon*.

Cheerful flames licked the owl andirons, their amber glass eyes glowing, as I drifted back to the afternoon when Morgan led me into a tiny glade of moss-covered stone slabs where pink and mint-green ribbons from her mother's sewing basket hung on twigs, fluttering like miniature banners. And so it was that we spent the rest of that summer pounding mica glass into fairy dust, casting spells upon all of Scotland's faceless boys from our very own *Brigadoon*.

Morgan wished to marry a bonny prince. And though I wished for nothing more than a wristwatch and a puppy, I happily followed her for years, caught up in the country of castles, pipes and warm-hearted people who burred like my grandfather. We wore matching tartan tams until we graduated from our rural Connecticut high school and went separate ways. But our friendship lasted, our lives remained entwined, even after Morgan married Ian and moved to another continent. Like sisters, we carried each other's history in our hearts.

Chapter 8

When the phone rang at dawn, I knew who it was. "Wake up. Troon calling," Morgan sang. "I couldn't wait any longer to tell you. Hamish moved up to Inverness years ago, but he remembers Laura and Andrew Macdade. They were publicans on the High Street before some juicy affair caused a divorce."

"Laura took up with a soccer player," I said, my voice still hoarse, and repeated the heart-rending story of Andrew's renting his historic manse to Edinburgh University to fund his children's private educations after the divorce.

"Hamish said when he left Brighton Place, the Macdade property looked a bit neglected."

"Wouldn't you think the university would take better care of such a landmark? Andrew will be sick when he hears. He hasn't been back since Paula died; this might give him a good reason to go."

"How long has it been?"

"More than ten years."

"Poor guy," Morgan said. "But that's how Scottish men are, true-blue. They make the best husbands. I can't believe he owned the Highclere. Our flat was only a few miles away. If you'd come over instead of going off to that girls' college, you would've run into him."

"I wouldn't have been interested at that point. Too busy with the books. Besides, he was married to Paula. After she died, he leased their house to Johnson & Johnson Corporation, sold the hotel and left for Jordan. Do you remember the house next to the Highclere?"

"You couldn't miss it, Anna; brick with black wrought iron gates and dahlia gardens galore."

"Once the lease is up, he'll sell it and make a half-million pounds, he says. More, if the market is strong."

"What about the wife? Will Andrew leave her after the mother dies?"

"I think so. He asked me to wait; at least I think he did. I've been floating on a cloud since we met, having imaginary conversations with him. Is that pitiful or what?"

"It's about time you let someone into your life. When you refused to meet Ian's friend last year, we were sure you'd become a professional widow. What does Andrew do in Chatham?"

"He calls himself an estate manager. We'd call him a handyman. Works for a dot-com couple who summer here. They fly in and out on a moment's notice and summon Andrew at all hours."

"That's a step down from owning the Highclere and managing a palace," Morgan said.

"True. But he needs flexible hours to look after Sheila's feeble mother."

"Just so he's not one of those hard-luck chaps looking for a free lunch."

"I suspect he's been strapped for cash since Paula died. He paid off the mortgage with the life insurance. And instead of investing the profit from the hotel sale, he bought his daughter a house in Kensington."

"So he spoils her even more than you spoil your kids."

"He's devoted to Andrina and her brother even though they've been estranged from him since he married Paula. Thanks to their mother."

"Sounds like you both deserve some happiness. Who cares if he's a handyman? You can afford to support him until his house sells."

"I know it's premature but I can see myself living in Britain some day. You did it. Maybe I can too."

"Bring your prince to Sanibel this year." She cackled the way she always did when hatching a scheme. "We'll drive over from Boca, talk Andrew into splitting the year between Scotland and Florida like we do."

"Oh God, Morgan. What if he's nothing more than a menopausal woman's fantasy? Do you think I should hire a private detective, have him checked out?"

Even as I asked, I felt like Judas.

"Don't waste your money. When we go to Sunninghill for the seniors' tournament, Ian will ask about him at the Wentworth. If Andrew's left any messes behind, we'll let you know. When did he win the Captain's Cup?"

"I think he said 1989 but he tied for it with a pro. He told so many stories in such a short time, I couldn't keep track. And I missed a lot of what he said; his brogue thickens when he's excited. Verra this and verra that."

"Ian's does, too." She laughed. "He's been eavesdropping. He says you should practice your putting before your new husband comes knocking at your door."

"I'd better go shopping and fix myself up first."

"Buy something other than a flannel granny gown, will you?" She cackled again, predicting a sooner rather than later Sanibel wedding.

Chapter 9

Had I gone back to church and seen Andrew again in the following weeks, I might have become less intrigued with him and the idea of living in Scotland. But I stayed home on Sundays, avoiding temptation. An affair would only burden us with guilt and ruin our karma.

Andrew apparently felt the same way. According to Mrs. T, he'd not gone back to church either. Nor did he "ring another time" as promised. Though I was disappointed, my respect and admiration for him grew. Instinctively, I knew he'd come to me after Sheila's mother died.

Summer had arrived. Generations of New England families and swarms of retired snowbirds returned to open beach cottages and summer camps. Come July, the crushing wave of tourists would gridlock our narrow winding roads with RVs, Land Rovers and Hummers.

Once-empty harbors suddenly filled with white sails and racing motors. Dinging trolleys shuttled day-trippers to village shops, to church fairs, and to Ryder's Cove for seal watching excursions on school bus yellow boats. Private planes and sleek corporate helicopters swooped over the eroding coastline of Lighthouse Beach before banking west to Chatham's

Stick'n Rudder airport, where startled VIPs alit to find Hannah Montana clones clutching Blackberries, connected to the *Boston Globe* celebrity hotline.

Unsuspecting tourists were delighted when horse-drawn buggies clip-clopped through the village carrying fairytale brides and their bridesmaids to steepled white churches. Pealing bells sounded the perfectly timed departures of *Just Marrieds*, swept away in stretch limousines to romantic seaside receptions. Misty-eyed shoppers clapped and caught confetti. Oftentimes I stood on the sidelines, wondering if my own dreams would come true.

No one threw a net over me during that long summer, so I must have appeared normal. When I chimed Andrew's praises in my new blond bob and hastily purchased pastels, friends said any woman over fifty with a glimmer of hope on the horizon would glam up. But I felt more like a possessed spirit than a mature woman as I trolled the aisles of the Village Market, listening for a brogue, hoping he'd appear.

Getting ready to get ready for Andrew, I organized closets, cleaned the basement and replaced old sheets and towels with European linens, feathering my nest to suit the standards of a palace manager. Lest he discover just how disparate our finances were, I purged file cabinets and burned old trust account statements and canceled checks, tucking those made out to Caribbean gift shops and a Boston florist between the pages of my journals.

Unlike Andrew, who'd remained faithful to Paula's memory until he married Sheila, I had dated an advertising executive soon after Sam died. Chandler's rakish good looks and dry wit ignited a physical passion I hadn't known existed. But only months after we met he was diagnosed with Lou Gehrig's Disease, succumbed to depression and took his own life. For years, I blamed myself for missing the warning signs. Now, as I caressed faded photographs and re-read his letters, I cringed at the thought of burdening Andrew with more sadness. I packed up all evidence of Chandler, along with stacks of journals, and shipped them to Morgan's Boca Raton address.

Andrew had admitted reading Sheila's diary; it seemed likely he'd read mine. Why wouldn't he? He'd been cuckolded twice.

Chapter 10

After weeks of studying the backs of broad-shouldered men at Chatham A's baseball games and at Friday night band concerts, I panicked. As young and old waltzed around the gazebo clutching glo-sticks and balloons, tears of exhaustion slid down my face. How could he remain invisible in such a small town?

Although I resisted the urge to attend Sunday services, I ushered at the church's summer concerts and hosted the West Point cadets. I also continued to volunteer with Mrs. T, serving lobster rolls, chowder, chips and brownies to long lines of frazzled families with hungry children in tow. Andrew never appeared. And Mrs. T had clammed up about Sheila's dying mother. The one time I asked, she clucked primly, "All in God's time."

In early August, Mrs. T confided she'd overheard our local doctor tell Pastor Gil that "despite the Scotsman's superb care, it's only a matter of days."

"What else did Doctor Bob say?"

"You know the doc. Scratched his head. Wondered how Andrew landed in such circumstances." Mrs. T dried her hands on her apron and looked me in the eyes. "He'll need a friend after all he's been through, Anna."

I felt woozy, wondering how I'd tell my children that a man they'd never heard of would likely move into our house in the near future.

ABOUT A WEEK LATER, Rumpus and I returned from an afternoon walk to find the soundtrack from Rushmore and a pail of wildflowers on the kitchen doorstep. The note said, "Dearest Anna, I cleaned the gutters while waiting to see you and pray you are well. Yours, Andrew XX." Another afternoon brought another note, saying he'd repaired a screen and was sorry he'd missed me.

I pictured him scurrying along the footpath to my backyard. Anyone in town could have pointed out my carriage house on the old Granger Estate, so I wasn't a bit surprised that he knew where I lived. But I was impressed he'd found the time to take on chores.

He never called or asked to see me, just appeared and disappeared in my absence. I began leaving notes taped to bags of oatmeal cookies. He answered with boxes of candy and lyrics to songs he'd written during the '60s.

The wait was almost over. I would welcome him into my home, shore him up and restore his faith in women. If our romance didn't pan out, at least we would have taken another chance at love.

In late August, I was on the phone with my one and only friend who seemed skeptical about my rave reviews of the charming Scotsman. As I regaled her with his latest good deed

– tying up my tomato plants – he pulled into my driveway in a vintage BMW convertible.

"Marta," I whispered, "gotta go."

Chapter 11

Sheila's mother had died. Andrew had been told to leave. "I did my verra best for them," he said. "I don't know where to turn."

Like old friends, we settled in, a grateful guest and his gracious hostess. We agreed to keep a low profile until his divorce was final. At Andrew's suggestion, we shopped and attended church services in nearby towns to avoid any awkward encounters with Sheila. He'd recently taken a part-time position in Orleans, with Baron von Mahler, to supplement the Damato wages. It would take a few months for Sheila to receive her inheritance. "I must support her until then," he said. "I gave her my last ten thousand dollars and my car."

The BMW he'd arrived in belonged to Mrs. Damato and was available to him only when running her errands. I offered him my station wagon and happily rode the blue bicycle he gave me to celebrate our new life together.

There were moments when I felt off-balance, unnerved by the abrupt changes, and thought it might have been better if he'd taken a temporary room instead of moving in with me. But on the morning of September 11, as we watched the Twin

Towers crumble, my doubts disappeared. We settled into each other's hearts and habits and never looked back.

Andrew planted dozens of blooming dahlias around the flagpole and designed a memorial rock garden complete with heather and Scottish moss. He hung his equestrian prints on the dining room walls. We arranged his horseracing memorabilia and biographies on the bookshelves and placed framed snapshots of his children on the piano, next to photographs of my family.

Weeks later, with my encouragement, Andrew left the employ of the Damatos. He continued to work for Baron von Mahler, and to maintain my house and yard. Considering the exorbitant costs of labor, the exchange seemed practical, one that would free him to winter with me on Sanibel Island.

His six-foot frame was bronzed and strong. He gelled his hair to camouflage a bump, the result of an injury he said he sustained ejecting from a cockpit during his RAF training. I discovered his vanity when I caught him preening before the mirror, plucking gray strays from his bushy black eyebrows and shaving silver threads from his temples.

Every afternoon I'd find an "Aily - XX" note propped against a dahlia on my dressing table. It took some time to figure out it meant "Anna, I love you – kiss kiss." Reading the fashion magazine *W* at the beauty salon, I learned in silent amusement that Aristotle Onassis had sent diamond "ily" bracelets to his mistresses for years.

Occasionally, Andrew grumbled about being a kept man. When I returned from shopping one morning, he reported he'd posted a letter to his Edinburgh solicitor, instructing him to deed me the centuries-old Admiral Macdade manse upon his death.

"Look at the life you've given me, darling," he explained, lifting the groceries from the car, eyeing the rolling lawns overlooking Gull Pond. "It's the least I can do until the Sunninghill house sells. You've saved me from misery. I'm calmer, sleeping better than I have in years. Even my nightmares have let up."

I was relieved that he'd broached the subject. After his first nightmare, I'd cradled him in silence, not wanting to burden him with questions. But the night I heard him keening Paula's name, I remembered. He blamed himself.

"Andrew," I said as we headed into the kitchen, "you're tormented. Your pillow was wet again this morning and you're exhausted from another night of thrashing."

He set the parcels on the counter and collapsed into the cushions of his wicker chair for his morning tea. "It's always pitch-black. I can't breathe. I can't find her."

"Why don't you talk to a therapist, dear? Or to Pastor Gil?"

"Therapy is an American indulgence, Anna. Nothing for a proud Scot."

"Twelve years is a long time to carry guilt over an accident you didn't cause."

He drained his cup, picked up his work gloves and lumbered toward the kitchen door.

"In the meantime," I added hastily, "why would you leave me your children's inheritance? You want to reconcile with them, not alienate them more. I'd like to write to Andrina and Drew, invite them to visit."

Astonishment flooded his face. "It would be too good to be true. Will you do this for me?"

Certain he needed them, I wrote impassioned letters to his children and prayed they'd respond. The next week, Andrina called from Kensington and Drew from his Edinburgh office. Andrew's voice trembled as he assured them that we wanted them to visit, in Chatham or on Sanibel Island, any time their schedules permitted. He was keeping well, he told them. He realized it had been a long time. And yes, we had e-mail.

The more I heard, the more I smiled. It was obvious his children were eager to see him and to meet me. Pleased for Andrew, I wondered if their mother had really turned them against him, or if he'd been so obsessed with Paula that he'd ignored them.

As the finalization of his divorce drew near, we entertained my close friends with dinner recipes he plucked from his food-spattered international cookbook, cataloging who'd eaten what, where, and when. Mr. Taubman, Sotheby's CEO, required a gluten-free diet. Pamela Harriman preferred seafood. Mr. Gore liked rare beef; Jane Fonda, cantaloupe sorbet; Senator Kerry, coriander risotto. And Mr. Bayley's bridge partner, Ambassador Annenberg, raved about the flaming cherries jubilee.

My own favorite was butterflied lamb marinated in spiced goat's milk and grilled to perfection. Andrew assured me I'd chosen well; that was also Queen Noor's favorite before she became a vegetarian.

He courted our guests with aplomb, teased their imaginations with palace intrigue and royal protocol. He'd had pheasant flown in from Harrod's for the elder President and

Mrs. Bush. "Must say, it was the highlight of my career to walk alongside him on Aqaba's beach."

Andrew had designed a garden of red anemones along the royal runway for Her Majesty's delight. He and Queen Noor had orchestrated King Hussein's surprise birthday party in the purple-hued wadi. Like excited children, Andrew's new friends wanted more: "Tell us again about the jeweled belly dancers, Andrew."

He obliged, humoring them with tales of red silk tents, belled camels and servants dressed like Aladdin carrying platters heaped with smoked sheep's eyes wrapped in maguey leaves. Only Marta remained aloof, unmoved by my Scotsman. She kept a steady gaze on him, her eyes skeptical, but Andrew never seemed to notice.

Sometimes during his stories – Saddam Hussein delivering water-skis, Margaret Thatcher elbowing her husband when she spied their framed photo on the palace piano – I studied the enormous sapphire ring he'd given me, wondering if the Jewish refugee who'd sold it to his father before the Nazis marched into Paris had made it to safety. Andrew found the ring buried in his mother's flour tin after she died. With it was a Van Cleef diamond brooch that Marta said looked like a cluster of rock candy. At his suggestion, our local jeweler removed some of the diamonds and designed earrings for Andrew's daughter and daughter-in-law. I never asked why he didn't have a pair made for me.

Chapter 12

My son and his wife surprised us with a weekend visit in December, just before we left for Sanibel. Andrew had soothed their initial concerns during Sunday evening telephone conversations, flattering them with solicitous questions, and they greeted him like a long lost uncle. We dined on Chateaubriand and lemon meringue pie, a menu Andrew said he'd served at one of the Bayleys' bipartisan fundraisers.

"Who was there?" James asked, taking a second slice of pie.

"I've forgotten most, but I do remember the lovely Pamela Harriman and your presidential candidate, Al Gore. He came looking for me in the kitchen, slipped me a crisp $50 with his card and told me to call after the election. Those were heady times, son." Andrew chuckled. "But I wouldn't change a thing, now that I've found your mother."

"To think we almost lost you to the White House," James said, laughing. "You're a culinary genius, but when can we hear your big hit?"

"Right away." Andrew dashed into the living room to play the *Rushmore* soundtrack. When he returned, tapping his fork to the catchy beat of *Concrete and Clay*, he said, "Pay attention to the words. Paula could always tell it was me by the way I sing 'clay.' My accent, you know."

"How did you make the big time?" Jessica asked.

He shrugged. "Fame by a fluke. I got a job as a session guitarist, the lead vocalist fell ill and they told me to give it a try. Shazam. I was a one-hit wonder." He grinned. "But it wasn't always easy. We played at plenty of rubbishy clubs before we hit the Marquee in Soho."

"Soho?" she echoed.

"The Tin Pan Alley of London. Everyone was there. Eric Clapton and Phil Collins. Little Reggie Dwight played piano in argyle sweaters and squinted through pink National Health glasses; he knew his name didn't have a ring to it so he changed it to Elton John. Rod Stewart dug graves until Python Lee Jackson's band heard him singing in an all night strip joint. They signed him up for a gig and *Rod the Mod* was off and running."

Jessica's eyes widened. "I'm a huge fan. Do you ever get comp tickets?"

Andrew nodded. "Rod's PR girl and I go way back. After her brother got out of rehab, I gave him a job packing up instruments."

James laughed. "I'm impressed. Do you keep in touch with any of them?"

"Not so much since Paula died. But I met Phil for lunch a couple of years ago, ended up sailing the Florida Keys with him on Jimmy Buffett's ketch. And Rod and I remain pals. He doted on my mum, loved her baked sweeties and Drambuie-laced haggis. Hold on. The *Evening Herald* ran a photo of me with Rod and his girlfriend, Kelly Emberg, at a *Hibs and Hearts* football match in Edinburgh. I called the press room and got a copy."

James shook his head as Andrew left the table. "Great guy, Mom. But what's he doing in the Chatham outback?"

"You and Jessica are young," I reminded him. "We old folks love it here."

Andrew returned and handed Jessica the photo.

Amazed, they passed it back and forth, contrasting Andrew's pin-striped suit with the rock star's open shirt and baggy slacks. "Why so formal?" James asked.

"Patrons always dress, son. Yes, indeedy. My father always said 'you can tell a successful man by the cut of his cloth.'"

James nodded. "It must have been brutal to lose your wife. And then to leave your family and fame in the U.K. Do you ever perform?"

Andrew stared at the Advent wreath's burning candles, snuffed one out and gave him a rueful smile. "Life is short, eh? After I sang *Bridge Over Troubled Water* at Paula's funeral, the music died for me."

My son affectionately nudged his arm. "We're pleased you're here, sir. It's been a long time since we've seen Mother so happy."

"Hoped you'd feel that way, James." Andrew sighed. "For I've asked your lovely mother to marry me. And I assure you I'll look after her until the day she dies."

Chapter 13

Palm Sunday came early that year, coinciding with Andrew's 58th birthday and our wedding on Captiva Island. The casuarina trees swayed in the soft morning breeze, seeming to nod as we hurried hand-in-hand along the sandy path to the Chapel by the Sea. Pastor Allen stood on the front steps, his black robe fluttering, and tapped his wristwatch. "You're late for your own wedding."

He chuckled, shepherded us through the door as the last bell pealed and pointed to our guests in the front pews. With sheepish grins, we slipped into the back row and waited for the call to worship.

"Listen everyone. Listen to the gulls. Listen to the surf. Listen to the song of the sea and be glad."

Week after week, Andrew's hand had clasped mine as we worshiped in the old whitewashed chapel. As the Palm Sunday service began, with its familiar haunting theme of betrayal, I reflected back on the first time we'd stepped through the chapel's doors. I'd been struck by the pure light; Andrew, by celestial visions. "A kirk set on a sacred island," he said, "far from the troubled past, where we'll exchange our vows without a fuss."

How easily he'd won my promise to marry him on his birthday. But now, I wished we'd held off until we returned to Chatham or at least until some of our children might have joined us.

"Once again Jesus comes to our hearts," Pastor Allen continued, "to hear our spoken and unspoken prayers, to weep with us, to hold us, to lead us on The Way. Let's stand and sing *Our Redeemer King*."

As always, Andrew and I shared a hymnal and sang with bursting happy hearts. Staring sideways at his handsome face, I stopped mid-sentence to listen to his sweet tenor. The altar's gold cross reflected in the surface of my sapphire ring and I prayed for the refugee who once wore it. As I was conjuring up an image of meeting her in a Parisian park and placing it in the palm of her hand, the pastor roared. "Your iniquities have separated you. Your lips have spoken lies."

Andrew flinched. I slipped my hand through the crook of his arm.

"Your tongue has spoken wickedness," the pastor thundered.

Andrew's jaw clenched. When the organ sounded the introductory chords for the recessional, he ignored the hymnal I held up. He stared at the altar throughout all three verses, worrying a thread loose from the cuff of his navy blazer.

Pastor Allen stepped into the center aisle for the benediction. He raised his arms and commanded, "Grope for the light during the long week ahead, as we mourn our Savior's crucifixion."

And then the pastor's tone softened. "As many of you know, Andrew and Anna are to be married today." He waved us forward. "They invite those of you who have shared their friendship to join them for the ceremony."

I nudged Andrew toward the aisle and clutched his limp hand. The organist played soft strains of *Ode to Joy* as we walked toward the palm-strewn altar, its candles flickering like tiny hopeful beacons. Ian nodded and Morgan smiled through misty blue eyes as we passed. A pretty, dark-haired woman, vaguely familiar, sat next to her.

The minister told Andrew to face me. Beads of sweat covered his upper lip. He recited his vows in monotone to the floor.

Pressure built in my chest. I couldn't get enough air. I delivered my vows to his bowed head. "I, Anna, take you, Andrew, to be my husband, to have and to hold from this day forward, for better, for worse…"

A wave of vertigo hit as Pastor Allen pronounced us man and wife and prompted Andrew to kiss me. My groom turned to the minister instead.

"I'm so sorry for this rush of emotion," he said. "I don't know what's come over me."

"It's the true spirit who is so touched, my son." Pastor Allen clasped Andrew's shoulder. "It's perfectly normal to be overwhelmed after years of suffering alone. Remember, Andrew, the Lord has sent Anna to love and cherish you. In time, the miracle of matrimony will renew and restore you. Now, kiss your bride."

Andrew puckered his lips and pecked mine, cast a *show-must-go-on* leer at the congregation, and took my arm. After our trip down the aisle, we posed for photographs at the back of the chapel, then emerged into a shower of rice and applause.

Dazed, I caught sight of Morgan's radiant face and Ian's shock of curly white hair. Relief rushed through me as Ian swept me into his arms, kissed my forehead, and pumped Andrew's hand. "Best be warned; I've heard my wife scheming with this lassie to move you back to Scotland for half the year."

"I've already put your names down for a unit at our complex," Morgan added, drawing the dark-haired woman closer. "Do you remember Kate Campbell from Portobello, Andrew? She ran the tea shop just down from the pub you owned, near the Village Café."

"Kate?" I hugged her like a long-lost sister. "Morgan's talked about you for years. Andrew, isn't this amazing?"

"Aye," he said, staring over Kate's head. "But after years in the Mid-East and in this grand country of America, Auld Reekie's a distant blur."

Kate smiled wistfully. "It's cold and dreike this time of year. You were lucky to get a green card. I'd give anything to live here, but Immigration won't allow more than a three-month visa. They pull me aside and interrogate me every time I…"

A couple broke in to shake Andrew's hand before leaving for our reception at the nearby Casa Ybell Resort. He seemed removed, perplexed even, as if he didn't understand their congratulations.

Chapter 14

Our wedding luncheon had been hastily planned a week before to include Morgan and Ian, Pastor Allen, and a half-dozen of my friends who were also wintering in Florida. Andrew seemed cut off from all of them, and I was relieved when the Pastor asked him about Edinburgh's archeological dig.

While the Casa Ybell staff circulated among our guests with silver trays of hors d'oeuvres and champagne flutes, I slipped away to arrange a place setting for Kate Campbell. At my heels, Morgan clucked like a mother hen. "Some of his friends should be here today. And where are his children?"

"Back home, like mine. I wanted to wait until they could all get away but Andrew was determined to be married on his birthday."

Absentmindedly, I picked a white carnation from the centerpiece on a side table. "And he refused to invite his best friend, Archie, that Portobello politician he raves about. Says he's a devout Catholic and wouldn't want to miss Holy Week in his own *kirk*."

Morgan rolled her eyes. "Sounds a bit sanctimonious. Wouldn't you think he'd invite someone? And why did he act like such a stiff in the chapel?"

I shook my head. "One minute he was warm and loving. The next, he was frozen."

"Until this morning, Ian and I thought he was perfect for you. But he's spooked. Kate's a watcher and she kept pinching me during the ceremony. Something's not right."

"Maybe he thinks he's betrayed Paula by marrying me. Did you hear me fumble the richer-poorer lines? I'm a wreck. Does it show?"

"You look poised and beautiful, my friend." Morgan smiled tenderly. "No one but me would ever guess how disappointed you are."

A few minutes later, in a private dining room, Andrew's dismay was obvious. He gave me a withering look as I rose unsteadily to thank our guests for coming.

"…You've all heard how Andrew and I crisscrossed paths in Britain years before we met in Chatham. But the arrival of Morgan's friend, Kate, straight from Andrew's seaside village of Portobello, is the most amazing coincidence of all. She's a golden link to his past and another bridge to our future. Welcome, Kate Campbell."

Kate stood, her violet eyes sparkling. "It's lovely to be here in the tropics. I came a wee bit early to escape the freezing temperatures at home, never dreaming I'd attend Anna's wedding, let alone that she'd marry one of Portobello's own."

She laughed and raised her glass. "May the best you've ever seen be the worst you'll ever see. May the mouse ne'er leave your girnal wi' a teardrop in its eye. May your lum keep blithely reeking 'til yer auld enough to dee. May you aye be just as happy as I wish you now to be."

Everyone chorused "Here, here!" as Kate sat. With an amused twinkle, she lilted, "Well, Andrew, you've come a long way from Porty."

Without a word, he stared through her. The waitresses appeared bearing shell-pink porcelain plates, each garnished with sprigs of purple bougainvillea. Glasses tinkled and laughter rippled around the table as my groom and I sat in silence.

I touched his damp face, now the color of putty. "Are you sick, Andrew?"

He shook his head as Kate excused herself to find the ladies' room. "She's a Nosy Parker. Drills me with questions in that awful voice."

His hostility shocked me. Kate was as warm and wonderful as I had imagined after years of hearing about her from Morgan. And her voice was lovely.

"As worldly as you are, Andrew, how could you be so put off by a few simple questions?"

"She's asking where the manse is, why it's rented, who I knew…"

"Why wouldn't she be curious?" I forced a smile and jollied him along, like a mother with a pouting three-year-old, promising it would be over soon.

"Then maybe you'll have a little time for me," he growled as a waiter appeared with our wedding cake. Andrew gave him a perfunctory nod and continued badgering. "You haven't said two words to me all day. I feel like a tailor's dummy but I'll play my part."

He stood, flashed a news anchor's smile and rapped his glass. "Anna and I met by chance at the kirk," he read from prepared notes, "and I pursued the lady with the Nantucket basket who has the kindest heart I've ever met. We both knew life's journey had brought us together. We have grown lovingly and spiritually in that time, and today as I reach another year on God's earth, my beloved and I are wed, bound to each other before the Lord…"

He sounded like Elmer Gantry thumping The Word. When he finally stopped, my friends clapped softly with lowered eyes.

At least it was over. In twos and threes, our guests trickled out to the parking lot. When Morgan, Ian and Kate turned to leave, Kate spun around and held up her camera. "Oh, Andrew," she called, "I'll have an extra set made up for your son and pop into his office next week."

"My son will see our wedding pictures when he comes to visit," Andrew replied stiffly. "He's a busy young man, Kate."

"Not to worry. I'll just leave them with his secretary." She waved with a laugh. "Cheerio."

Andrew saw me to the car and slammed the door. I crumpled behind the tinted windows as he cautiously pulled away from the resort.

"What the hell is wrong with you, Andrew? You've ruined the day. How could you take such a menacing dislike to Kate Campbell?"

"I left that cold country and its ignorant people after Paula died," he blustered. "That busybody will run around Porty, blethering on, telling everyone she saw me."

"What is wrong with being seen at your own wedding?"

He didn't answer.

I swallowed hard as we crawled along. "Until now, Andrew, you've spoiled me, showered me with too many presents, a sentimental Romeo in hot pursuit. But today, you've given me nothing but misery. No affection, no warmth and no wedding present."

"I'm your present. In Scotland, the bride and groom don't exchange gifts."

"You should have warned me of that mean custom, saved me the time and expense of selecting one for you."

He'd seemed pleased with the oil painting of Sanibel's mangroves I'd given him the night before and had hinted at giving me a gold Nantucket basket charm. Defiantly, he continued to creep along; the normal twenty-minute drive took a grim forty-five.

Nestled in a blaze of tropical flowers, *Little Palm Cottage* awaited, a pink and green stucco dollhouse. Andrew switched off the ignition and tossed a small box in my lap. "You've got one of everything, Anna, but I do the best I can. I found this yesterday in a Fort Myers pawn shop."

Speechless, I gingerly opened it to find an antique gold cross inlaid with bloodstone, carnelian, jasper, and banded agate. Missing a square stone in its center, it was nonetheless exquisite.

"It's Celtic, isn't it?" I asked.

He nodded. "Now you have something to brag about. Happy?"

"It's beautiful, Andrew. But what did I do to deserve such a heartbreaking day?"

"You called the shots today, my dear, and I guess you always will." He slammed the car door again, leaving me alone, believing I'd gone stark raving mad.

Chapter 15

The wedding was over and we were unhappy for the first time since we'd met.

I changed into a pair of shorts and a sweatshirt, then grabbed the dog's leash. "Would you like to come?"

He clicked on the television and stared at the horse racing results from Gulfstream Park.

"A walk would do us good."

No reply.

I softly latched the lanai's screen door and slipped away, ashamed of him.

THOUSANDS OF SHELLS jingled in the late afternoon surf while I kicked the sand, lost in wracking sobs. Then I remembered a friend who had married a religious widower who insisted on separate bedrooms. After sex, he crept out of her bed and into his late wife's, to repent. On their counselor's advice, they sold his house, moved into a new one and lived in harmony from that day forward.

And so will we, I swore. *Worse* is part of the deal. I marched home with a plan to bide my time, to smother him with sympathy until Paula was a distant memory.

Rumpus shook himself dry, spraying sand and salty water all over Andrew. "Did you and Mummy see the dolphins on your walk?" he asked. He picked me up, grazed my lips and whispered in a trembling voice, "Never let it be said that this brave heart didn't carry his wee bride over the threshold."

The man I thought I knew had returned and peace was mysteriously restored. We had a light supper of wedding luncheon leftovers and watched an Inspector Morse mystery on PBS about the strange disappearance of an Oxford University student. I thought of Paula's years of study there.

"Which school did you say Paula graduated from, Andrew?"

"Magdalen College. High honors all the way."

"But the student who disappeared in the movie went there. It's a men's college."

He shrugged, stood and clicked off the television. "Maybe Magdalen is where her father, Sir Robert, taught the classics. And now, if you're through cross-examining me, I'm going to bed. To sleep."

The slam of the bedroom door echoed like a gunshot. "Sadistic little shit," I muttered, clicking the TV back on. Rumpus cocked his head and followed me across the room to retrieve the blue and green tartan throw Morgan and Ian had given us that afternoon. Huddled under it to stop the shaking, I felt crazy.

Mocked by tinkling laughter from the neighbor's pool party, I realized Andrew was even more fragile than Pastor Gil had warned. I should have been on the lookout for red flags. Instead, I had played Lady Bountiful and ushered him into my home the moment he left Sheila. I convinced him to semi-retire, dressed him up, gave him an ATM card and then congratulated myself for landing such a catch.

Andrew had shadowed me like a puppy, finished my thoughts when I was flustered, opened doors, pushed our cart through the supermarket and carried the parcels. When I struggled to open a jar or to pull a weed, he appeared like a faithful servant. Unlike Sam, who'd grown impatient with my long-winded telephone calls, Andrew served hot coffee, bowed and retreated. He was a splendid host, courteous and dapper, though his habit of announcing "madam, dinner is served" mortified me. I often implored him to stop behaving like a maitre d', whereupon he'd give me a hangdog look and duck out the door, returning hours later with flowers or a bucket of steamers.

I wondered just how fractured he was. So often, he deflected specific questions about his past with a sad smile or a wrenching plea to "move forward," moving me to tearful apologies.

He knew when to elicit sympathy and when to turn on the comedy. A pantomime of Charlie Chaplin, a lusty grope, or an overdone impersonation of Sean Connery's "What now, woman?" would crack me up and I'd forget my question.

But those antics wouldn't work with Kate Campbell. She was all too familiar with the Celtic charm of her countrymen. Maybe she was nosy. Maybe I should have seated him next to Pastor Allen. It would have been such a simple accommodation for someone who seldom asked for anything. Except constant attention.

Chapter 16

Dawn's pink light crept through the Venetian blinds. Wind rustled the palm trees and their fronds slapped the living room windows. Tropical birds screeched and swooped from limb to limb. I shuddered, longing for Chatham, as I tiptoed into our bedroom.

Slipping into bed, I spooned against his back.

He snuggled closer. "I'm so sorry, heartsweet."

"Me too." Scalding tears ran down my face.

He rolled over, tucked the sheet around my shoulders and rocked me.

"Talk to me, Andrew. From your heart. Tell me how to make us right again."

Brushing my eyelids with butterfly kisses, he ran his fingers through my tangled curls. "Morgan shouldn't have brought an uninvited guest to our wedding."

"But something was wrong in the chapel, before you met Kate."

"Shush, my love. Broken dreams and death make a man anxious. I was upset and acted badly. Kate triggered too many memories."

"Isn't it time you go home? Face the past and put it all to rest?"

"Never. The Scots carry grudges to their graves. The lads have never forgiven me for making it big in America. Kate's just like them. Surely you saw her face when she learned I'm an alien resident. As green as the card itself."

"Kate was curious, not jealous." I was stunned by his animosity. "And what do you mean, the lads haven't forgiven you? You said Brian, Archie and Bosworth are loyal mates."

"Archie is. The others are daft from drink, nattering on about nothing but other people's misfortunes. Believe me," he warned, "if Kate asks about me, they'll give her a dirty earful."

"So you punished me because you wound up sitting across from Kate, giving her the opportunity to pry."

He exhaled, relieved that the dim child had finally caught on.

"Lucky for me, I guess. I thought you regretted marrying me."

"But darling, you're my light, my reason for living. I'm a better man since I met you."

"Then renew your passport. Morgan and Ian expect us to visit. I want to see the Macdade manse, the Ravelston, your grandfather's racetrack. And I want to meet your friend Archie."

"I can't go back," he insisted. "I raged and cut everyone off after Paula's death. I should've been on the slopes with her that morning. I could've saved her. But I went to the bar for a cooked breakfast, braced myself with brandy to join her for a noon run, forgetting about the effects of alcohol in high altitudes. By the time the house doctor found me, I was so drunk he had to help me walk. It was terrible. She was all laid out in a black body bag. I removed her rings and kissed her warm lips one last time."

He shuddered. "I can still hear the sound of that zipper. I passed out cold from shock and drink. Haven't touched a drop since."

Alarmed, I remembered an altogether different account. The day we met, he told me that he'd slept in the morning Paula died, that the ski patrol roused him from a deep sleep to notify him of her death. And he'd said he quit drinking in Philadelphia, not Switzerland. I bit my tongue and let him continue.

"After the funeral, I ripped out a wall in a third-floor bedroom at the Highclere, stashed some of her belongings under the eaves for safekeeping until I returned from Jordan, and then worked all night, re-plastering."

I didn't remind him that he'd told me he sold the hotel before he left. "Did you ever go back for them?" I asked.

"There wasn't time."

"We'll go to Sunninghill together," I said, "and retrieve it all. Then maybe you'll find peace."

"Let it go, Anna. None of it was worth much; costume jewelry, old Steinbeck paperbacks and a purple Armani suit I gave her for her 40th birthday. Besides, I did such a grand job we'd need a demolition crew to tear that wall down."

"What about Paula's parents? Why didn't they store her things?"

"Oh, they did. Lady Margaret and her maid arrived at my front door with an estate wagon after the funeral. They loaded up the Clarice Cliff pottery, the antique chimney pots, Paula's books, jewelry and most of her clothes."

"You just stood and watched?"

"Lady Margaret said I'd never been good enough for her daughter. A few days later, she sent a man from the London Aquarium to take Paula's Koi from the pond I'd dug by hand in our backyard. She's a vindictive woman with a long arm. I didn't want you to know how much she hated me."

I leaned closer and told him what he wanted to hear. "What a despicable creature."

"And Kate Campbell is just like her. For the sake of our marriage, Anna, I beg you to call Morgan this morning. Tell her to stop that bloody woman from butting into my private affairs."

I reminded him that Kate had merely offered to drop our wedding pictures at Drew's office.

"Kate is common." He sniffed. "I won't have her pushing her way into my son's office like some char back from a grand holiday. Make that call. Please, darling."

I nodded, wanting to scream. Our wedding was a disaster but this twist was beyond comprehension.

He sat up and fixed an empty gaze on the pillows. "Anna, I don't know how to begin."

"There's more?"

"I'm a proud Scot. I've worked hard all my life. Yesterday, I felt worthless, the same way I felt when Paula forced her toffee-nosed friends on me."

"You own a house in Porty and another next to the Highclere. How can you feel worthless?"

"Because until that albatross sells, I'm at your mercy. You pay for most everything."

My patience had left the room long ago. "So what? If you need more money, manage a country club or start a catering business. You're talented, Andrew. You can do anything."

His face lit up. "Mrs. Damato called. She wants me back. And the Baron will be home from Klosters in May. Did I tell you about the time he hosted Martin Scorsese and the famous rabbi for dinner?"

"Many times. Now, tell me how Mrs. Damato got this number."

"I sent her a postcard."

"She took advantage of you, Andrew. Perhaps you should apply at Chatham Bars Inn."

"Or we could start a non-profit for shut-ins. You and me, Anna. We'll sell soup and creamy custards, drive the old dears to their appointments, call ourselves Mariners."

"You be the Mariner. Count me out."

He laughed. "In the meantime, if you don't need me tomorrow, I'll take in a few races at Gulfstream, dearest."

"Of course." Resentment tightened in my chest. I'd married a child.

We held each other for a long time. I remembered a winter day at my desk, watching a pair of cardinals in the garden. The male hopped over and pecked his mate's beak and I realized he was feeding her. She gave him the ultimate gift: trust.

I had trusted Andrew. I had loved him and thought we'd spend a lifetime together. But now, I didn't know which end was up.

"Let's put aside the glums," I said with feigned lightness. "We'll bicycle to Lighthouse Café for breakfast and spend the day on the beach. I'll e-mail Morgan while you shower."

I opened my laptop only after I heard the shower door close.

Morgan, sorry to burden you, but I think my new husband needs a psychiatrist. Please ask Kate if she'd be willing to make discreet inquiries about him when she goes back. And tell her to steer clear of Drew's office.

Morgan responded immediately.

I suspect there's someone in that office Andrew doesn't want you to know about. Send me a list of all his relatives. Kate and I will check him out at Edinburgh's Registry of Births, Deaths and Marriages when Ian and I go over in June. Be careful, my friend.

I read her answer and then deleted both messages. Andrew claimed to be computer illiterate, but I no longer knew what to believe. Hiding behind a cheery smile, I kissed him and assured him that Kate would not butt into his "private affairs." He shrugged as if I'd commented on the weather.

Chapter 17

After filling up on blueberry pancakes and homemade sausage at Lighthouse Café, we pedaled to the beach, staked the umbrella and spread our towels. Nearby, a sunburned dowager in a floppy hat weighted with fishing lures was bent over collecting shells. We passed a pleasant hour examining her treasures. Later, we acquired the "Sanibel stoop" too, becoming daily collectors. Our bond was evident in the photo she took that day: tanned lovers, elbows entwined, huddled under a bright blue umbrella with hopeful grins. We'd survived our Palm Sunday wedding.

But Andrew's irrational fear of Edinburgh gossip troubled me. Almost as much as the inconsistent accounts of Paula's death.

Pastor Allen called on Monday, inviting us to join the final session of his Lenten study group. We gathered under the casuarina trees on Wednesday afternoon to open our minds to the mysteries of faith and spiritual growth. Andrew was reticent at first, but soon astonished even the minister with his knowledge of Biblical verse. The group murmured "Amen" when he told them he'd ushered at Billy Graham's Glasgow Crusade and had been "saved by the great man himself."

Pleased to see Andrew so popular, I relaxed until he announced that Pontius Pilate was Scottish, "the only son of a Roman slave billeted in Edinburgh." He was about to embellish the story, but I pinched him.

Andrew was such a star, the pastor asked him to read the Easter Sunday scripture, which he did masterfully. Later, he wondered if he should apply to Harvard's Divinity School.

My granddaughter's spring break, and her annual trip to Sanibel, followed Easter. From the moment we picked Emma up at the airport, Andrew doted on her. He figured her math sums as quickly as he calculated horse-racing odds, helped her paint sand dollars we scavenged from the beaches, and bicycled with us to Pinocchio's for Sanibel Crunch ice cream.

Emma adored Granddad Andrew. She giggled and pedaled faster when he called, "Go, Girl. We're on the hols." And she mimicked his brogue, shouting "Cheerio" and "Jolly hockey sticks" at every opportunity.

Andrew's tender affection for my granddaughter softened my heart and gave me hope, yet something wasn't quite right. I worried all the time, watching him for signs of a nervous breakdown. I was relieved that his sunny disposition lasted through the week. Emma gave her new granddad a hug and a kiss before we put her on the airplane back to Boulder.

Andrew seemed content, with me and our daily routine. Tuesday and Thursday mornings we bicycled along Periwinkle Way, past fluttering kites and wafts of frangipani, to Sanibel's Big Arts Center. I painted smoky clouds or salmon-pink sunsets, depending on the day. Andrew discovered a natural gift for drawing and wrote a colorfully illustrated storybook about his granddaughter's adventures with her globe-trotting parents. Since Andrina, Tom and Fiona were due within the week, I found a local printer and surprised Andrew with six bound copies.

He soon changed his mind about leaving the past in the past. He filled notebooks with stories of his youth, tales that took him back to *Auld Reekie*, to the Edinburgh he knew before the Thatcher years. And he mailed letters and wedding photos to his old pals in Porty. Perhaps he'd grown more confident, I thought, and was willing to reach out to those from his past. Or maybe he was gloating to his mates about his easy new life. Most likely, with his daughter's visit imminent, he was trying to convince me of his commitment to the *miracle of matrimony*.

Chapter 18

Anticipating Andrina's visit, Andrew stocked the refrigerator with fresh fruit, assorted cheeses and white wine, while I rented a crib and a highchair for Fiona and made a list of local pediatricians.

Tom and Andrina pulled up to Little Palm Cottage two hours behind schedule, weary from the Heathrow-to-Miami flight and the bumper-to-bumper traffic. We heard the booming beat of *Cheeseburger in Paradise* before we saw them, climbing half-naked from a metallic gold convertible. Eager for an instant tan, they had changed into shorts and tank tops for the long drive to Sanibel; they looked like buttered lobsters. Luckily for them, we had an aloe plant in the backyard.

Grinning, Tom introduced himself to his father-in-law, then pointed to the cottage and gave him a thumbs-up. I lagged a step or two behind, studying his daughter. Tall, sleek and blond, Andrina was the antithesis of her Falstaffian husband. She looked around approvingly. "Lovely, Dad, lovely," she said, and thrust a heavy brown bag at me. "We would have come to the wedding, Anna, if you'd asked."

"But your father said you couldn't because…"

Andrew interrupted, wedging himself between us and gently lifting Fiona from her car seat, saying hello to his granddaughter for the first time.

Dinner was festive and noisy. Tom had been made a full partner at Price-Waterhouse and Andrina had been promoted to supervise its Human Resources Department. Andrew beamed as I unwrapped the crystal vase, then he yammered on about meeting the legendary glassblower Chihuly at a MOMA reception with "Mighty Al" Taubman.

Delighted with the vase, I tilted it toward the light, passed it to Andrew, and caught Andrina staring at my sapphire ring. Smiling, I slipped it from my finger and handed it to her. "It must have dazzled you when you were a child sitting on your grandmother's lap. Andrew has told me how close you were. When I'm gone, it'll be yours to pass along to Fiona."

A flicker of confusion crossed her face. "It's nothing I'd wear, Anna, but you enjoy it." She dropped it on the table, changing the topic to outlet shopping.

Fiona began fussing, alerting us it was time for her bath and bed. Andrew and Andrina went to find her bubbles, leaving Tom and me alone at the table. An intelligent man full of droll remarks, Tom realized quickly that he and I shared a love of good books. I was thrilled to have him to myself, to discuss literature and its more infamous characters. Almost at once, he delved into *Krapp's Last Tape* by Samuel Beckett, a work I hadn't read.

"Krapp is a broken-down old man who does nothing but boast about his past," Tom explained. "He's absurd; his life was meaningless."

"Sounds like a French twist on Arthur Miller's *Death of a Salesman*. I'll read it and report next visit."

In time, I would realize that Tom had dropped a literary pearl in my lap.

Topping off his glass of wine, he nodded toward the bathroom and Andrew's lilting tenor. "Maybe he'll make a good grandfather, after all. He sure wasn't much of a father."

"Oh Tom, cut him some slack. Andrina and Drew turned their backs on him when he married Paula."

His head jerked up. "Who?"

Andrew appeared with Fiona, fresh from her bath, and passed her to me to read *Goodnight Moon*. Tom's *Who?* got lost. Until it boomeranged back a few weeks later.

Their holiday was somewhat awkward. Andrina kept me at arm's length, huddling with her father for hushed, serious conversations. Tom seemed restless, talked about being lonely and drank more wine than Andrina liked. Andrew routinely diverted conversation from his historic manse, his hit record and our wedding. I hid my disappointment and led them around the island like a cruise director.

For a farewell adventure, I chartered a Captiva fishing boat. We reeled in our quota of sea trout and grilled them that evening under the stars. After dinner, Andrew presented Andrina with a pair of diamond earrings made from her grandmother's brooch. She flushed and slipped them into her pocket. Dismissing her muted reaction, I regaled them with the story of her father finding the diamond brooch and my sapphire ring years before in his mother's flour tin.

Only Tom was amused.

Chapter 19

A few days after Andrina, Tom and Fiona departed, Andrew offered to pedal to *Rosie's Place* for sandwiches while I packed up for the long haul home. Hours later, he burst into the kitchen with two cold pastrami subs and an invitation to spend the summer at a cabin near Lake George.

"The owners are grand people, Anna," he assured me between bites. "We'll rent your house until Labor Day and next winter return to our honeymoon nest."

With some reservations, I left a deposit on Little Palm Cottage for the following year.

Andrew insisted we take the blue roads "to enjoy the rural sights" and we crawled along at a snail's pace. The second night, at a funky 1950s mom-and-pop motel in Natural Bridge, Virginia, he shook me awake.

"I dreamed of Paula," he cried. "Listen, Anna. She came to me wearing a luminous gold robe. Told me to obey the First Commandment, to remember her words and share them with others. Am I being called?"

I yawned. "If you want to study theology, do so, dear. Didn't I tell you souls connect through dreams? Perhaps you're more at peace now, more receptive."

In the morning, Andrew asked me to drive so he could record every detail of Paula's message. He wrote and erased, concentrated and wrote again, mile after mile. He read his notes to me repeatedly, each recitation more jubilant than the last.

"Be true to Anna. Love her with all your heart. Seek truth and forgiveness. Stay on the twelve dry stones for the rest of your life. One more challenge awaits but I will be there to lead you to safety."

When I asked how he felt about the challenge ahead, he replied, "She's released me to love you, darling. Why ruin it by talking about feelings?"

He amused himself for hundreds of miles retelling stories I once found fascinating: his lonely hospitalization for pneumonia after racing his grandfather's thoroughbred, Coronation Baby, to the finish; the award he received from the Duke of Edinburgh for founding the city's first soup kitchen; the shelters for battered women he funded. But one story was new - and startling. He suddenly became disappointed in Paula; she was sexually cold and neurotically hygienic.

Just like you, I thought.

On and on he droned, all the way to Chatham. I mentally cataloged every word.

The message machine's red light was blinking when we got home. I pressed *play* and a gravelly-voiced woman belted out *I Will Survive*. As I watched the color drain from Andrew's face, I wondered how he'd found time between his divorce and our marriage to break anyone's heart.

Chapter 20

May 15th was a glorious sunny day. Tender green shoots of spartina swayed in the sparkling saltwater pond across the street. Seagulls circled and swooped, dropping quahogs from the sky to crack on the tarmac below. Pink-and-white petals fell from festooning cherry trees, blanketing the freshly mowed lawn. Andrew left early, to place a bet at Suffolk Downs Race Track en route to Logan Airport. I cut flowers, filled vases and provisioned for the next British invasion.

Drew and Jill were a handful. They informed me they ate only the finest organically grown food and I gladly accommodated them for Andrew's sake. Jill resembled a young Audrey Hepburn and I worried about her race to the bathroom after each meal. Drew was a handsome, hearty bloke with a booming voice and an arrogant sexy swagger. I suspected they liked me well enough because I spoiled them.

Several days after their arrival, we celebrated Jill's 30th birthday. Andrew prepared a pyramid of poached salmon, asparagus and lemon grass infused with a complex sauce. I bought a three-layered coconut cake from Luscious Louie's, Chatham's emporium for serious foodies, and served it along with a silver box of diamond earrings. Drew chuckled as I retold the story of Andrew's great find in his mother's flour tin. Jill fixed the diamonds to her ears, leapt from the table and cooed into the mirror over the sideboard. What a contrast to Andrina's glum response.

Drew raised his glass. "Here's to you, Anna, the most generous woman we've ever met. Thank you for sharing my grandmother's diamonds." Pointing at his necktie, he reminded me of his November birthday.

I laughed, rising to refill his coffee cup. "A diamond tie tack it shall be, Drew."

Andrew was especially tender that night. He seemed genuinely grateful to be reunited with his son. A much-needed peace washed over me as I fell asleep in his arms.

Morning broke and the men left in high spirits for a round of golf at Chatham's Seaside Links. Jill and I lingered over a late breakfast, then spent the afternoon swimming at the health club. When we returned, I lit a small fire, brewed a pot of strong coffee and opened a box of shortbread cookies. We sat in yellow wing chairs alongside the fireplace in compatible warmth.

"You've made such a beautiful home for Andrew," Jill said, glancing up at the oil painting above the mantel. "That horse was his pride and joy. Drew said Andrew was so sure Selena's Dream would win that he had a suit custom-made to match the gray in her coat."

"Oh yes. I've heard all about it, many times. He even clipped bits from her mane to make sure the tailor got the right hue. Andrew hung the painting there soon after he moved in. And I'm sure Drew recognizes his father's equestrian prints, old brasses and silver stirrup cups in the dining room. Now we call it *The Stable*."

"You're so good to him." Jill smiled softly. "And you seem so comfortable and complete in yourselves. Drew says he's never seen his father so tranquil."

"We had our share of baggage to sift through," I told her. "Poor lamb suffered for years with nightmares and depression."

"I didn't know Andrew suffered from depression." She frowned. "Drew is never down. Neither is Andrina."

"Paula's death almost destroyed him."

Jill stiffened. Her hazel eyes widened. "Who is Paula?"

Time stopped. Icy fingers crept up and down my spine. I remembered the Sanibel dinner table, Tom's surprised *Who?*

"Really, Jill, this is absurd," I said evenly. "Paula Barnett was Andrew's second wife. She died skiing in Switzerland."

Her mouth opened but she said nothing, just shook her head in disbelief.

I stared back, waiting.

"I have never heard that name before this minute," she said at last. "And neither has Drew."

"That's impossible," I argued. "Completely impossible."

She met my frantic eyes with stony silence as Andrew and Drew called out from the kitchen door.

Jill startled.

I bolted to the bathroom.

Chapter 21

Death is public. It entails obituaries and funerals. How could Drew and Jill not have heard of Paula? The room spun.

Dry heaving over the bathroom sink, I caught a whiff of lime aftershave a split second before Andrew's reflection appeared in the mirror. "Jill said you were sick." His tone was menacing. "What's brought this on, Anna?"

I raised my palm, bent my head toward the steam rising from the running faucet. "Too much excitement," I mumbled, "too much rich food."

"You're well enough to go out, aren't you? This is their last night."

"Of course," I assured him. "I'm looking forward to the film. I'll order something light at the café. Just give me a minute. Please."

Muttering "Can't live with'em and can't live without'em," he took care to close the door quietly when he left.

Children raised in troubled homes learn to stuff reality into invisible brain boxes, to pretend all's well. I became adept at disassociating from terror at an early age, when my father flew into furious fits and my mother retreated into impenetrable silence. Faced with a long night ahead, I resolved to act as if nothing unusual had happened.

In a trance, I brushed my teeth, blushed my ghostly cheeks and glossed my lips. Still woozy, I grabbed a bottle of perfume and inhaled its familiar fragrance. If Andrew had lied about Paula, then I was the naïve victim of some depraved scheme. I prayed for a logical explanation but reality bested hope. I was in terrible trouble.

In the living room, Andrew and Drew swung invisible golf clubs, boasting about their drives to Jill, who was engaged and composed.

Andrew swanned across the room and pecked my cheek. "We're having a little party, darling. What would you like?"

"Cola, no ice, dear. I'm still queasy after such a... stimulating day." I glanced at Jill, hoping for a flicker of compassion. None.

She held up *The New Yorker*. "*Monsoon Wedding* has great reviews here. It would never fly in Britain, not since the bloody Pakis took over."

"Would you rather not go?" I asked.

"Of course we'll go, Anna," she replied. "It's only a couple of hours and it'll be interesting to see that Cape Cinema you rave about."

THE DARK THEATER gave me a break from their superficial chatter and a chance to think. I knew Andrew was planning to spend the next afternoon at Suffolk Downs, after dropping Drew and Jill off at Boston's South Station to catch the train to New York. I'd have hours to unpack the bulging briefcase he kept in his closet. It had always piqued my curiosity.

Jill and Drew didn't like the film or the menu; they whispered through the movie and picked at their food with noblesse oblige. Andrew engaged Drew in lively conversation about the stock market, another inconsistency; he'd professed complete ignorance of it to my trust officer the week before. I was floored by their references to my trust fund's investments, and by Drew's offer to take over my portfolio, to increase its annual yield.

No one seemed to sense that I was a ticking time bomb.

Chapter 22

Fog and drizzle matched my mood the next morning as I jollied them into the car, silently bade them all sweet good riddance and bolted to Cumberland Farms for the first pack of cigarettes I'd bought in more than a year. Finally alone, I reheated my coffee, sank into Andrew's favorite wicker chair in the kitchen and lit a Marlboro, something I'd do thousands of times in the long months ahead. Through the window, I stared at the gnarled roots and anthropomorphic shapes of the old guardian tree, planted generations ago to ward off evil spirits. It had let me down.

Shivering, I stood, then stumbled through the living room into our bedroom, opened the closet and looked up at Andrew's worn brown leather briefcase. As I reached for it, knowing its contents would change my life, a jolt of thrilling revulsion shot through me. It burst open, showering dozens of photographs to the floor.

A twenty-something woman with long black hair and a Louis Vuitton bag smiled at two little girls in Easter bonnets. A busty ponytailed blond in striped pajamas showed off an ornately decorated Christmas tree. A mahogany tanned woman with a sagging midriff and cornrows leaned against the Sanibel Lighthouse. Was she the gravelly voiced diva who *Will Survive*?

A series of 5x7 photos showcased a topless redhead with pendulous breasts posing on a rumpled bed in a lacy black garter belt and fishnet stockings. Her painted wrinkled face and wistful smile made me sad, then enraged. Printed internet pages of vaginas spread apart by someone with a French manicure made my flesh crawl.

The memory of our first night together flashed before me. His voice had actually trembled when he confessed, "I'm a verra inexperienced man, darling. Please be gentle."

His innocence had moved me. I'd kissed his tears in the dark, assuring him that after years of celibacy he was simply out of practice.

Hatred for him and disgust with myself whipped me into a rampage. I carried the sordid pile into the living room and dumped it on the sofa. My choirboy was a porno freak.

A letter from the owners of the Highclere Hotel caught my eye. It was a lukewarm job referral for Grace and Andrew Macdade, who'd co-managed the place. Andrew had never owned it. And his manager's salary wouldn't have financed a half-million pound house in Sunninghill.

Another letter, addressed to Mr. and Mrs. Andrew Macdade, was signed by the administrative assistant to the Royal House of Jordan. "Dear Grace and Andrew: I regret to inform you that the managers' positions cannot be offered to you at this time."

He'd never served Queen Noor, never walked the beach in Aqaba with President Bush, never procured pheasant from Harrod's for him. He didn't swim in the Dead Sea, wasn't cut and poisoned on its coral reefs, hadn't been given top security clearance or signed the Official Secret Acts Document. The gaps in his stories weren't because he'd been sworn to secrecy. He wasn't there. He and *Grace* didn't get the job.

Morgan said Andrew's first wife was Laura. Who is Grace? Who are the little girls in bonnets? How many secret wives and children does he have?

Tucked into a fold in the briefcase was a faded 3x5 of Paula's gravestone. "In Ever Loving Memory: Paula Barnett OBE, Professor of Medicine, Died October 2, 1989, Aged 42. To Live in the Hearts of those we Love is not to Die."

I'd seen that quote meticulously printed under P in his address book. Acting on instinct, I hid the photo behind a framed portrait of my grandmother.

Glamorous photos labeled *Paula* looked like publicity shots from a model's portfolio. She posed under cascading fountains in designer bathing suits and sported foul-weather gear on a yacht. In one close-up, she showed off a lacy white Victorian costume, complete with parasol. There were no letters to her or from her, no photographs of them together.

Snapshots of the interior and exterior of my house had been taken only recently, his equestrian prints and stirrup cups prominently displayed in the dining room. Andrew Macdade had married into a fine piece of real estate.

And I had married a stranger.

Chapter 23

A honk from the driveway reminded me of Mount Holyoke's alumnae luncheon. Edith Troy had arrived to pick me up. A psychology professor at Cape Cod Community College, she liked Andrew. And so did her husband. "Anna," she called from the kitchen door, "we're going to be late."

Still in baggy blue sweats and reeking of cigarettes, I threw open the screen door and pulled her in. "You're not going to believe this, Edith."

She stared at the pile on the sofa in silence for a few moments before her outraged eyes met mine. "He's a con artist, Anna. You've got to get out of here. Pack a bag. Stay in our guest cottage until you get rid of him."

"I'm not leaving my own house. I'll face him. Back him into a corner. Make him explain."

"I don't like this," she said uneasily. "Aren't you afraid?"

"Yes. Afraid I've married a nut case. I'm going to get inside his crazy head."

"I'm telling you, he's going to be enraged," she warned. "Promise me you'll come to us after you confront him."

I promised.

Piece by piece, I carried the evidence into the dining room and arranged it carefully on the polished table that once showcased Andrew's gourmet feasts. Now it seemed like a mortician's slab.

When I finished, I stood under the hot shower until the water ran cold, its pulsating spray doing little for my injured pride. Makeup and clean clothes didn't help either. Regret overwhelmed me. He had deceived me and every friend I had. Except Marta.

The telephone rang. Andrew, prompt and considerate as always, was on the line. "Hello, heartsweet. I've just crossed the Sagamore Bridge and will be along in about thirty minutes."

"Yes, Andrew."

"You sound upset."

"I am."

"Is it one of the children?"

"No."

"Have I done something?"

"No, Andrew. You've done quite a few things." I hung up without waiting for a response.

Peering out the dining room window, I wept at the futility of it all. My station wagon crawled up the driveway like a hearse and I knew precisely what Emily Dickinson meant when she wrote, "I felt a funeral in my brain."

Chapter 24

Andrew rested his head on the steering wheel for a minute before he switched off the ignition. Rumpus bolted through the kitchen door and out to the car. I lagged behind, counting the cracks in the brick walkway. By the time I reached the driveway, Andrew was leaning against the station wagon, staring at the sunset over Gull Pond.

Something beyond reason moved me closer to him. "Magical, isn't it?" I said, my voice breaking. "Sad, too. This is where we stood, cherishing the same view, the evening you proposed."

"What's stirred you up this time, Anna? You couldn't wait to get home and now you're a wreck. Everything was fine this morning. Can't I go off for a few hours without you…"

"Your briefcase, Andrew. I went through it."

He stiffened. "It was locked."

"No, it wasn't."

He spun me around to face him. "How did you get the combination?"

I wriggled free of his grip. "I pulled it down and it burst open. I wanted to know why your kids have never heard of Paula ."

His eyes glinted. "What did Jill say to put you in such a flap?"

"She's never heard Paula's name. And Tom nearly choked when I suggested your children shouldn't have turned their backs when you married her."

"I told you their mother turned them against Paula. They refused to meet her."

I glared and headed inside.

Meekly, he followed me into the dining room, exhaling at the sight of his photographs, papers and pornography spread out on the table. "Who else knows about your little snoop-fest, darling?" he asked lightly.

"Edith. She came to collect me for the Mount Holyoke luncheon and found me nearly hysterical."

He winced.

"You lied to me from the moment we met, Andrew," I said, pointing. "Who the hell is Grace?"

"I should've pitched this stuff," he mumbled.

"What?"

"We came together too fast. I didn't have time to get rid of it."

"Time? You didn't have time to marry Paula, to live with her in a half-million pound house next to a hotel that you and your wife Grace managed, not owned."

Pointing to the odalisque cupping her breasts, I hissed, "She has nothing to do with time. Who's this secret?"

"Sheila," he groaned. "Pictures her toy-boy took before we were married, or maybe after. Sweet Jesus, Anna. How dare you rummage through my tattered life."

"How dare you bring this filth into my house," I screamed. "You're a pervert."

He snorted. "I am not. I was going to use those pictures against Sheila if she caused trouble."

"You were going to blackmail a demented woman whose mother just died?"

"She's vicious. Accused me of the unthinkable. Kicked me out when she caught me sponging her mother's corpse. I planned ahead to protect us."

Visions of him spoon-feeding the old lady flashed before my eyes.

"I trusted you, Anna. More than I've ever trusted anyone. In time, I would have told you everything. But I had to get you to love me first, so I could have you, darling."

"And I swallowed your pathetic widower's story. When I opened your briefcase, I expected to find remnants of your life with Paula, photos of you together, love letters, an obituary. Instead, I found cheesy pin-ups of Sheila, a never-before-mentioned wife, Grace, and a young mother with two little girls in bonnets. Who is she, Andrew?"

He clutched his chest and collapsed into his chair at the head of the table. "Please, darling. I think I'm having a heart attack."

"Then have one, damn you. How could you lie about being widowed?"

"I was widowed. Paula is buried behind the kirk in Sunninghill. I have a picture somewhere in this pile to prove it."

I froze, watching him search for the faded Kodachrome I'd hidden, relieved when he threw the stack down.

"So you combined your years with Grace and Paula?"

"Aye. Paula died on our first anniversary, not our third."

I waved the letter from Jordan's royal administrator under his chin. "And the years in Aqaba were fairy tales."

"I went over after that letter was written, once things calmed down in the Mid-East."

"But you weren't ducking bombs, waiting for the king's helicopters to swoop in and save you, when the Gulf War began."

Nothing seemed real. Except the perverse pleasure I felt watching him squirm. I scowled. "Tell me about Grace."

Blubbering, he swore upon his mother's grave to tell the truth. Grace, he said, was his second wife, a mistake he made after Laura.

"Nice kids you have, Andrew. They never once mentioned her." A surge of fury seized me. "Where does she work?"

He flicked the tip of his tongue back and forth over his lips. "Drew felt sorry for her and gave her a receptionist's job."

"And if Kate had gone to his office with our wedding pictures, she'd have met Grace head-on."

"If you want the truth, Anna, you'll get it, by God. Then, with my luck, you'll kick me out, replace me with another."

"A novel idea, Watson. Start talking."

"I had to have you, Anna. You're the woman I adore, my earth angel…"

"I know the song. And you didn't write it."

"I'd sooner die, but I'll walk away if that's what you want."

"Not before you tell me about Paula, you won't. From the beginning."

He launched into another convoluted account of meeting Paula. In this version, he didn't stumble upon the emerald-eyed Grace Kelly look-alike in London Clinic's car park.

"Paula was my childhood sweetheart, the crème de la crème of Lady Erskine's School for Girls. When I went to London, she followed and entered Oxford's medical school. A year later, my father's lungs went brittle; my mother summoned me home to run the Ravelston."

"And Paula stayed behind, trusting you'd return?"

"I had promised to marry her after graduation. I'm a one-woman man, Anna. I remained faithful. Until New Year's Eve, when Laura got me drunk."

"Got you drunk? Forced it down your throat, did she?"

"This is where it gets bad, darling. Should I continue?"

"It got bad a long time ago, Andrew. Keep talking."

"It was just a quick shag in the hotel's wine cellar. But she got pregnant. Who knows if I was the father? I married her on April Fool's Day, thinking I'd lost Paula forever."

He glanced at my stricken face and continued through muffled sobs. "*Concrete and Clay* was climbing the London charts and there I was, running the Ravelston, about to become a father. It was the end of my music career and the end of Paula. I wrote and told her. Andrina was a good baby and I accepted her as my own. Then Drew came along. Laura had her kids, got a house and dumped me for another after twenty-three years."

Nodding gravely, I berated myself for allowing such a rat into my life. "What happened next?"

"After my mother died, I found twenty-three dress shirts wrapped and tucked in her hall closet, all from Paula, each with a birthday card with the same verse: 'If it takes forever, I will wait for you.'"

Exasperated, I hummed a few bars of the popular '50s song. "How romantic. One for each year you were married to Laura." I wondered if that was the day he found the diamond brooch and sapphire ring in the flour tin. "Why no pictures of you and Paula together?"

"How many times do I need to say it? I left those things in Sunninghill. When Paula was in medical school, she modeled part-time to buy textbooks. I kept a few glamour shots."

He rambled on while I scribbled. *Laura, Grace, Paula, Sheila...*

"If Paula was your third wife, I'm your fifth. Yet you signed our application for a marriage license saying I was the fourth. You swore to it."

"Stop, Anna. I'm sick and lost. I need help, not contempt."

I wasn't finished with him. Not even close. "Maybe we're not legally married," I said happily. "And the will my attorney crafted to provide you with a comfy old age isn't worth the paper it's printed on."

He gasped. "I'm not after your money."

And he was not going to get it, I resolved. "I should call my lawyer anyway," I said. "Find out whether I'm married or not."

"No attorneys. We'll figure this out ourselves."

"But you two got along famously. He's still waiting to see King George's tin cup and that photo of him drinking tea with your grandfather."

Silently, I vowed to match wits with Andrew from that moment on. Neither his greed nor his madness would diminish my lifestyle. And he wouldn't see a dime of my children's inheritance. "Rupert's a dear," I said sweetly. "What are you afraid of?"

"Nothing. But if you bring on the lawyers, I'll leave now."

"Then I'll go on-line for answers," I lied. His expression relaxed as I maneuvered the discussion back to Paula. "Where was Dr. Barnett when you discovered those shirts?"

"At the Peak Hospital in Hong Kong," he said proudly. "The day I found out about Laura's affair, I popped into a pub and ran into Paula's brother. He told me, man-to-man, that his sister had never gotten over me. I hopped a British Airways flight the next day."

"To Hong Kong?"

"Aye, flew first class," he said, massaging the bump on his head. "Thanks to BA's policy of upgrading injured vets. Paula was cool toward me at first, but since I knew she'd never stopped loving me, I…"

"So twenty-three years later, she was still waiting?"

"Not exactly," he said. "She blew hot and cold, one day promising to marry me, the next punishing me, worried that she'd missed her chance to have children. After five weeks, she asked me to leave. My heart was shattered but I felt I got what I deserved. I went back to Edinburgh a broken man."

"Let me guess; you met Grace and she fell for your *poor me* routine."

"True. If Grace hadn't gotten me a job at the Royal Hotel, where she managed housekeeping, I would've packed up my guitar and tried…"

"Why didn't you work at the Ravelston?"

"My brother sold it after my father died. Swindled me out of my share."

Andrew was making a fool of himself. I wanted to keep him talking. "How long did you and Grace work at the Royal Hotel?" I asked.

"Not long," he said. "A few months after I started, a bloke came 'round scouting for a stable married couple to be live-in managers of the Highclere. Paula had left the Peak by then and had taken up her former post at the London Clinic; it was my last chance to have her. I convinced Grace to marry me so we could get the job. She was an orphan, had no one but a famous half-brother in Sydney. She needed me to look after her."

"Who is her famous brother, Andrew?"

"Jethro Tull."

"The hillbilly in that '70s TV show?"

"No, Anna. He's a musician, plays the flute in a band. His real name is Ian Anderson. I met him once with Grace after he performed at the Palladium."

I stared at him over my granny glasses, then added yet another name to the list. "Where were you and Grace married?"

"At the Edinburgh registry. A cold affair like the first, with Laura."

"And even though it was a business arrangement, you lived as husband and wife."

"It wasn't admirable of me; I loved Paula. But I was a slave to my hormones before I stopped drinking."

"Was Grace happy with you?"

"Not particularly. She ran off most weekends with her little friend." He winked. "Judy."

I pantomimed horror. "A lesbian, Andrew?"

He nodded. "Rumor had it she was engaged once but no one I knew had ever met him. What could I think? I've respected you. You're a verra straight-laced lady. I didn't want to subject you to such things, darling. But now that you know everything, I'm relieved."

He struck a match, torched the picture of the young mother and her two little girls and tossed it into the fireplace, visibly pleased when the kindling burst into flames. Sucking in the smoke, he asked, "How 'bout a cuppa before I take you out to dinner?"

Tongue-tied, I cursed myself. I should have hired a detective.

Chapter 25

Andrew bustled in from the kitchen with our Sanibel mugs and a pot of tea, his smug expression telling me he thought he was off the hook.

"What about Paula?" I asked wearily. "When did you next see her?"

Once again, he took his seat at the head of the table. "I tracked her down a month or so after I arrived at the Highclere, told her I'd taken the position to be near her and invited her to lunch. In time, she forgave me and we bought the house next door."

"Just like that? Poor Grace."

"Remember, darling, it was a deal we made to get the jobs. Actually, Grace was quite relieved to be rid of me. We split our savings and she took off for Durban with her girlfriend. Happy as a lark, she was, until she ran out of funds and came back, begging Drew for work."

"When did you marry Paula?"

"1988. In Edinburgh, at Duddingston Kirk."

His words were stilted, as if he'd rehearsed them.

"Why weren't your children there?"

"I told you. Their mother turned them against me. And besides, Paula didn't want them around; they reminded her that I'd deprived her of having her own. We set the date to coincide with Andrina's walk-about in Australia and Drew's internship at Goldman Sachs in New York."

"And did you really honeymoon in Tenerife with Paula or was it with Grace?"

"Both. It suited Grace well enough, so I took Paula." He flashed an unconvincing grin. "You sound like a KGB agent. Next, you'll shove splinters under my fingernails."

"How could you afford a house next to the hotel on a manager's salary?" I asked.

"Paula bought it. I said I owned it, and the hotel, to impress you."

"Were you happy together?"

"After the first blush, it became a rather empty marriage. She had little time for me, except for an occasional cruise down the Thames on the *Hey Paula*."

I laughed, unable to keep a straight face remembering the '60s hit.

Andrew took my hand in his. "Wish she'd been more like you, my little homebody. But she worried obsessively about her patients. I watched her read, review gory medical videos and sleep. How romantic was that?"

He paused as if he expected an answer and then shrugged. "After the funeral, I stayed drunk for weeks before I managed to pull myself together for the interview in Amman. They liked me, my references cleared and I went over for eighteen months, not three years."

"That doesn't explain why there isn't even a letter from Paula, or a picture of you two together."

"I've already explained."

"Right, Heathcliff. You hid her things at the Highclere. Is her obituary there, too?"

"It's all there, Anna, just like I said. Her professional accomplishments were vast. So vast that the *Times* gave her a half-page."

"Did she leave the house to you?"

"Of course she did. I was her husband. Just like I'm yours, my love."

My eyes fell on the fire, where all traces of the slender woman standing next to her two little girls had vanished. "Who was the woman in the photo you burned?"

"A single mother who lived in the apartment next to mine in Philadelphia. I felt sorry for her, looked after her girls on my nights off while she took medical shorthand classes. When I realized she was trolling the bars, I had nothing further to do with her."

He was married to a doctor, a pharmacist, and most likely the young stenographer. He must have a predilection for women in the medical profession.

"What's her name, Andrew?"

"She used me," he whined. "Everyone always takes advantage of me. Except you. Please, Anna, I'll burn this rubbish and we'll move forward."

"I want her name, Andrew."

"Debbie, or maybe Denise. I can't remember."

"I'm waiting, Andrew."

"Darby." He grinned crookedly. "She called herself Darby."

"Darby what?"

"Darby Hamilton."

"Where is she now?"

"In Michigan. With her parents, I think."

"Did you know her when you worked for the Taubmans?"

He shook his head. "I didn't meet her until I took the position in Philly. She was just a kid who lived next door."

"You said you lived with the Bayleys."

"I did. I had quarters above the garage. They sprang for a townhouse while their painter took his time doing the dump over."

"Oh." I wondered what Laura, Grace, Paula, Darby, Sheila and I had ever done to deserve him. Rising from the table, I told him Frank and Edith Troy were expecting me.

He leapt from his chair. "The secrets were killing me, Anna. I probably left my briefcase open, hoping you'd catch me and help me. I wanted to tell you everything but I was scared you wouldn't want me."

I paused just long enough to drop the internet pornography on his lap before walking out the door. "I'm not sure I do."

Chapter 26

As I sped along Route 6A, I thought of all the thrillers about gigolos and con artists who burrow into their victims' hearts. But no book or movie had prepared me for Andrew's deceit. I had believed what I wanted to believe, had seen what I wanted to see, to fuel my romantic dreams about him and Scotland. Moaning useless "what ifs" one minute and hurling bitter threats the next, I numbly pulled into the Troys' long winding driveway.

Nestled in a copse of scrub pines alongside the main house, the guest cottage had always reminded me of a Kincaid home-sweet-home painting. I pushed against the swollen door, glanced at the potted geraniums on a bureau and locked myself in for the night, grateful for Frank and Edith's hospitality. I fell into bed, snuggled under the quilt and dropped into a fitful sleep.

At first light, panic-stricken, I focused on a knot in the pine paneling and breathed deeply. Had I overreacted? Should I have stayed home? Had he killed himself during the night? Or called a taxi and skipped town with my credit cards? I lay frozen until anxiety pulled me under. Moments later I came to, cold and clammy, and curled into a fetal position as the horror of it all returned. I knew women had endured betrayal since the beginning of time. But I wasn't one of them.

Certain that he'd demand a hefty sum in any divorce proceeding, I pictured him casting himself as a contrite foreigner who'd been pressed into retirement to caretake his wife's property and to indulge her whims to travel.

I slid out of bed and spied Edith's note taped to a jar of instant coffee on the kitchen counter. *Come for breakfast.* Mortified, I took the old copper kettle from the stovetop, SOSed it to its original luster, filled it, lit the gas burner and waited for its whistle.

A dusty laptop on the desk actually worked and I went on-line to e-mail my attorney, Rupert Kendall. I told him every last detail about the undisclosed marriages and the phony employment history. "I'm shaken, Rupert. I should have listened to you, should have insisted on a prenuptial agreement. The thought of Andrew Macdade walking away with a share of my assets makes me sick. My children would never forgive me. Extricate him from my life. Please."

The kettle whistled as I finished and I filled a Mount Holyoke mug. Cupping my icy hands around it, I mourned the inevitable end of my marriage and wondered how I'd break the news to my children. James would fly home, physically remove Andrew from the premises and probably get arrested for assault and battery. Sally would descend from the mountains of Colorado to protect me, a responsibility she didn't need.

And what would I tell my friends? I'd be Chatham's laughingstock.

My thoughts were interrupted by a ding from the laptop announcing an incoming message. My good friend Rupert had wasted no time in responding. "An annulment is your best bet, Anna. Since you've only been married a few months, I believe the court will grant one, particularly if Andrew agrees to it. We don't want him to seek counsel, so don't say anything to alarm him. Maintain the status quo for now, and see me as soon as possible."

"Maintain the status quo," I said aloud. "I can do that."

I marched across the lawn to face Edith, Frank and whatever breakfast I could swallow. They opened the door before I knocked, wearing flannel bathrobes and worried faces.

"How was the showdown?" Edith asked as she filled three juice glasses. "What did Andrew have to say for himself?"

Detached, I heard myself repeat every sordid detail in a hollow voice. It wasn't necessary, or even appropriate, but I had to say it in order to believe it. They listened, wide-eyed, nodding sympathetically, until I asked Edith if she would recommend a counselor.

She glanced at her husband's alarmed expression. "Anna, do you really want to pour money and effort into someone who conned you into marriage?"

"No. But my attorney says I should maintain the status quo for now, and a therapist might help."

My hosts looked uneasy.

"I just e-mailed him," I added, nodding toward the cottage, "using your laptop. I'll see him before we leave for Lake George."

Edith paused, her glass midair. "Jesus, you're not still going to that isolated cabin?"

"I have no choice. My house is rented for the summer."

After another glance at her husband, Edith asked, "Does Andrew have access to your money?"

"I added his name to my checking account about a month after he moved in." I winced, adding lamely, "He offered to pay the bills."

"Can he get his mitts on larger sums?"

"No. Everything else is beyond his reach."

This information seemed to do little to allay their concerns. After a tense silence, Edith said, "Frank thinks he's a compulsive gambler."

"I'm sorry, Anna," Frank said sadly, "but I think at some point you'll find unexplained withdrawals from your account. Gamblers play the odds. Stealing and lying are part of the thrill."

I scoffed, reminding them that Andrew had mucked stalls and groomed his grandfather's trotters since he was a boy. "Racing is in his blood. He knows breeding, form, and fetlocks the way we know boats and nautical charts. It's not the gambling that attracts him, Frank. It's all that horse flesh and the stories swapped with jockeys and trainers. Besides, it gets him out of my hair once a week."

"Be careful," Edith warned. "If I were you, I'd kick him out today. Is he home waiting for you?"

"Who knows? I humiliated him by coming here."

"Andrew seemed so honorable, an old-world gentleman, a perfect companion," Edith said. "But Frank and I aren't entirely surprised. You always see the best in people. Unfortunately, that trait attracts predators."

"What can I say? Another foolish woman got what she deserved."

"Don't be so hard on yourself. He's a smooth operator. He fooled all of us. Just watch your back and guard your money."

"I trusted him," I said as I stood. "That's what hurts most."

When I reluctantly left, they waved me off with half-hearted smiles.

I crept along scenic Route 6A, remembering how perfectly matched Andrew and I had once seemed. Passing our favorite restaurants, antique shops and art galleries, I wept irrationally. I still cared for the man he'd pretended to be.

Chapter 27

From the front yard, I studied him through the living room window. Strikingly handsome in a brown tattersall shirt, burgundy knit tie and chinos, he sat on the edge of the couch facing the fireplace, hands folded loosely on his lap. He looked like a hotel guest waiting to check in. Or maybe out.

I rapped on the window. He started, leapt up and dashed for the kitchen door. "Darling, you're home," he cried, wrapping his arms around me. "I couldn't face going to church alone but I walked the dog and lit a fire for you."

He patted my bottom and nibbled my lips. His breath was odorless; without the familiar scent of Royal Lime, he could have been anyone. He has no smell of his own, I realized for the first time, no earthy maleness.

I inched away from his embrace and tried to lift his chin so his eyes would meet mine, to no avail. "Smothering me with kisses isn't going to fix anything, Andrew."

He grabbed a spiral notebook from the telephone table and presented it with a flourish. "My true life story is right here," he said, looking quite pleased with himself. "And I burned all those pictures that made you so unhappy, heartsweet.

You shouldn't have seen such things. I'm sorry I brought them into your home."

He paced in circles, glancing at his watch like Alice's white rabbit. "Now I'm no tattletale, but since we have no more secrets I can tell you that those vile internet photographs belonged to Mr. Bayley. He was always on the prowl. Did I tell you his wife called him 'Pussycat?'"

"No, Andrew. And I don't want to hear it now. Leave the poor old man out of this." Tapping the notebook, I asked, "Was it hard for you to write?"

"Aye, but I did it for us."

A pale blue envelope from London's Dorchester Hotel fell out, my name written on it in black curlicues. Wondering who footed the bill, I asked if he'd enjoyed the hotel's amenities.

"Paula and I stayed there after we saw *Phantom of the Opera* a month before she died. Oh, you're frowning. Nothing I do is right. I only wanted to write on fine stationery. Just read the letter. Please."

My Darling Anna,

I am dreaming about our love tonight. For the first time in my life I feel secure – in your love, our bond.

As I hope to live forever with you, you must know what happened in my life. In the beginning, nothing came out clearly. Only two people ever knew what you are about to read and one is now gone.

Please forgive me. More than anything, I want to wake up in your arms on Christmas morning, as Christmas won't be Christmas unless I spend it with you.

I will love you eternally.

Andrew XX

Wee-witted soul makes no sense, I thought sadly. "It's May, Andrew. Is this from the Christmas song you wrote for Rod Stewart a few years back?"

"Aye. I thought it was a nice touch."

"And Paula is the person now gone?"

"Of course. Speaking of her, I couldn't find the photo of her gravestone. It was in a side pocket of my briefcase. Did you see it?"

"No, Andrew." I kept my head down as I flipped through his notebook, finding no reference to a wedding at Dudddingston Kirk. "Where exactly were you and Paula married," I asked, looking up. "The truth, this time."

"It was a cold, impersonal ceremony at a London Registry. We went alone. Her parents loathed me and my kids were upset."

"Where were they when Paula died?"

"Andrina was in New York on business. Drew was training in Germany; his water polo team made it to the Olympics that year."

I mentally gave his tall tale an F. Either he was slipping or I was getting better at culling fact from fiction. "Did Paula really break her neck skiing?"

"Aye. Just a year after I got my girl to the altar, she was taken from me. We never had a chance; everything and everyone was against us. Now you know why I thrash all night, crying for her."

"I insist on a psychiatrist, Andrew. I've asked Edith for a referral. Either we go or you pack your bags."

"But we leave for Lake George in a month, darling. How can I start psychoanalysis and stop midstream? I'll be frustrated, sicker than I am now. Can I start when we come home in September?"

Taken aback, I agreed, and immediately regretted it.

His eyes gleamed. He believed himself masterful. "I want to be your husband and move forward without Paula's ghost. I can be a better person with your help. You'll give me a second chance?"

"If you stop lying, Andrew. But I assure you more questions are coming."

"Fire away, Anna Banana. I'm an open book." He laughed, throwing a log on the fire.

Relieved that he agreed to counseling, I suggested we give Rumpus a run on the beach.

He rushed off to collect the leash and biscuits from the mudroom but returned empty-handed and picked up the remote. "I just remembered. I have a wee bet placed on the race. Would you mind if we go later?"

"No. I'll make lunch and we'll watch it together. I didn't know we had the sports channel. Did you order it?"

"Some time ago. Do you mind, darling?"

"Not a-tall, Andrew. But if there's a race next weekend, be prepared to miss it. You promised to take me to Mount

Holyoke's commencement. And I have a big surprise planned for you."

"Hang it, Anna. I can't get the house ready for tenants and fritter away my time with people I've never met. What's the surprise?"

"Queen Noor is the keynote speaker," I announced. "And my friend, Ruth, is organizing her schedule. Write a letter; Ruth will deliver it personally and you'll have an audience with your favorite royal."

His face went slack. "You arranged all this without asking me first?"

"Small world, isn't it?"

I laughed, placing my own wee bet on the odds that Queen Noor had no idea he existed.

"Well, now…" He grinned sickly. "Next weekend, is it?"

Chapter 28

Don't forget I'm your best boy," Andrew called, pulling a long face as I hopped into my station wagon. Eager to take off for Monday morning's yoga class, I impatiently adjusted the seat and rearview mirror, peeved that he didn't want a car of his own.

He whistled.

I poked my head out the window. "What?"

"Since you planned a big surprise for me, I have one lined up for you. It'll be waiting when you get home." He ruffled Rumpus's thick coat and headed toward the tool shed.

Dismissing him with a wave, I drove off brooding over the Troys' warning to watch my back.

Chanting "Om" during the ten-minute drive across town calmed my nerves and allayed my fear of falling apart in class. "Breathe," I whispered as I parked. Plastering a serene smile on my face, I slipped into the hushed, eucalyptus-scented room, bowed *Namaste* to each yogi, then eased into a seated lotus position. The candle's flame helped me to focus and eventually, to surrender mind and body to the ancient discipline of being present.

When I got home a few hours later, Andrew was flat on his back, motionless, next to a towering pile of brush.

Screaming his name, I ran across the lawn and dropped to my knees to palpate his neck for a pulse.

"Gotcha!" He shot up and pointed proudly to butchered stumps and ripped-out roots. "Now we can see Gull Pond better, darling."

"It looks like a bomb site," I hissed. "You've chopped down fifty years of growth. On my neighbors' property."

"But, dearest, it was an eyesore."

"Not to anyone who cares about wildlife. I've warned you. Everything beyond their red markers is off-limits."

The retired general next door was a loose cannon. He habitually patrolled the estate's mishmash of subdivided plots and irregular property lines with his fisheyed wife. I'd earned a modicum of respect from them only after I bailed out his sinking sailboat during one of their trips to the commissary. Even so, he'd kept me mindful of the boundaries and wary of his wrath for years.

"He won't know," Andrew said. "It's too far from their house."

"You see those little black boxes on their roof? Surveillance cameras, you fool."

"But look at the view, Anna." He swept his arms toward the pond. "I've increased your property value by a hundred K, maybe two. We'll sell it for ten times what you paid, then buy a spread in Vermont."

I reeled. "Vermont? You told me you love Chatham."

"I do. We would have lived here forever if you hadn't aired our private affairs." He stroked my cheek. "I'll be my own man up there, have a small holding, grow vegetables and board horses. We'll make a fresh start in a new place."

"The only new place we're going to see is the inside of a courthouse, when the general has you arrested and sues me."

"I've been clipping that stuff since last fall. He never noticed."

"Pruning is one thing, Andrew. Hacking down a thicket full of birds' nests is another."

"Those rubbishy vines were choking that old hornbeam," he argued.

"It's not my tree and it's none of your business."

At that moment, General Granger stepped out from behind the hornbeam. I approached him, my hand extended, hoping for clemency. "I'm so sorry…"

"Not sorry enough, Anna Wells." He charged past, waving a roll of orange surveyors' tape in my face. "I'll get you and that smirking foreigner."

I looked around for Andrew. He'd disappeared.

The general's wife stumbled through the bushes, clutching a bundle of wooden stakes and a video camera. Dropping the stakes, she aimed the camera at me and demanded a check for seven thousand dollars.

Speechless, I froze as a cruiser pulled into my driveway and two red-faced uniformed officers chugged across the lawn. To the Grangers' smug satisfaction, one handed me a no-trespass order.

My offer to hire a professional landscaper to repair the damage was met with contempt and sly grins as the general and his wife cordoned off the site with the orange tape. Frantic, I looked again for Andrew. He was in the driveway tossing sticks for Rumpus. When the telephone rang, he sprinted inside.

The officers exchanged knowing looks and one gently advised that I should notify my insurance agent and retain legal counsel.

Mrs. Granger sniggered as the cruiser rolled down the driveway. The general flung Andrew's muddy work gloves from the pile of brush while his wife filmed: my house, my lawn, me and the rubble. The fragile tolerance we'd achieved was shattered. After casting a bitter look at them and their yards of day-glow plastic tape, I stormed into the kitchen.

"That was my Edinburgh solicitor, Mr. Bryce," Andrew said gravely, cradling the telephone against his chest before hanging up. "Mrs. Bayley is dead. A fatal stroke last evening while in flight from Barbados. Her memorial service is this Sunday. I'm expected to attend." He spoke with the brevity of the bereaved.

"I'm sorry. I know you were fond of her. But you left me out there to fend for myself. Why did you desert me?"

"It's your property. And your neighbors have treated me like hired help since I took over your dirty work. Not an ounce of respect. Besides, I'm a guest in your country. The last thing I need is trouble with the law. Forgive me, darling, but when the phone rang I bolted."

"You bolted long before it rang." I was appalled by his cowardice. "And why would you be expected to attend a high-society service?"

"Mrs. Bayley left written instructions," he said, shooting a balled paper towel into the wastepaper basket. "We were like mother and son. Mr. Bayley respected her wishes and tracked me down through Mr. Bryce."

"How would Mr. Bayley go about contacting your solicitor?"

"He must have phoned Claudette Colbert's secretary. Mrs. Bailey paired us up every time they came to visit." He grinned, subtracting ten years from his mud-streaked face. "Her solicitor and mine have the same surname. See?"

"No I don't, Andrew," I said, suspecting I'd find the woman's name in his little black book. I offered to drop him off at the bus station on my way to Mount Holyoke.

"Dandy plan, Anna. I'd only be in your way at commencement with all those lesbians hovering around."

I recoiled. "What are you talking about?"

"Thanks to Grace, I learned all about those women. Pegged your girlfriends for dykes the minute I saw their pictures."

I felt certain that Grace's take on that subject would be quite different.

"Your own son told me he was relieved when I came along. Said there hadn't been a man 'round here since you went off to that girls' school."

"If you'd rather rendezvous with Miss Colbert's secretary than see your beloved queen, say so, Andrew. But this kind of talk is beneath you."

"Pestering Her Majesty for an audience was a brash American idea, my love. It's simply not done."

THE "TREE SITUATION" redirected the tension between us; I was preoccupied with being sued. Andrew assured me that money from his Scottish Equitable Pension Fund would be forthcoming to help with legal expenses. He also tried to convince me that the incident was an omen; we should look for property in Vermont.

A few days later, the Grangers erected a six-foot spite fence, blocking both the view and the salty breezes from Gull Pond, leaving us becalmed in a dead zone.

I was relieved to escape to Mount Holyoke on Sunday, driving off-Cape as hordes of Memorial Day visitors were driving on. And oddly, Andrew had had a change of heart. Rather than attending Mrs. Bayley's service, he insisted on escorting me to commencement.

Chapter 29

Andrew and I strolled along the maple-shaded sidewalk toward the towering wrought iron Mary Lyon gate, which had admitted generations of women from all over the world to the college before me. Stately elms, flowering dogwoods and fragrant lilac bushes covered the campus. Students lugged coolers across vast green lawns, stopping to greet friends or fling Frisbees.

American parents clutched strings of balloons and bouquets of red roses. European mothers cradled spring flowers. Japanese women held pretty umbrellas to protect their delicate complexions. The dauntless spirits of Muslim women radiated from beneath silky hijabs and pastel burkas. African fathers looked like kings in saffron and fuchsia Kinte cloth robes.

Scattered groups of graduates huddled in fluttering black gowns, pinning ropes of ivy and silver stars to their mortarboards. When the tower clock tolled, they hurried toward the gymnasium to line up for the processional march.

We found an usher to lead us to Ruth's faculty seats in the packed amphitheater. Scanning the crowd, I waved to a classmate, listened to the blend of foreign tongues and smiled at the women behind us, mothers and grandmothers wrapped in shimmering saris.

A hush fell as the first triumphant chords of *Pomp and Circumstance* resounded. Memories of my own happy college years erupted. Blinking back sentimental tears, I studied the procession of graduates, faculty and honored guests, their caps and gowns denoting their universities: Yale, Harvard, Smith, Wellesley and so many others.

The applause was deafening when Queen Noor appeared. Wearing Princeton's colors, she was tucked into the middle of the long chain of scholars. Andrew tensed, then stood and aimed his disposable camera as she glided past.

"Isn't she grand? Slimmer since the king died. Verra close, they were. I used to see 'em riding dirt bikes 'round the palace grounds. There's Steve Norris, her security guard," he announced loudly, pointing at a lanky man wearing aviator glasses standing in the shade under a tree. "Spent many fine hours with him outside the palace gates at the Holiday Inn, the only place that served alcoholic beverages. Muslim rules," he explained and saluted Steve.

Steve didn't react.

"Saw him for dinner in Texas years ago. Good friend, but he's got his hands full with this mob."

"Sit down, Andrew." I tugged at the hem of his blazer. "You're blocking everyone's view."

"You were right, dearest. I should have written that letter. She would've seen me, I'm sure."

He continued snapping shots of Queen Noor as she addressed the graduates. Her poignant call for tolerance and universal peace moved me to tears. She inspired me to face what might have been had I finished my master's degree and taught, instead of chasing romance and building a marriage on quicksand.

As our beloved President Liz took her place at the podium to pass out diplomas, I glanced at Andrew's blank, bored face. *Ignorant*, I thought.

When the ceremony was over, Ruth met us at the front entrance as planned. She said she understood Andrew's decision not to impose on Queen Noor, graciously accepted his invitation to join us for a day of racing at Saratoga Springs and then turned to me. "My friend, you've been away from all who love you far too long." She gave me a piercing look as she bade us farewell.

Andrew took my hand as we jostled through the crowd to the parking lot. "Lovely lassie, our Ruth is," he said. "I'll show her a grand time at the track, give her a tip or two and get to know her better. Would that please you, darling?"

"Of course. But why don't you have any friends, Andrew? You must like someone well enough to enjoy a round of golf, see a ballgame or spend a day at Suffolk Downs."

He patted my knee as we pulled out of the lot. "Why would I need friends? You're my best pal."

Lucky me. I steered the conversation to the tree situation. "The Grangers are about to sue and I don't know what to do about the spite fence. Don't you think we should see Rupert?"

"Hope you'll make it clear that it was a mistake I made," he grumbled. But he didn't threaten to bolt as he had when I suggested contacting Rupert about the validity of our marriage license.

"Won't you be coming along?" I asked, hoping he wouldn't.

"We'll see. There's a lot of work to be done before the tenants arrive. But my blood boils when I think of the fuss that bully next door has made over a few branches. I assure you, Anna, if my old mates Peachy Keen and the Rock got wind of this, they'd hop the first plane and shut him up for good."

"What kind of friends did you have over there?"

"Loyal mates. A hotelier meets all kinds. Some lived on the fringe and some dined with the nobs."

"They sound like comic book thugs," I muttered.

Reclining my seat, I wondered how I'd gone from academic splendor to life's lowest common denominators.

Chapter 30

A week later, I left Andrew in bed nursing a sudden toothache, drove to the Barnstable park-and-ride and took the bus to Boston. Rupert's turn-of-the-century brownstone on Newbury Street stood diagonally across from the Ritz-Carlton. He buzzed me in and the scent of cherry pipe tobacco triggered a flood of fond memories as I ran up the stairs. In his office, colonial maps and sagging bookshelves lined hunter green walls; casebooks, history journals and museum catalogs spilled out onto worn Turkish carpets.

"Oh my. What a mess." Rupert clucked absentmindedly as he saw me to an upholstered chair. His wispy white hair and tortoiseshell glasses made him look like an addled professor. "You look exhausted, Anna. Are you all right?"

"My life is a hornet's nest, Rupert."

"Does Andrew know you're here?"

"Yes. The coward has a convenient toothache. Invented or not, that suits me fine."

He collapsed into a vintage Eames chair, lit his pipe and handed me a file. Inside were Xeroxed copies of Andrew's many marriage certificates, including one from Michigan proving he had married Darby Hamilton, as well as contact information for Mr. Bayley in Philadelphia, "Mighty Al" in Michigan, and a half-dozen domestic agencies. Rupert had done his homework.

"Clearly, Andrew is a pathological liar," he said. "And you're going to have to tell a few whoppers yourself, while we gather the evidence needed to secure an annulment. Blame your bank. Blame your beneficiaries. Tell him you must be single at sixty to collect your late husband's social security payments."

He paused for a tug on his pipe. "I'll dig into all this while you're in the Adirondacks. We'll file with the court when you return, and then it will take two months to get a hearing. Can you endure him that long?"

"To send him packing without a dime? You bet I can."

Rupert frowned. "I liked Andrew. Believed his stories. Even made an embarrassing wager with a colleague about the king and his tin cup."

I reached into my purse, pulled out the photo of Paula's gravestone and handed it to him. "Why would anyone take such an eerie picture?"

He shook his head. "Andrew told me of his sad loss at Locke-Ober's last year, when you introduced us. You left the table between dinner and dessert and he described the accident in detail, right down to the black body bag's zipper. Now that I think about it, he was far too eager to dredge up a twelve-year-old tragedy. But one doesn't question grief; I never gave it a thought. It's going to be a long summer for you, Anna."

"I wish I hadn't rented my house."

"If you're not up to it, we can take our chances in divorce court."

"No. He's not going to get a penny more than I've already given him. And whatever he's skimming from my checking account."

"Let him skim," Rupert advised. "Don't change a thing. Let him think he's getting away with it. Remember, maintain the status quo."

"He's impulsive and destructive. He filled the car with diesel one night and we had to be towed; that fiasco cost hundreds of dollars. And don't get me started on the spite fence. It's the talk of the village."

Rupert furrowed his brow. "These things divert your attention from Andrew, don't they?"

"Meetings with surveyors, landscape architects and insurance adjusters will consume me for some time."

"Maybe we haven't given him his due, Anna. Maybe he's more clever than we realized."

"Are you suggesting he vandalized the Grangers' property to distract me?"

"I think it's likely," he said, reaching for his tobacco pouch. "He's keeping you off-balance. Be careful. Normal squabbles are okay, but don't push him too hard. And stay in touch with me."

An hour later, I boarded the bus and braced myself to face the mess I'd made of my life.

Chapter 31

Speckled with dark paint, Andrew bounded across the lawn as I drove up my driveway late that afternoon. "I found seven gallons of ultramarine blue at the thrift shop, made three round-trips on your bicycle and did up the whole basement."

"I thought we agreed on off-white."

"You've been poormouthing me since we got back from Sanibel. I thought you'd be happy I saved you a few dollars."

"I'd be happy if my checkbook made sense. When you started paying the bills there was always a surplus. In the last few months, it's disappeared."

"But you have a windfall coming, Anna. You've rented the house for the whole season. And let me remind you, my little miser, your profit would've been cut in half without my labor."

"That's true, Andrew," I said softly as we walked through the kitchen door. Once inside, I got down to business. "Rupert had a widowed client, who remarried before she was sixty and lost her widow's benefits. Had she waited, she would've collected $1,000 a month from her late husband's social security."

"Is Rupert suggesting you should've chosen extra spending money over marriage?"

"He simply informed me of my options." I smiled angelically. "Maybe we should have our marriage secretly annulled and then secretly re-marry the day after I turn sixty."

"Rupert's a shyster to promote such a thing. He wants to annul me out of your life for a lousy grand a month?"

"Twelve thousand dollars a year is a lot of money," I said as I settled on the couch. "If you can't sell one of your houses or produce cash somehow, what choice do we have?"

"I'd go back into service before I'd let you go. You're my life, Anna. Put this crazy idea out of your head. I'll nudge Drew again about my pension. In the meantime, since you're penny-pinching, Drew has again offered to manage your investments."

Nice try, I thought. I patted his hand and picked up the needlepoint canvas I'd bought on Newbury Street that afternoon, a decoy to distract him from the deceit in my eyes.

"What's that you're making, heartsweet?" he lilted.

I smiled. "A Christmas stocking for our wee Fiona, darling."

He breathed a sigh of relief. "And now my dear, I'll tidy up the house and make it palace perfect. Everything will be tickety-boo. You'll see."

FROM DAWN TO DUSK, our days were filled with hard work. We detailed everything from the telephone to the garbage cans, packing up personal belongings and stuffing them into locked bins in the basement. Andrew took stacks of newspapers and magazines to the dump while I sorted through our clothes, making a pile to donate to charity, another to toss. Before throwing out his moth-eaten tweed jacket, I checked the pockets and found two dainty emerald rings in one.

In the palm of my hand, the fiery stones seemed to pulsate. I felt certain I was holding the rings that Andrew had removed from Paula's fingers before kissing her lips one last time. I was even more certain that Paula's spirit was near.

Assuming Andrew had forgotten the emeralds, I carried them to the basement and tucked them into the folds of a blanket in an old cedar chest. Overwhelmed, I sat on the chest and cried.

Chapter 32

A few days later, friends e-mailed to invite us to join them for a leg of their summer cruise from Fort Ticonderoga to Canada. I was eager to accept the invitation but Andrew refused, humbly confessing seasickness.

"What?" I exploded. "You said you and Paula cruised the Thames."

"Only when she needed rest from her busy practice. Besides, the Thames is a verra different kettle of fish from the choppy waters of Lake Champlain, Anna."

His once endearing brogue now grated on me. "What about sailing the Florida Keys on Jimmy Buffett's ketch? How did you manage your seasickness then?"

"I endured, Anna. It was my chance to get back into the music world."

"How'd that work out for you?"

"You know I'm a has-been. But you loved me so much that I started to believe in myself again. Why are you making fun of me now?"

"My world has turned upside down. I don't know who you are."

He stepped close and held me. "Aye. It's all my fault. I should leave, make my own way. But I'm a coward, Anna. I'd ache forever for the sight of your beautiful smile."

Tears came from nowhere. Against my will, I leaned into him.

"Also," he continued calmly, "your friends' sailing schedule conflicts with the Traverse. I'm not going to miss Saratoga Springs' biggest race to throw up before strangers."

"Maybe they'll tie up for a night and at least we'll see them. What's this new aversion to socializing? Once you won the hearts of everyone you met."

He stroked my hair. "We do best on our own, my little one. Aren't I enough for you anymore?"

Before I could respond, he shifted gears. "Drew called while you were at the post office. My pension fund is fat enough for him to send twenty thousand pounds come autumn."

"That's good news. Rupert reminded me that if I ask my trust officer to dip into principal, I'll open a can of worms."

"What are you talking about?" He sounded genuinely alarmed. "It's your money."

"It's not mine. It's only for my benefit during my lifetime. My children and Sam's are also beneficiaries. If any of Sam's three kids gets wind that I've been supporting you, I'll be looking at another lawsuit. Disgruntled heirs make bankers' knees weak. They've guarded the family trust like it was their own for years, made me account for every cent I've spent."

Pretty sure I had his undivided attention, I continued. "This is nothing to fool around with, my dear. Banks are in business to make money; mine makes less if I invade principal.

Sam's social security checks would keep me from having to do that."

I let him digest that information and kissed his cheek. "I'll pack our suitcases and stack them by the kitchen door."

"Don't forget my Duke and Duchess of Windsor books. I'm going to buckle down, get my musical written this summer, the greatest love story Britain has ever known."

And one of the most horrific scandals to rock the royals in modern times, I thought.

He carried on, sturdy and confident again. "Also, Anna, it will free up space for Rumpus if we ship our golf clubs. You were right; I should find a friend or two of my own. I'll join a men's league at the Ticonderoga Country Club."

"Wonderful, Andrew."

"Off you go then, my angel." He laughed as I left to UPS our clubs to Cabin #7 at the Trout House Village Inn on Lake George, a few miles from the 1920s summer retreat of Georgia O'Keefe and Alfred Stieglitz and an easy ride to the famed Adirondack Museum on Blue Mountain Lake.

At last the house was sparkling. We left a note propped against a bottle of good red wine for our summer visitors and stopped at the realtor's office to drop off keys and our cabin's telephone number. Our car looked like it belonged in a gypsy caravan.

As we crossed the Sagamore Bridge, I searched the Cape Cod Canal for a lone sailboat, an omen of safe travel, my personal Saint Christopher. Not one boat in sight.

Chapter 33

Connecticut friends had invited us to spend a night. The Carters had been mesmerized by Andrew from the moment they met him and they extracted each story from his vast repertoire with aplomb. Eager to please, he held court, savoring a cup of tea and Scottish shortbread Marybeth Carter had baked in his honor.

"Queen Noor would call from Amman, tell me which VIP would arrive in Aqaba that week. I was gobsmacked when the Italian president arrived with his film star mistress. She sunbathed topless, causing an uproar; the maids refused to change her sheets and threatened to quit. When I instructed her on Muslim etiquette, she left in a fury…

"Then there was the wizened little Arab whose sole purpose in life was to walk across the desert each year to trim the king's palm trees. Refused to come inside to eat with the staff. Slept on the ground for a week. I delivered a hamper and blankets to him each day. I felt obliged, you see…"

I left them all whiling away the afternoon and went strawberry picking. Returning a few hours later with trays of juicy red berries, I found Marybeth flustered and fanning herself. Well-traveled friends had popped in unexpectedly and when she invited them to stay for dinner, Andrew left without a word, isolating himself in the guest room. Crestfallen, she asked me to intervene.

"I'll try," I told her, and went upstairs.

"Andrew, Marybeth says you're upset. What's wrong?"

"I'm tired. And bored. You left me here alone."

"I asked if you wanted to come berry picking. You said no; you were going to write to Rod's PR agent, find out if he was performing in Saratoga this summer."

"I'm not a Trivial Pursuit game. Those people do nothing but quiz me. I'm sick of it. If you find time, bring me a supper tray."

"As you wish, Andrew. I'm not going to try to change your mind."

I suspected his bluster was a smokescreen, erected to avoid interacting with the other guests, and wondered why they posed a threat. Maybe he had a sixth sense about the kinds of people he could - and couldn't – bamboozle.

The next morning, we cheerfully ate breakfast with our hosts, pretending Andrew's inexcusable rudeness had never happened, and then headed for the nearby home of Lucinda Wells.

MY LATE HUSBAND'S elderly aunt fixed her piercing azure eyes upon Andrew and held out her alabaster hand.

"A great honor, Madam." He bowed so low I thought he'd fall over.

She withdrew her hand and gave him a charitable smile. After seating us on the patio overlooking the lake, she left to prepare a tea tray I knew would include a bunny bowl of animal crackers.

I hadn't told Andrew about the extent of the family fortune. Or that most of it had been lost in the '70s, when Top the Texan convinced Aunt Lucinda's late husband to invest in oil wells. She and Sam became closer after the scandal, often speculating about the idiot wildcatter with diamond cufflinks. They remained devoted to each other even after we left Connecticut, and she deeply mourned Sam's passing.

I admired Lucinda's resilience, appreciated her pragmatic advice and was grateful that after a quarter-century she still considered me a member of her family. Had I been thinking clearly, I would have called her, put off our visit until my own idiot wildcatter was gone.

Andrew's head swiveled, taking in the boathouse and log cabin across the lake. "What's going to happen when she dies? Do you still have a claim on it?"

"Shush, Andrew. We'll talk in the car."

"You signed off on this when your husband died?"

"Later, Andrew."

Aunt Lucinda appeared, carrying a tray filled with a silver teapot, embroidered napkins, Quimper cups and saucers, and the anticipated bunny bowl. My heart fluttered with affection. Sam and I had enjoyed many a cup of tea from that whimsical French pottery.

"Andrew," she trilled, "do you like my park?"

"It's verra impressive, Mrs. Wells. It reminds me of Henley-on-Thames, where my late wife and I used to take our launch on summer weekends. It's so lush, so grand."

"My husband's people created it during the mid-1800s, dammed the lake to generate power for the old paper mill. We lost the chestnuts in 1919 and blight hit the hemlocks last summer. The dam needs repair and miles of stone walls are crumbling. Perhaps you'll buy it all when I'm gone, infuse it with new money."

He gazed at her adoringly. "I'd love to. I'd close the deal today. But I don't think I'll ever wrench Anna from Cape Cod."

Lucinda smiled. "She does love her village and her friends. And now that she has you, Andrew, her life seems complete. I've worried about her, alone all these years since my nephew died, raising two children without a father's strong arm to rein them in. I applaud her spunk."

"Aye. She's made me a verra happy man. And she's won the hearts of my two university-educated children." He looked heavenward. "All since my dear wife departed. Dr. Barnett, God rest her soul."

I held my breath, afraid he might genuflect.

Lucinda reached down and lifted a canvas tote from under the table. "I found these Staffordshire dogs tucked away in a closet the other day," she said, handing the pair to me. "Thought you'd like them, dear. You were always fond of my collection."

"My goodness, Lucinda, they're exquisite. You'll have me in tears."

Andrew took one into his shaking hand. As he studied it, he began stuttering in fragmented phrases about shooting porcelain dogs at his grandfather's stables. "Gordon made me... we lined 'em up... then finished off dem Wally dogs wit BB guns."

Lucinda and I stared at each other in stunned silence. She stacked our teacups on the tray and I stood to help. The visit was over.

Lucinda graciously ushered us out and waved from behind the screen door, which I assumed she'd locked securely behind us.

"I couldn't stop myself, Anna."

I shook my head, unable to speak.

"It just came rushing back. I was a bairn. Gordon was bullying me. He made me shoot all those dogs."

"Do you want me to drive?" I managed.

"No. I'd rather concentrate on the road than think about the things Gordon forced me to do. More reasons not to go back. Please don't make me."

I closed my eyes as we drove in heavy silence toward our next stop, my mother's nursing home. Andrew was more damaged than I had imagined. I realized that stringing him along, feigning devotion with just enough outrage to be credible, would take some doing.

Chapter 34

We headed west along Connecticut's industrial maze, passing the exits Sam and I took so often before we fled suburbia for the quaint villages and windswept shores that had whispered my name since childhood, when I first heard Patti Page singing *Old Cape Cod*. I looked at the Nantucket basket my grandparents had given me and winced at my ridiculous notion of predestined meetings. Had I not carried the status symbol to church that spring morning, Andrew probably wouldn't have given me a second glance. Recalling Darby Hamilton's Louis Vuitton, I wondered if he kept a lookout for expensive bags.

As we rang the nursing home's bell, *I'll Never Smile Again* wafted through invisible speakers. Inside, patients were scattered about the lobby, some wearing curlers and swaying with the music, others engaged in animated conversations with imaginary friends. Hearing the thump and drag of a walker and my mother's cough, I stiffened. "Here she comes."

Andrew moved me aside, glided across the room and kissed her cheeks. "Hello, my heartsweet. You're as lovely as your daughter. We've a grand lunch planned for you at the Hawthorne Inn. Now come along, we'll order you a nice split of champagne. Will it be roast beef or lobster today, madam?"

She nodded absentmindedly, patted his hand and turned her brown rheumy eyes to me. "It's been a year since I've seen the ocean."

"I know, Mama, but the last time you visited, you fell and ended up in the hospital."

"You forgot to give me my sleepy pills."

"Oh Mama, you took too many."

Andrew jumped in like a magician waving a wand. "Dearest lady, your daughter and I plan to spring you from this place for a nice long weekend. Isn't that right, Anna?"

This was news to me. I bitterly wondered how he could be so thoughtful and so full of deceit.

"You'll come to Chatham in October for your birthday," he continued, "and we'll take you to the ocean every day."

"Baked Alaska?" she asked, her eyes wide. "Like they serve on the QE II?"

"Aye, my angel. Fried clams, crab cakes, scallops and whatever your heart desires."

Throughout our lunch at the Hawthorne, he fawned over her. I was warmed to see my mother smile and proudly share the secret ingredients of her Armenian recipes. All too soon, our visit was over. Mother returned to her bed beside a grated window and I went back to the car, shackled to Andrew's deceptions.

Was it really the money that drove me to follow Rupert's advice, to pursue an annulment rather than pay the price in divorce court?

No, I realized. It was morbid curiosity about Paula. I was haunted by the inconsistent accounts of her death, and by the image of her gravestone. I had to know more.

Focused on the task ahead, I asked, "Andrew, will you level with me this summer? Tell me the truth about your life?"

He adjusted the rearview mirror and took my hand. "Can't we just enjoy the holiday, darling? Stop looking back? I said I was sorry."

"But until we understand each other, our lives remain superficial, like one never-ending, exhausting date."

"Why would I ruin this life of leisure? I hated being servile. My employers were unreasonable. Mighty Al insisted I wear a uniform. Old Man Bayley wanted to know where I was every minute, actually timed every errand I ran. They all used me. Even Paula. Did I tell you she had me up doing breakfast at 4 a.m. on surgical days?"

"Let me guess. You cooked hot porridge to sustain her through long operations."

"Aye, and soft scrambled eggs."

"Sounds like you doted on her."

"I hardly ever saw her, Anna. We were star-crossed lovers for years and when we finally married, well, you know the rest."

"Didn't you say she wanted children?"

"We were going to call our first-born *Skye*. I wrote a ballad for the child. I'm sure you've seen it in my songbook," he snapped. "You've seen everything else."

I ignored the jab and reminded him that he'd shown me the tartan-covered book, told me Paula had given it to him just before they left for Switzerland. "*Ode to Skye*, subtitled *The Day Before*, was dated September 25th. I remember because that's my birthday. Did Paula miscarry the next day?"

His face lost color and he clenched the steering wheel. "Bloody hell," he shouted. "If you don't stop prying into my late wife's personal life, I'll pull over and walk. What's wrong with you? Where's your respect?"

"Sorry," I said, and let the dark moment pass.

We settled into the monotonous rhythm of the journey. I worked on Fiona's stocking, dozed for a while and then read the map he'd highlighted days before. His mood improved as I called out the names of towns he'd circled along Route 87.

"Look, Anna, there's the exit for Saratoga Springs. We'll reach Hague and the Trout House in no time. It'll be an easy drive to the racetrack. It doesn't open 'til the 14th, but I'll suss it out this week. I haven't been here since my Williamstown won. A champ, he was; I wish I hadn't sold him."

"Too bad," I mused. "Where did you stay that year?"

"Too bad, indeed. It's good to be back. Sheila wouldn't let me out of her sight long enough for a trip like this. My life is much sweeter now."

"But where did you stay the year Williamstown won?"

"There you go again, wanting every detail. I can't re-member where I stayed. What difference does it make?"

I put down my needlepoint canvas. "None a-tall, Andrew."

"Until I met you, I'd never had so many adventures. Summer will be grand, old girl. I'll light the woodstove and unload the car. While I do the blue jobs, you can do the pink."

"The pink?"

"Aye, heartsweet. Make up our bed and heat the chicken potpies. All set for cigarettes, my little chimney?"

"I have a pack. Why do you buy me cartons at a time? You don't like smoke and I'm trying to quit."

"For your little emergencies, darling."

I wondered if he was hoping to kill me.

RELAXED ON ADIRONDACK CHAIRS, the owners of the Trout House Village Inn waved us up to the veranda overlooking Lake George. Scott and Alice and their four lively kids had met Andrew months before, when they all queued up to buy sandwiches and newspapers at Rosie's Place in Sanibel. When he told them he'd written *Have I Told You Lately* for Van Morrison, Scott all but gave us a cabin for the summer. He thought it was a God-wink, for he'd been rehearsing that song to sing at his nephew's wedding.

Alice handed us the key and told us to follow the winding, rutted road three miles to the mountaintop. Twenty minutes later, we arrived at our one-room pine cabin, yellow gingham curtains at its mullioned windows, two café chairs and an old enamel table on its porch. In the distance stood a barn and a lopsided bathhouse. Andrew called it a "shunky" in his Sean Connery accent.

"Haven't I done well to find this for you, Anna? I'll set up your tent under the trees and we'll run an extension cord from the cabin. You can read and paint in there to your heart's content."

Enchanted, I rested my head on his chest and declared it perfect.

He pulled me closer. "The world is our oyster, my sweet. Tomorrow, I'll carve our initials in that tree beyond the berm.

Then we'll tie the tartan, promise to love each other forever, just like William Wallace and his true love in *Braveheart*."

Tender moments like this had once charmed me, but I now knew his words meant nothing.

I set the porch table for two, lit the pinecone candle and we endured the first of sixty camp dinners. After beating me at Scrabble, he went off to shower in the shunky, whistling all the way. When its door opened and closed fifteen minutes later, I grabbed my towel and met him on the moonlit path.

He embraced me. "I haven't seen so many stars since I was a boy in Porty. And look at that moon, Anna. Can you see his face? It's a good omen, you know."

Millions of plump, twinkling stars lit up the old man's face. But it wasn't the benevolent face he wore during my childhood. In the shunky, I found that Andrew had drawn our initials in a heart on the steamy mirror.

Showered and dusted with bath powder, I dawdled along the pine path, at one with the forest and its spirits. Lingering in the sweet balsam scent of the hushed night, I felt embraced by a warmth, the same pulsating heat that filled the palm of my hand when I held Paula's emerald rings.

Again, I knew her spirit was near.

Chapter 35

We slept later than usual and awoke to sunshine and growling stomachs. Andrew announced he was taking me out to breakfast and then to shop "in *Ti*, local lingo for Fort Ticonderoga."

Teams of retirees wearing bright green jackets greeted customers at the doors of Wal-Mart. Disabled shoppers scooted around on motorized carts and elderly ladies in purple smocks hovered, eager to help. A Dorsey swing number filled the air, giving me a carefree moment. I held out my hand to Andrew. "Take a twirl?"

"You know I never learned to dance. I was on stage."

"What a pity."

We collected two cartloads of groceries and a walk-in tent, my summer asylum, then explored Ticonderoga's Main Street looking for a restaurant. Andrew lit up when he spotted an off-track betting parlor. "Do you mind if we nip in here, darling, check out the set-up?"

"You want to eat in a betting parlor?"

"It looks decent. We'll have a sandwich. I'll catch up with the racing news."

"You said the track doesn't open until the 14th."

"True, but racing is everywhere; Belmont, Del Mar, Hollywood Park, and my old stomping grounds in Philadelphia. Here I can watch all the races at the same time."

I felt uneasy. "Do you plan to spend the summer rushing from betting parlors to the race track?"

"I ain't bettin'."

"Ain't?"

"I like the buzz. And besides, don't you want to paint pictures and read books? What am I supposed to do while you're busy in your new tent?"

"You were planning to write your musical about the Duke and Duchess of Windsor," I reminded him. "And weren't you going to join a men's league at the Ti Country Club?"

"I changed my mind."

"The man who played with the pros should enjoy tougher competition than his wife."

"This is my holiday, Anna. I'll do what I want. When you're available, we'll golf. I'm too rusty to play with anyone else. Now let's order lunch at the bar."

The long line of televisions blared race results and sports scores as we ate turkey clubs. Wearing dark plastic visors, the bartenders hustled drinks and bets. Andrew sizzled. I'd never seen him so charged. I feigned interest, watched him banter with a local barfly, and knew Frank Troy was right. Andrew was addicted. I pictured his clever routine, handing me a crisp C-note after each "win." He'd probably debited my credit card for every one of them.

My misgivings about Andrew spending the summer in betting parlors vanished. I knew his weakness would buy me the time I needed. I'd learn the lingo, encourage him, and he'd be off and running while I ostensibly painted and read.

"Close finish, could've made a bundle on that long shot," he said, sliding off his stool and waving to the barkeep. "I'm ready to go."

We dropped our clubs at the Ti Country Club, set a tee time for five the next afternoon and headed back to Hague.

THE POSTMISTRESS WELCOMED US and set us up with a mailbox. We explored a shop called Old Glory Gifts and Antiques, then went next door to the Island View Café for homemade chocolate ice cream with sprinkles. As we headed back to the car, the scent of roasting beef and garlic drew us to the Public Market, its flaking white wooden porch festooned with Fourth of July banners and balloons.

We went in and ordered take-out for supper. We'd heard that the guitar-playing owner was once famous and that at night the market became a musicians' haunt. Dozens of guitars hung from the rafters. Andrew blew the dust off one and whistled.

"Why don't you buy it? Jam with the boys after dinner some night?"

"I told you my guitars are stored in Porty."

"Most men would enjoy jamming with the boys."

"I'll send for my own when I'm ready, not before. So stop blethering on about things you don't understand. Now let's head back to camp."

HOURS LATER, we admired the sturdy tent sheltered under tall pines. Andrew seemed pleased with his work, but without warning his mood soured. "Now that your sulk house is set up," he said, "I'm going to have a cuppa and watch the news." As he trudged up the hill, I wondered if he enjoyed poisoning each good deed with a biting slur.

A 1950s metal table retrieved from the barn gleamed after a good scrubbing. I hauled it into the tent and topped it with an old Mason jar filled with wildflowers. The Bakelite radio beat out a country reel and I hummed along as I hooked up my laptop to e-mail Morgan. After filling her in on recent developments, I confided, "I'm furious with myself for ever believing a word he said."

Not ten minutes later, a male voice announced "You've got mail" through the tiny speaker. I jumped and switched off the volume. E-mail threatened Andrew, made him sweat. He couldn't eavesdrop.

Morgan and Kate had been busy at the Edinburgh Registry. "All bad news," Morgan wrote. "You married a rat."

The Macdades never owned the Ravelston Hotel. The men were all coal miners. Mr. Macdade never went to war. Classified Reserve Occupation, he was needed at home to supply fuel. Nor was Andrew in the RAF; he didn't bump his head during flight training. The only thing he ever ejected from is reality.

Andrew's first marriage certificate says he's a 'coal lorry driver.' Laura Macdade owns the house he's promised to you. The Highclere owns the house he claims Paula left to him.

Laura divorced Andrew in 1988 and he promptly married Grace Jamieson, who divorced him in 1993. Both Laura and Grace are listed in the telephone directory.

Paula Barnett may have died on October 2, 1989 but she and Andrew couldn't have been married unless he's a bigamist. Kate and I are still searching for her birth certificate.

I wasn't surprised to learn that Laura owned Andrew's "historic manse." Nor was I the least bit fazed to learn he was a poor coal miner's son who'd reinvented himself. His obsessions with cleanliness and dress, his bombastic speech: all evidence of his delusions about the upper-class. But if Mr. Macdade had never gone to war, where did my sapphire ring and diamond brooch come from?

I replied to Morgan at once. "Information about Paula is out there somewhere. It's just a matter of dissembling Andrew's stories."

My hands shook as I lit a cigarette and reread the e-mail. When I heard the cabin's screen door bang shut, I deleted Morgan's message and printed one from Andrina inviting us to join them in Montreal during the third week of August. On the spot, I decided I'd take that opportunity to tell her everything I knew about her father.

He unzipped the tent's flap and walked in. "E-mailing again, my little computer whiz? I thought you were setting up your easel," he purred. His dour expression gave me a fright.

"We're off to Montreal." I waved the invitation. "Isn't this wonderful? We'll see our Fiona again before you know it."

"E-mail is a good thing, eh? Now, is madam ready for our evening swim?"

Chills ran up and down my spine as he stroked the back of my neck.

Chapter 36

That night, after listening to him breathe for what seemed like hours, I inched across no man's land and spooned against the arch of his back. "Are you awake?" I whispered, stroking his damp head.

"Aye. And juddering at whatever scheme you've been brewing over there."

"I've been thinking about us. Praying you'll have the courage to speak the truth."

Without warning, he rolled over and pinned me. "What do you want of me, Anna?"

"You're crushing me."

Disgusted, he rolled off and lay on his back. "What now?"

I gave him just enough information to force a response, telling him I knew that he was from a coal mining family and that the Macdades never owned the Ravelston Hotel. "Morgan and Kate went to the Edinburgh Registry, Andrew. Public records don't lie."

He sat up and switched on the lamp. "Look at me, Anna," he demanded. "You've married a coal miner. Is that what you wanted? I could have been an architect."

Tears streamed down his face. "I won first prize for drawing. But my father made me quit school the day I turned fifteen, to drive the coal wagon pulled by an old nag named Dick. I pretended he was a racing champ and I a famous jockey. I hauled two-hundred pound sacks of coal on my back. The Ravelston Hotel was on my route. When I came to America, I made myself believe we'd owned it."

"And now it's time to face reality, Andrew."

He stared into space, then muttered, "I don't know how much more meddling I can take."

"You're chained to fantasy. Does your brother Gordon make up stories, too?"

"He never had to. He got it all; looks, personality and brains, yet he was always jealous of me, abused me no end. Our parents never once put a stop to it."

"Such a heartbreaking story." I cradled him in my arms until he fell asleep, thinking I'd like to meet Gordon Macdade.

WE SETTLED INTO CAMP LIFE and tiptoed around each other with exaggerated civility. Twice a week Andrew went to the racetrack. On alternate days, we hiked, golfed, swam and kayaked. We Scrabbled for hours each evening, to postpone bedtime and the mechanical gymnastics of sex. And though we presented ourselves to everyone we met as devoted newlyweds, my thoughts were elsewhere. I suspected his were, too.

Andrew left camp each morning to pick up racing programs, newspapers and muffins at the market. He returned from one trip with a stack of Vermont real estate listings. "I went to Bolton Landing and met a nice lady who will show us a house in Manchester this very afternoon."

He handed me her business card. "It has a big vegetable garden, a pond, and can be had for half of what we'll make on your place."

"Let's look around when we get back from Canada," I suggested, "not today. If you're bored, go see what's happening at Saratoga Springs."

He blew me a kiss. "You're the best wife a man could have, heartsweet. I'll place a few bets and book a table with Duncan at turf side. Have you e-mailed Ruth?"

"No, but I will. Who's Duncan?"

"The club manager, a fellow Scotsman. I met him at Gleneagles, where Paula and I spent our wedding night."

He may have spent a wedding night there with Laura or Grace, but certainly not with Paula. I laughed and kissed him good riddance. "Tally-ho, Andrew."

My station wagon turned right toward Saratoga Springs and I leapt with joy. I kneaded bread dough, marinated lamb chops in garlic vinegar and hastily filled a canvas with a rough impression of Georgia O'Keefe's *Night Sky*, in case Andrew asked what I'd been doing all day. The remaining hours were mine to send e-mails and make telephone calls.

I e-mailed Ruth, confessed I'd married a con artist and enlisted her help. She was a techie and I asked her to search Oxford University's database for Paula Barnett, the *Times* archives for her obituary, and Switzerland's 1989 newspapers for a London surgeon's fatal skiing accident. I added, "Please come up for a day of racing as planned. The more friends who visit, the better. He'll see himself as an integral part of my life."

It was then that I noticed the dough caked under my fingernails and remembered the summer Morgan and I baked forty loaves of bread each day and delivered them on our bicycles. It beat sewing sticky tobacco leaves in a hot shed. By the end of August, we'd saved enough to buy fabric and patterns for A-line skirts and a year's subscription to *Seventeen*.

Smiling at our resourcefulness, I smelled the yeast on my hands and looked through the flap of my tent at the field of wildflowers. A whippoorwill sang, a cardinal answered, and for a brief moment I forgot I was Andrew Macdade's wife.

I PROPPED THE 3x5 of Paula's gravestone on the table and studied it through a magnifying glass. Her headstone was surrounded by older, moss-covered tombstones in a fenced area behind an 18th century brick church. I squinted at the lettering on the stone, wondering why it was inconsistent, then shrugged it off and pedaled down the mountain to enlarge and copy it.

I brought a picture of my granddaughter to use as a decoy, worried that someone from the tiny village would tell Andrew his wife had been photocopying a gravestone. He'd know exactly where it came from. But the young woman behind the shop's counter barely looked up. Glued to her cell phone, she waved me to the back of the empty store, where I made the enlargements without a single witness.

Shaking, I paid the clerk and biked to an empty bench in a secluded corner of the beach, where I took one of the 5x7s from the bag. Paula's name, date of death and credentials were crudely lettered, not chiseled like every other word on the gravestone.

Had Andrew placed paper or cardboard over someone else's headstone and written a phony inscription? I felt nauseous. Only a psycho would do such a thing.

Adrenaline propelled me up the mountain after I mailed an enlargement to Troon. In no time, the bread was baked, the table set, and dinner ready. Andrew would arrive home to an idyllic scene. But I smelled like cigarettes and garlic. He'd keep his distance.

Chapter 37

At precisely seven, Andrew rolled into camp full of joie de vivre. Tanned and dusty, he pressed a crisp hundred into my palm as he kissed me.

"Great day, honky-tonk. Seven modest returns and $1500 in the last trifecta. We'll claim it tomorrow with your ID and take in a few races."

"Why can't you collect your own winnings?"

"Because my passport is expired." He went on to remind me that circumstances beyond his control had forced him to work under the table in recent years. "I haven't filed a tax return since leaving the Bayleys. I'd tip off the IRS, cause trouble for my employers."

And more than a little trouble for himself. "My financial advisors won't be pleased if they see gambling income on my tax return."

"But Anna, racing is the sport of kings and the verra upper class. Just queue up at the winners' window, give the cashier my ticket with your driver's license, and sign."

"I'll do it this time, but don't ask again. Now tell me what you did, and who you saw, at the racetrack."

"Spent most of the day in the paddock with my former trainer. His new filly was sired by Williamstown. I shoulda bred him myself instead of selling him off to support Sheila and her sons."

"And to get her name tattooed on your ankle," I added.

"Jealous?"

I stared at him.

He grinned slyly. "I saw your favorite jockey and got his autograph for you."

Before I could ask who that might be, he continued at breakneck speed. "Princess Margaret's cousin was there with his luggage heiress. They want to meet you, my beauty. I told them you're my goddess."

More like your Medusa, I thought.

"The stupendous Joan wore a smashing blue and brown Chanel suit to match the racing colors of Manhattan Skyline, who still keeps old Jack in champers and Cuban cigars. They've invited us for drinks."

"Glad I packed my linen dress."

"Add a posh hat from Saratoga Trunk and you'll fit right in with the owners' wives. They're always dressed to the nines; a hat is de rigueur."

I stared at him again.

"It's the done thing," he explained pedantically. "I picked up those French expressions from the Taubmans' masseuse. Did I tell you about the time I crewed on his corporate jet? We flew to Palm Beach to meet with Jack Kemp, then to New York to get Mighty Al's wife a pair of shoes. She was a former Miss Israel, a frequent guest of Queen Noor's."

Here we go again, I thought. His friend the queen.

"Did I mention Her Royal Highness recognized my ear for languages? Had me speaking Arabic in no time, to control the natives."

"Natives, Andrew?"

"I mean the staff. Now as I was saying, tomorrow we'll go to Saratoga, collect my winnings and find a bonny hat for you."

"We're not owners," I reminded him.

"But I was." He pulled a tattered badge from his wallet. "This gets me into the paddocks and the club. Tomorrow, the security guard will wave us through the main gate and we'll breeze into the owners' parking lot."

He revolted me. I thrashed most of that night, counting his duplicities instead of sheep.

Proximity to the glittering hub of stars gave Andrew the details that lent credibility to his stories from the beginning. The Highclere Hotel stood smack in the center of the Royal Borough of Windsor and Maidenhead. Morgan and Ian told me that rockers, publicans and punters lived back-to-back with royals and landed gentry. On any given day, Andrew could have passed Wentworth's champion golfers, Elton John, Eric Clapton or Queen Noor herself. He may have seen Fergie in the butcher's shop, Princess Diana at the polo grounds and the Queen Mother's chef placing a bet at Ascot.

According to the letter from Queen Noor's administrator, Andrew had interviewed to manage her summer palace. If he'd been hired, he might well have met Jordan's notorious neighbor Saddam Hussein, Prime Minister Thatcher and President Bush. And if he'd had royal references, America's domestic agencies probably would have placed him among the elite.

Aside from his one-hit wonder saga, he'd cast himself as a humble servant. Someone had to wait on the rich and famous. Why not Andrew? He'd sprinkled fairy dust from his bag of fool's gold upon every gullible American he'd met. The biggest fool of all had married him on his 58th birthday.

Hours later, it was Paula keeping me awake. I brooded about her that moonless night, listening to the helpless cries of small nocturnal creatures. Andrew had said that he felt responsible for her death. He was a good liar. And like all good liars, he constructed each story around a grain of truth.

Chapter 38

At the track's gate the next morning, Andrew flashed his dog-eared badge at the security guard. "Top of the day to you, my good man." He waved and zipped into the restricted lot.

I marveled at how easily he was able to disarm and manipulate with his grandiose airs.

Freshly painted red and white, the Saratoga Racing Park teemed with people in T-shirts and shorts. Beach chairs, umbrellas and coolers made it impossible to walk a straight line. We jostled through the crowd to the cashier wearing our Sunday best, as Andrew had insisted.

"Why are we overdressed?"

"Anna," he scoffed, "those people can't afford any better." Pointing heavenward, he crowed, "Next week we'll be in the clubhouse with the swells. Don't worry your pretty head. I've arranged everything."

We queued and I collected his winnings, feeling like a moll. Happy with a wad of crisp hundreds in his wallet, Andrew squired me to The Saratoga Trunk, an emporium of regal Ascot hats.

The shop was a delight and I modeled one exquisite creation after another. Years later, when I read *Love, Loss and What I Wore*, I thought about the hat I chose that day, pale lemon trimmed with sea green grosgrain ribbon and porcelain buttons. It dipped on one side and its wide, soft brim gracefully brushed my right cheek.

Full of high energy, Andrew carried my hatbox to the car. "Come along, milady. I'll drive you past Jack and Joan's summer place."

Humoring him, I asked, "Do you really think they'll have us over for drinks?"

"Why wouldn't they? They'd have been at our wedding, but Joan's father took ill."

I didn't comment. He hadn't invited one friend to our wedding. I thought it unlikely that he'd received an RSVP from Princess Margaret's cousin and his luggage heiress.

Lush rolling lawns and 19th century mansions lined North Broadway, reminiscent of Newport's Cottages. "They're wonderful, Andrew. What's with the lawn jockeys?"

"Yardells," he said. "Painted with the owners' racing colors, they tip off the public to who's who each season."

"I've a lot to learn about the sport of kings, Diamond Jim. Let's stop at the bookstore for a browse and a bite. I'm a bit peckish."

"Your wish is my command. I'll fetch tomorrow's racing program and meet you at the sidewalk café."

SEATED UNDER A RED AND WHITE striped umbrella, I studied the colorful horse statues lining Saratoga's historical Broadway. Andrew figured the odds and scribbled between slurps of tea. Taking a long sip of lemonade, I picked up the *Times Union*, finding it chock-full of racing tips and society gossip. The newspaper's articles were peculiar, but entertaining:

"Macho Uno sticks tongue out at Buster's Dream at the finish line..."

"The country offers so many opportunities for two-year-olds these days..."

"Wicked Will wins by a nose in a head-bob at the wire..."

"Among the opening-day crowd at Saratoga was Andrew Macdade from London, who owns a hotel (Highclere) a mile from the famed Ascot racetrack..."

My heart beat faster.

"Macdade said he plans to 'be here the whole six weeks and see quite a bit of racing. I want to do the whole thing. Opening day is a big part of it.' Macdade, who is staying at the Sagamore Resort in Bolton Landing, is not new to Saratoga. In 1997, his horse *Williamstown* finished second in the Ballston Spa handicap."

I flew from my seat, hyperventilated through the store to the restroom and sluiced icy water on my face. Proof in print that Rupert was right. Andrew is a pathological liar.

The mirror stopped me short. I was looking at a muttering madwoman.

I paced the black-and-white marble tiles, wondering why he didn't trot out Paula's OBE to punch up the story. I folded and refolded paper towels into tiny squares, creasing them with my nails to steady my nerves, then forced a deep breath. Still fuming, I walked slowly back through the store, running my fingers over stacks of tabled remainders.

The heat of the street hit me hard. When I sat at the table, Andrew put down his program. "Are you right-side up, Anna?"

I didn't answer.

"What's wrong now? One minute you're okay and the next you're like a wee tattie bogle flying about in a frenzy. The minute I saw yer face I knew you'd gone off again."

I threw the newspaper at him.

"Oh, I forgot to tell you. The track's roving reporter interviewed me yesterday."

I glared.

"Darling, she couldn't understand my accent, got things all wrong."

"No, you half-wit. You lied about who you are and where you live. If you want to check into the eight-hundred-dollar-a-day Sagamore Resort, pack your bags, Mr. Big Shot."

Like any other liar caught red-handed, he backpedaled. "But I used to live in London. It was all a joke, Anna. Just a joke."

"Well I'm not laughing."

"Stick with me. Please, Anna. I got carried away yesterday. She was just a kid. I wanted to help her career. Let's go home and have that leftover pot roast, forget about today. I shouldn't have said that rubbish. I'm sorry if I hurt your feelings."

He clutched my hand during the drive back to camp. Drained, we went to bed after dinner and read, side-by-side, each very much alone.

Chapter 39

After a strained breakfast of stale cereal, Andrew left camp to market in Ti and place his bets on the afternoon's races. Happy to be rid of him, I called Ruth at her office, confirming our date at the track on the first Tuesday in August. She wasn't at all surprised by the news of Andrew's deceit. "We'll put the bastard in his place," she said matter-of-factly. "In hell and away from you."

When I turned on my computer, I found a message from Morgan. Kate had stopped for a drink at Laura's dockside pub, snapped photos of the Admiral Macdade manse, and reported that I shouldn't lose any sleep over my lost "inheritance."

It was ten o'clock, three p.m. in Troon. Morgan picked up on the second ring. "Hope you're not broken up over losing the Admiral's manse," she said, laughing.

"No," I told her. "I'm too distraught over learning that the one-hit wonder never recorded *Concrete and Clay.*"

"Hah. Bet he's never strummed a guitar."

"He says the music died with Paula."

"Speaking of Paula, if Andrew dummied her headstone, whose grave is it?"

"Good question."

"Ian leaves for Sunninghill next week. He'll check out the Captain's Cup winners on the Wentworth's trophy board."

"Tell him not to bother. I'm certain Andrew never tied for any cup. He stinks. He's short even on basic etiquette."

"Ian and I are worried about you. You shouldn't be alone in the woods with that nut. The Paula thing scares me, Anna. No one in his right mind tampers with a tombstone to prove he's widowed."

The cold blue eye of my five-carat sapphire mocked me as I slowly returned the receiver to its cradle.

An hour later, after a long downhill trek to the Hague Market, Rumpus stretched out next to a Springer spaniel at the never-empty ceramic trough on the porch. I bought a bottle of lemonade and settled on the stoop next to them, Morgan's words weighing heavily.

The Trout House kids appeared, looking like happy clowns with smudges of red Kool-Aid on their tanned faces. "Dad sent us over to see if you want to go water skiing, Miss Anna."

"If you kids will look after Rumpus, I'd love to."

Ten minutes later, I dove into the clear water of Lake George.

"Come on, Anna," Scott hollered as the boat drew alongside. "Let's go skiing. How long has it been?"

"Only about twenty years," I yelled over the motor's roar. "Hit it."

I rose from the water and gleefully high-fived a cheering gallery. Andrew appeared at the shoreline, his arms akimbo, scowling.

I signaled for Scott to circle the lake again, swearing I'd live long enough to see Andrew Macdade shackled in a deportation line.

Chapter 40

Whatever inexplicable resentment Andrew felt while watching me water ski evaporated the second I joined him onshore. After a light supper and guarded chitchat about everything except water skiing, he set up the Scrabble board on the porch for our nightly competition. I collected the dictionary, citron candle and our stash of licorice. He was an enthusiastic player and a worthy opponent. His eagerness to learn new words had once touched me; I was sorry he'd been deprived of a higher education. Now I knew he'd have used it only to pull off bigger scams.

Waiting for him to take his turn, I pictured a hungry, envious youth carrying coal on his bent back to the Ravelston Hotel. Andrew's imitation of Oliver Twist, begging "more food, sir" had once endeared him to me. Now it was evident that that performance was the nearest he'd ever come to revealing his bleak past.

He played the word *tahini*, proud of himself. "That's something I'll never eat again. All that couscous and tabouli at the palace made me long for fish and chips."

"Great word, Andrew. Good for you." I smiled, playing *axe* on a double word tile.

"It's a close game, my dear."

He Scrabbled on a triple word tile for eighty-three points and won the match. "How's that for a boy from Porty?"

I lavished him with praise and then reached across the table and took his hands in mine. "We need to talk about your property, Andrew. Are you up to it now or would tomorrow morning be better?"

Stone-faced, he looked across the field at my tent.

"Your first wife, Laura, owns the Admiral Macdade manse; it's not leased to the university. The Highclere Hotel owns the house you claimed Paula left to you; it's not leased to the Johnson & Johnson Company. You were wrong to deceive me, but you were a fool to lie to my financial advisors, especially in light of today's technology."

He flung the dictionary over the porch railing.

"Listen up, Andrew. You met my trust officer, my accountant and Rupert early on. We all believed you owned real estate worth a half-million pounds."

"So?"

"You promised to send them copies of your deeds and leases for our financial planning. I typed those requests for you months ago, but we've never heard a peep. Did you deep-six them?"

"I sent them," he insisted, "through Drew. Maybe he grew suspicious when you refused his offer to oversee your accounts. Or maybe my solicitor, Mr. Bryce, thinks my affairs are none of your business."

"You know I have a moral and legal obligation to keep the trust intact for future generations."

"We Scots do things differently. Under Scottish law, I'm not required to disclose my personal holdings."

"That may be," I said through clenched teeth. "But you lied to my advisors, putting us both under a microscope. You have no holdings."

"Oh no? Ask Drew about my royalties from *Concrete and Clay* and about my pension. I told him to protect me until I could see which way the wind was blowing with you. Just last month, he reinsured my collection of guitars and equestrian paintings, all stored in the Admiral's manse by the sea."

"Laura owns that house, Andrew. The registry records prove it."

"I was in a bind after Paula died, couldn't pay the taxes. Laura said she'd help and then moved in behind my back."

"Listen carefully, Andrew. We're in trouble. If Sam's kids learn I'm supporting a penniless husband, they'll sue the fiduciaries for mismanagement. My monthly allowance will be withheld indefinitely and I'll be penniless too."

"I'll get a job and support you."

"You couldn't earn enough to support me. I'm not about to forfeit my security because you're a liar. Only an annulment will get us out of this mess."

"Are you still on that kick? What would I tell Andrina and Drew?"

"We won't tell anyone. We'll carry on as we are. The bankers won't have anything to balk about and we'll continue to receive that generous monthly check."

"Is this a trick?"

"No, it's a solution." I turned a radiant smile on him. "We'll continue to live together, and I'll be able to collect my widow's benefits."

"And everything else between us will stay the same?"

"Absolutely. Except we'll be richer."

Brightening, he volunteered to go back into service. "You can rent the house and live with me in staff quarters, study your books while I work. We'll save for a Sanibel cottage."

The hour was late and my nerves were frayed. "Perhaps I've misjudged you, Andrew, but your lies make you look bad. Bankers are like pit bulls when it comes to safeguarding trust funds. Annulment is the only way out."

"Anna, I've hated being a kept man. I'll make you proud, just wait and see. I'll contact my domestic agencies tomorrow. The Regal will place me in a minute; Joe Biden wanted me to buttle and Jane Fonda asked me to run her Georgia horse ranch before I took the Bayley position. Stanley at New York's Pavilion Agency tapped me for the Revlon estate. Everyone loves a Scottish servant. I can write my own ticket."

Andrew was again flying through never-never land. Maybe he was keeping the farce alive. Or perhaps he lived to lie. But he was a survivor. His future with me was finished. And he knew it.

Chapter 41

The next morning, he lay in bed grumbling about the bank. "We just got married. I've never heard of such poppycock. This wouldn't happen in Scotland. Does money mean more than love?"

"No. Unfortunately, you bought more than you bargained for when you tried to dazzle the money-men. It's one thing to spin a tale at the racetrack, quite another to lie to a bank officer."

"Would you have married me if you'd known?"

"I'm a coal miner's granddaughter, remember. You should have leveled with me."

"What a bother," he groaned. "Anna, I swear I'll never tell another lie."

I laughed. "You and George Washington. Now let's move forward, as you're wont to say, and plan our trip to Montreal."

"It's a week off," he snapped. "I don't want Andrina or Drew to know about this annulment business."

We avoided the topic as the days passed, focusing instead on a fictional future. Andrew painstakingly updated his resumé in longhand and studiously composed urgent cover letters to domestic agencies, begging them to reply "posthaste."

Each day as noon approached, he fussed and rushed to the post office lest he miss the early afternoon collection.

He spent more and more time away from camp, gambling at the betting parlors and the track. I volunteered at Hague's Black Watch Library on Tuesdays and ran the Trout House Inn's reception desk on Wednesday mornings, to keep busy and to be seen.

My boating friends dropped anchor near Fort Ticonderoga, dinghyed ashore and collected us for a few strained hours aboard. When they waved farewell, I suspected they were happy to be rid of us. Andrew had monopolized the conversation – until he flooded the head.

ON THE FIRST TUESDAY IN AUGUST, we met Ruth in Saratoga Springs at the Circus Café. When Andrew went off to organize his bets, my friend leaned over her cappuccino. "You're gaunt, Anna," she said. "I'm worried."

Her concern released a storm surge of tears. "It's humiliating to have married such a slimeball but it will soon be over." I filled her in on the disgruntled beneficiaries/annulment scheme and then asked about Paula.

Ruth shook her head. "I've searched the Oxford database; nothing. And I've combed the *London Times* archives; not a trace. No OBE, no skiing accident and no obituary. Mark my words, Anna, this man is a lunatic."

The lunatic's sudden appearance made me jump. Feigning delight, I squeaked, "Oh, it's you. Aren't we supposed to meet at the clubhouse in thirty minutes?"

"I didn't think you'd find your way. The grounds are more crowded than usual."

"Did Duncan get us a good table?" I asked. "We're dying to meet Jack and the stupendous Joan."

He shrugged nonchalantly. "Duncan's off today and Jack left word at the paddocks that he had business in London, flew out this morning." He chuckled. "So it's just the three of us for lunch, ladies. Duncan told Manny to set us up. We'll be sitting pretty."

ANDREW USHERED US UPSTAIRS and slipped a $50 to Manny, who led us past impossibly close tables to the kitchen's entrance, where he seated us with a flourish next to the rubbish bins. The chairs were rickety, the table tiny, the garbage cans stank, and the chef yelled at the help. No one was dressed up. And only Ruth and I wore hats. We burst out laughing.

Andrew posed, stony-eyed, fingering his faded Hermes necktie and flashing his gold Rolex. Intermittently, he scanned the crowd below us through binoculars, announcing the names of VIPs only he could see. Nudging Ruth, I rolled my eyes.

He pointed to the finish line. "Manny's given us a fine table, eh girls?"

I snorted. "We look like extras on a *My Fair Lady* set."

Andrew stared at the menu.

The waiter scribbled our order, caught me sniffing the garbage, moved the bins an inch and bowed. Our lunch arrived in no time and Andrew gallantly rose to help. The massive tray held a pitcher of iced tea, three bottles of mineral water and three plates of salmon garnished with pickled beets. Most of it landed in my lap.

Andrew nimbly caught a boat of dilled mayonnaise, inadvertently knocking my hat into a garbage can. Wide-eyed,

Ruth and I watched it sink into a pool of grease and floating French fries.

Nothing original could be said. We reeled in gales of laughter, wiping and mopping, tears streaming down our cheeks. If Andrew was ruffled, he hid it well. He left to place a bet just as Manny bore down on us with wet cloths and limp red and white roses.

Ruth collapsed into her chair. "My knees are weak, Anna. He's like the emperor in the fairytale."

I nodded, drying my eyes, not yet able to speak.

"Listen to this," she continued. "Yesterday, I interviewed a woman at the college who crewed on Mr. Taubman's corporate jet about ten years ago. I asked if she knew Andrew."

"Let me guess. She never heard of him."

"Bingo."

"I don't think he ever met the man."

"He's such a pig, Anna. I hate to leave. What more can I do to help?"

"Call often. Talk to him if he answers. We need to make him think he's in the loop."

LEAVING RUTH THAT AFTERNOON to join Andrew for the ride back to camp, I felt I'd been sentenced to hard labor. My frustration grew when I opened Andrina's e-mail that evening. She expressed sympathy over my friend's death, wished us a safe trip to New Jersey. "Fiona and Tom and I look forward to seeing you in Sanibel next winter."

What the hell had he done? Rumpus's former owner was ill but she was expected to make a full recovery. I flew out of the tent and thrust the printed message in his face. "What's going on?"

His smile was melancholy. "You've been concerned about your friend, dearest. I called Andrina from the track today, told her we'd see them another time."

"My friend is far from dead, you idiot," I shouted. "Why didn't you consult me? I was looking forward to seeing Fiona."

Smug as the cat who swallowed the canary, he replied in little more than a whisper. "It's not exactly a good time for us, is it, my little one?"

I stalked off with Rumpus and marched down to the lake, Rupert's words ringing in my ears. *Maybe he's more clever than we realized.* Andrew had neatly sidestepped my plan to confront Andrina privately.

Reality came in for a crash-landing. He's on the lam. Afraid to cross the border, he never intended to go to Canada in the first place.

Andrew hadn't filed a tax return since he left Philadelphia. He refused to renew his expired passport. He carried an old international driver's license and rigidly drove under the speed limit. He had no car, no post office box, no checking account and no credit card. He was a non-person. Invisible. Untraceable.

Did Scotland Yard want him? Interpol? He'd been flying under the radar for more than a decade, hiding behind the skirts of American wives.

Chapter 42

The next morning, I burrowed my head under the blankets, sick of scheming and more than sick of Andrew. Standing naked and erect over me, fresh from a shower, he yanked the blankets to the foot of the bed. He'd never been aggressive about sex before. He normally wore a dressing gown or wrapped a towel around his waist before lilting "Hormone time, darling."

"No way." I retrieved the bedcovers and pulled them up to my neck. "I'm miserable."

"You've brought it on yourself," he snarled, grabbing his trousers. "You made me retire, promised we'd be together forever. Where am I supposed to live if you annul our marriage?"

At that moment, I lost my cool. "In a sink hole on Devil's Island."

"See?" he cried. "I know you're trying to get rid of me. But I'll love you to your dying day, Anna."

In a fit of rage, I shot out of bed and socked his shoulder. "Love? You don't know the meaning of the word. Your filthy lies have ruined everything. Have you never loved anyone enough to stop lying?"

He licked his lips and stared at the John and Yoko poster he'd hung over our bed. "I'll tell you what I want you to know and no more," he said flatly.

Regaining my composure, I reminded him that he'd always told me and everyone else only what he wanted us to know. "It's long past time to put down roots, Andrew. You've reconciled with your children. They look up to you."

He seemed disinterested, almost bored.

"Don't you want something more than a transient life?"

"You're just like all the rest of them greedy women who trapped me." He glowered and inhaled, setting off a coughing fit.

I thumped his back. "Greedy? I've supported you. Grace got you a job at the Royal Hotel, moved to Sunninghill and helped you manage the Highclere. And how can you classify Paula, a philanthropic surgeon, as greedy?"

Lost in the world he created, he stumbled through another variation on the *woe is me* theme.

"I told you. Laura was a tramp, Grace a lesbian, Sheila a nympho. And Paula was a selfish tease. She promised to teach me to ski the day she died, but then took off early with her fancy friends." In a feral voice, he added, "She got what she deserved."

"Stop it. You don't mean that."

"Oh no?" He smirked. "If she'd kept her word…"

"And what am I, Andrew? Another day at the races?"

"At first, you seemed different. You listened to me, made me feel good. But now you're like the others, always butting into my private affairs." He stomped out the door, calling for the dog to follow.

Rumpus stayed put.

I made my way to the bathhouse and stood under the steamy shower. How long had it taken Laura, Grace, Paula, Darby and Sheila to realize he was an amoral man? His contempt for Paula made no sense. Why would he mourn a woman who *deserved* to die?

I drew hearts on the mirror because he expected them and then stiffened my spine and erased them, ready to go another round. Rumpus was waiting outside the shunky door and we headed back together.

We found Andrew reading the newspaper in the Adirondack twig rocker he claimed he found by the roadside a week before. The packrat had turned the porch into a junkyard, full of ripped boxes, cracked stained glass, rusty iron gates and a black-faced yardell. I stepped over a box of old tools and patted the bump he didn't get during RAF training.

"Hello, dearest," he said pleasantly. "Refreshed and ready to hear my plan?"

"Another one?"

"I've been looking at real estate in Manchester. We should leave a few days early and go take a look, stay at that B&B up the road from the outlets. Would a shopping spree suit you, darling?"

Stunned that he believed I'd move to Vermont with him, I asked, "Do you really want to leave Chatham, Andrew?"

"Change would do us good, my dear. A small holding overlooking a pond, rolling hills and starry nights. I'll grow vegetables and board horses. We'll have a wholesome life. Once your bankers hear I'm working, they'll leave us alone."

Next he'll ship a crate of carrots to the Trust Department to prove he's a man of substance, I thought. "There was a time when I would have followed you to the moon."

Andrew tossed the newspaper aside. "Still planning to give me the boot, eh? Should I go now, call it a day?"

"We're taking the business out of our marriage, not the love."

"Is that so?" he said, pulling me onto his lap. "Do you promise we'll live together until the end of your life?"

I resisted the urge to remind him again that his lies had shattered our lives. "With luck, therapy will help. Let's focus on the present rather than my old age."

He looked hopeful. "Maybe we'll find a perfect spot and live off the land. I stopped drinking and swearing. I can stop telling stories, too. I have a verra strong will."

Faking a smile, I agreed to pack up early, wondering what he might "will" for me.

Chapter 43

We settled up with Scott and Alice a few days later. I fought with my guilty conscience as we cheerfully promised to see them in Sanibel the next winter. I knew our friends would never see us together again.

Red silos, white spires and herds of Jersey cows dotted Vermont's lush green hills. At noon we stopped at a Dorset bakery and sat among falling yellow leaves savoring hot crusty bread, cheddar cheese wedges and tangy cider. In the warm rustling wind, I found myself amused by Andrew's real estate prattle and grew curious to see more of the area.

Oddly, he insisted on scouting out the property listings alone and dropped me off at the outlets. Two hours later, he loaded my shopping bags into the car and eagerly drove me up a long, winding road to a glossy red Greek Revival. With a huge barn, perennial gardens and two small ponds, it was storybook perfect.

"You have a connoisseur's eye, Andrew. Who lives here?"

"A couple in the village bought it last year as an investment. They plan to list it next month; perfect timing. She's a lumber heiress from British Columbia and can afford to be choosy about who buys it. Get your annulment and sell your house. We'll live here eight months of the year and winter at Little Palm Cottage the other four. How's that for good planning? Are you happy, my darling? Do you want to go inside?"

"No one is here, Andrew. We can't just walk into someone else's house. Where are the owners?"

"At the conference center, where I left them viewing Linda McCartney's retrospective on the Beatles." He grinned. "They told me to take you right into the house. We'll either see them at the center or catch them tonight for supper at the local diner. You're always telling me to make friends, so I did."

Against my better judgment, I walked the stone-walled boundaries with him and then poked my head into the well-swept barn. Afternoon sun streamed through the open door across bales of hay and a long row of stalls. A thin layer of dust covered tools, tables, chairs and wooden boxes. Andrew climbed the ladder, disappeared into the loft and came down with an oil painting of someone's ancestor tucked under his arm. Two antique children's chairs dangled from his fingers and a small brass telescope stuck out from his back pocket.

"Look what I found that no one wants," he said, stacking the loot in a dark corner. "I can make a quick quid on this stuff at Bob's Back Door in Chatham."

I froze, glaring at him. Oblivious, he darted in and out of the stalls, searching for more. This was a man who fancied himself a soldier of the Cross, a paragon of Christian morality.

"Put them back, you fool," I hollered, "or you'll burn in hell."

"But they're just going to rot here, Anna. I'm saving them."

Saving. Protecting. Helping. Always a justification, an excuse. I walked over and gently took a carpenter's plane from his hand. "Andrew, we don't belong here. Let's have a peek at the exhibit before dinner."

He nodded sheepishly, thanked me for reminding him to "be good" and said, "Maybe Linda caught me in one of her photographs. Now wouldn't that be a coincidence?"

AT THE CROWDED CONFERENCE CENTER, Andrew reminisced for all to hear, placing himself in several photos, a tiny unrecognizable speck, and just outside the frames of others. I cringed when an awestruck Midwestern family asked for his autograph.

"T'was John there that I knew from Soho," he said as he signed each of their programs with a flourish. "Saw Paul from time to time at Ascot and verra grateful he was for my lyrics. Aye, those were grand days, my friends." He laughed, waved to his fans, and ushered me to the exit.

The lumber heiress and her husband were nowhere to be seen. They didn't show at the diner that evening, either. What a surprise.

Chapter 44

We arrived in Chatham just as an early afternoon thunderstorm rolled over Gull Pond and out to sea. The spite fence had been whitewashed and forty Leland cypress trees had been planted along the Grangers' property line. It seemed they'd had nothing to do all summer but bedevil the landscape.

Even so, I was happy to be home. My house was still standing and friends were within easy reach. We unloaded the car together, then Andrew offered to pick up a pizza. The second he was gone, I called Rupert and learned he'd unearthed a treasure trove of damning evidence.

"Right on schedule, Anna," he said as soon as he heard my voice. "I'm relieved. I finally heard from Mr. Bayley yesterday. I'll Fed-Ex a copy of his file today, but not to your house. You'll need a safe place to receive correspondence from now on."

I didn't hesitate. Marta had been leery of Andrew from the beginning; her reservations had caused a ripple in our twenty-year friendship. I gave Rupert her address and phone number and then asked, "Why did Mr. Bayley take so long to answer?"

Rupert sighed. "His secretary had surgery. The temp stuffed my letters into a seldom used in-box. If Mr. Bayley hadn't grabbed one to write on during a conference call last Saturday, they'd still be sitting there. He's terribly sorry, wants to help in any way he can. Seems like a fine gentleman. He faxed extensive information and the bottom line is, Andrew is more devious than we thought."

At that moment, the line beeped. Andrew was trying to get through. I ignored him.

"What do you mean, Rupert?"

"You mustn't let down your guard. You'll understand when you read the materials. In the meantime, burn your will and jot down a replacement, leaving everything to your children. I've prepared a new one to that effect and will put it in the Fed-Ex package."

"When do we file?"

"He'll have to be served first."

"Served?"

"A sheriff will deliver official notice to the house, put the papers in Andrew's hands."

"A uniformed sheriff will terrify him. He'll bolt. Why can't I get the forms at the courthouse and give them to him myself?"

Rupert hesitated. "Try it," he said at last. "If he doesn't retain counsel, we may get away with it. Remember, his signature on the affidavit must be notarized. Do you know a notary public?"

"Yes, my bank manager. I'm sure she'll help."

"I'll tell the courthouse clerk to expect you tomorrow afternoon. Review the forms and then call me. Don't forget, Anna, we still have a two-month wait for the hearing."

I thanked Rupert, hung up and dialed Marta. When her voicemail picked up, I hurried through an apology for avoiding her, said she'd been right about Andrew all along and told her that a package from my attorney would arrive at her house by noon the next day.

Suddenly, I heard her voice; the warmth in it flooded me with relief. "Anna, I'm on my way out. I'll see you here tomorrow. I'm sorry, but I knew something was wrong with him. I don't trust anyone who won't look me in the eye."

Desperate to account for the time I'd spent on the phone, I dumped our suitcases in the bedroom and flew to the basement to stuff clothes into the washing machine. Back upstairs, I turned on the kitchen lights and heated the kettle. Andrew appeared behind me just as I slipped the *Rushmore* soundtrack into the CD player, hoping to humor him.

"I called. Why didn't you pick up?"

I smiled brightly. "I was talking, silly boy. I'm a woman. Women talk on the phone. I called Marta and left a message, telling her we're home. I've started the wash and put the kettle on. Set the pizza on the counter and I'll get plates."

"I thought you were at odds with Marta," he said suspiciously. "Why did you call that old hippie? I like Jackie better. She knows her place. Handles herself like a proper woman."

"I called her, too," I lied. "We're having lunch in a few days."

"So soon?" he grumbled. "What am I supposed to do?"

"Aren't the Damatos expecting you? And don't forget to ask Baron von Mahler if he needs a fall clean-up."

"Yes, madam. I'll ring the Baron today. And I'll make arrangements to call on the lovely Mrs. Damato as well."

I ignored his taunt. "I've asked Marta to give me drawing lessons on Wednesdays," I said, picking a piece of sausage from the pizza. "I promised my Sanibel teacher I'd be ready for January's intermediate class."

In what I hoped was a nonchalant tone, I added, "You're an artist, darling. You know it's all about training the eye to see beyond the obvious. Where better to brush up on perspective than Marta's studio? I start at noon tomorrow."

Chapter 45

Marta waved the double-taped Federal Express envelope at me as I got out of the car. I hugged her, took it with shaking hands and followed her into the dining room, where the curtains were closed. I was grateful for the precaution, for the cool quiet and for the carafe of coffee on the table, centered between two schooner-sized ceramic mugs. I ripped the package open while Marta poured.

On top was my new will, which I slipped into my handbag. Below it was a letter to Rupert from Richard Bayley, enclosing a typewritten chronicle of his experiences with Andrew Macdade; an insurance claim form; the report of a private investigator who'd been hired by Darby Hamilton's mother; and a letter from Darby to the Bayleys. I passed the cover letter to Marta, took a sip of strong, steaming coffee, then delved into the pile, beginning with Mr. Bayley's narrative.

The Bayleys had employed Andrew for about fifteen months when they found him one morning asleep on the back porch. He told them his wife, Darby, had cleaned out the apartment and had gone home to Michigan. They let him live in their servants' quarters above the garage and loaned him one of their cars.

Andrew soon met a medical student, Kristen, and "began spending nights with her," Mr. Bayley reported, "returning in time to make breakfast."

"Another medicine woman," I muttered.

When Andrew told the Bayleys he was going to his daughter's wedding in Edinburgh, Mrs. Bayley gave him an $8,000 bracelet to take as a gift. But not long after, the local chemist showed Mr. Bayley her wedding band and announced that she'd married Andrew. Sheila Peters was wearing the $8,000 bracelet.

Andrew later explained to Mrs. Bayley that Kristen had refused to marry him, so he proposed to Sheila, used the bracelet as bait, and missed his daughter's wedding to go on his honeymoon.

I passed each page to Marta as I finished. We both read in silence, pausing occasionally to let it all sink in.

Andrew terminated his employment with the Bayleys in 1998, telling them he was divorcing Sheila and going home to be with his children. "He sent us a postcard, wishing us well, with a return address in Woodstock, England," Mr. Bayley wrote, "but it was postmarked Philadelphia."

Shortly after, Sylvia Stone contacted the Bayleys, saying she'd been involved with Andrew four years earlier and that he frequently brought her to their house when they were in Barbados. "He told her he was renting, thinking about buying the place, and that the Mercedes in the garage was his. Somehow, he'd learned the combination to the safe. He opened it, showed her precious jewelry and bank statements reflecting substantial deposits; all his, he said. Sylvia thought he was a

British Airways pilot; he wore a shirt with pilot's stripes to the nightclubs and called himself Captain Andy. She also thought he was once married to a doctor, named Paula, who died while skiing."

The Bayleys knew Andrew gambled at the Philadelphia Race Track. They suspected he was also a bookie. He left boxes of betting slips and racing forms behind.

The final page of Mr. Bayley's account contained just two sentences. "While in our employ for four years, Andrew Macdade simultaneously had two wives and two girlfriends. That we knew about."

I handed it to Marta and stared as she read.

"Good God, Anna," was all she said.

The next document was a copy of Mrs. Bayley's 1998 insurance claim for stolen jewelry. When I gave it to Marta, she actually half-laughed. "Hope you brought along his family heirlooms, Anna."

I had. Using a magnifying glass, we studied the serial number on each piece. Both matched. The sapphire ring and the diamond brooch belonged to Mrs. Bayley. They had never been covered with flour in any Portobello pantry.

"A jewel thief, to boot," Marta said.

Next was the private investigator's report. In an effort to stop her daughter's ill-fated marriage, Darby Hamilton's mother had hired a PI to check out her prospective son-in-law. She learned that Andrew Macdade was never in the RAF, never worked for the prominent Taubman family, and was wanted by Interpol for theft in Sunninghill. He wore a British Airways uniform to Michigan bars, telling everyone who'd listen that he was an undercover CIA/PLO agent and spoke fluent Arabic. His favorite drinking establishments were *Scuzzy's* and *Fingers.*

This time, Marta hooted. "You couldn't make this stuff up."

She was right. I had to laugh, too. But our levity faded when we looked at the last document, Darby Hamilton's letter to the Bayleys, handwritten in beautiful script. She apologized for her inability to warn them about Andrew, explaining that when they married, she was 26, he was 49, and her daughters were four and two. Within a month, the beatings began.

Andrew punched her and threw her around the bedroom "because I was late getting home from work or because I forgot to pick up the mail or because the weather was bad." He'd beg for forgiveness each time, then get drunk and "rough her up" again. He'd routinely "grab me by the neck," she wrote, "lift me off my feet. The last time, he chased me into the bathroom and strangled me until I passed out. My children ran to a neighbor, who called the police. My girls and I left Philadelphia the next morning."

"Paula died of a broken neck," Marta whispered.

"And I'm beginning to think Andrew is capable of anything."

"You're not safe with him, Anna. What are you going to do?"

I lit another cigarette and ground the smoldering one out. "I'm going to drive straight to the Barnstable Courthouse to pick up the annulment forms. Then I'm going to convince the bastard to sign. Today."

"Not today. You're wired. Chill, before you do something you'll regret."

I shook my head. "I've waited long enough."

She pressed her hand to her throat, her eyes worried. "Remember, Anna, revenge is best served cold."

Chapter 46

When I arrived home, I found a note from Andrew saying he'd gone for a walk to town. Rumpus wouldn't go with him. The ninety-minute round-trip to Barnstable had given me the opportunity to realize Marta was right. I needed time, to convince Andrew that the annulment was a mere formality and that we would continue to live together, before I presented him with the papers.

The next week, as I rushed out the door, ostensibly to meet Jackie for lunch at the Optimist Café on Route 6A, I found Andrew on a stepladder alongside the Grangers' fence, pruning branches. I screamed, "Stop."

"It's legal to trim anything that hangs over your property," he said, and continued cutting.

"That may be, but the Grangers will call the police, report that the foreigner is at it again. Stop it. Now."

"Yes, ma'am. Right away, ma'am." He slowly climbed down and bowed.

I scoffed, kissed him goodbye, and walked briskly to my car. Five miles away, I parked out of sight behind Marta's barn.

She greeted me with a mug of coffee and a glazed expression, the Fed Ex package in hand. "I've read this thing three times. It's frightening."

I nodded. "And I'm guessing it's the proverbial tip of the iceberg."

I used Marta's phone to call Rupert. "Listen to your intuition, Anna," he said. "Strike when the time is right. Where are the papers?"

"In my handbag."

"He must admit his misrepresentations and consent to the annulment in writing. Did I tell you all that?"

"Yes, but my head is jumbled. Tell me again why the documents have to be notarized."

"To authenticate his signature."

"Does Andrew have to attend the hearing?"

"No, better that he doesn't. He could change his tune at the last minute, claim coercion and demand counsel."

"I'm shaky, Rupert. It's even harder living with him now, knowing what I know."

"Tell Andrew that all your friends sympathize with him. Tell him I'm outraged that the bank has such a hold on your personal lives. We'll coddle him, string him along, and be rid of him in about two months. If need be, I'll come down to the Cape and reassure him."

Later than afternoon, I found Andrew dozing in his favorite spot, sans the Gull Pond view and breezes. He awoke when I sat across from him and then asked pleasantly if I'd enjoyed my lunch with Jackie.

"Yes and no, Andrew." I placed my manila file on the table between us and spun yet another story. "Jackie saw how troubled I was. I told her about our problems and Rupert's plan. She was saddened and sends her love."

"Bloody hell. You told Jackie? You said it was just between us, Anna. Why did you tell her? Marta knows too, doesn't she?"

"They both knew something was wrong. We need support, Andrew. Friends will help us cope."

I took a deep breath and plowed on. "The psychiatrist will help, too. Edith says he's a Harvard man who specializes in conflict resolution and has an office in Provincetown."

Andrew glanced nervously at the folder.

I pointed to the spite fence. "That's a constant reminder of your skewed thinking. Your impulsive behavior is about to freeze my trust."

"Jackie sent her love?" he asked. "She's not mad at me?"

"No," I said, realizing I lied with the grace of a saint. "And Rupert isn't either. He told me how to proceed with this miserable thing. And with the doctor's help, we can get back to where we were before this bank mess reared its ugly head."

"When did you talk to Rupert? I'd like to speak with him and explain myself."

"Oh, don't worry," I said. "You'll see him soon enough; he wants to visit. He's enamored with Scotland and its history, wants to hear more about your grandfather and King George. Now, I've brought home some fresh scrod. Do you want to see a movie tonight or play Scrabble?"

Chapter 47

Andrew held my hand during the hour-long trip to Provincetown. His demeanor puzzled me. He seemed confident, perhaps even excited. Either he was worried and covering it up, or he was thrilled to have an opportunity to con a psychiatrist.

He droned on about one of his favorite topics: people from the past and how he'd helped them improve their lives, yobs and nobs alike. I took the cue, praising his good deeds as we passed through Harwich, Orleans, Eastham, Wellfleet, and Truro. My head was pounding by the time we reached the office of Dr. Willard Whitney.

The waiting room was cold and sterile, with orange plastic chairs lining the walls. Weathered lobster pots held stacks of self-help magazines and informational brochures on everything from AIDS to xenophobia. A radio talk show camouflaged the muffled voices of patients in session behind flimsy hollow doors.

Dr. Whitney reportedly had served as a mediator during the Clinton administration and held a chair at Harvard, where he lectured and authored treatises on conflict resolution. Now over seventy, he'd semi-retired in Provincetown and counseled only a few privileged patients. He'd agreed to see us as a professional courtesy to Edith Troy.

We'd been waiting about twenty minutes when a tall, lean man walked into the waiting room wearing a starched khaki uniform. His tanned, bald head looked like an elongated walnut. He waved us up to his second-floor office, a well-appointed room filled with charcoal line drawings, Navajo rugs, brass lamps and framed diplomas and citations. An exotic lap dog slept by the woodstove. Andrew and I settled side by side on a soft brown leather couch.

Dr. Whitney sat in a Boston rocker across from us, picked up a pen and a legal pad, then took down our names, address and dates of birth. Looking over his rimless half-glasses, he announced, "We are strictly a cash operation. My fee for couples is $350 per fifty-minute session. You've booked a double session today and I will accept your check at this time."

I gasped. "Don't you take Blue Cross?"

"Insurance? That's between you and your company."

I was desperate. I wrote the $700 check.

Money business done, Dr. Whitney looked at us with renewed interest, smiling benevolently as if we were errant children in the principal's office. He leaned forward and confided, "You've come to the right place, Mr. and Mrs. Macdade. We grow souls here."

He then told us about his political connections, his professional achievements and his success treating troubled marriages. Perhaps he was trying to gain our respect and trust, but I was anxious. He was spending my money, touting his curriculum vitae, at a rate of $7 a minute. *Cha-ching* rang in my ears. When he finally asked why we were there, I pounced.

"Dr. Whitney, Andrew has told so many lies he's placed me in a legal bind. My financial advisors have demanded that our marriage be annulled. We need help to deal with the fallout."

Nodding sagely in his General Patton uniform, he scribbled on his legal pad. "And Andrew, why are you here today?"

"Well, Doctor," he said earnestly, "I misrepresented myself to my lovely wife to get her to marry me and now things are strained between us. I've admitted I was wrong but she can't stop blaming me. She's my life. I don't want to lose her. So I'm here for you to fix me, Doctor."

Dr. Whitney vaulted from his rocker, strode across the room and grabbed two paperbacks from a credenza. "Here's just the thing. I've had brilliant success using this scholarly treatise for role-playing. You two need to bond, to create a lasting emotional intimacy, and I'm just the man to help you."

He handed each of us a copy of *Partnering: How to Love Your Mate Without Losing Yourself*. "This will teach you how to listen, how to really hear and understand each other."

I glanced sideways at Andrew, saw he was eating it up, and groaned inwardly as Dr. Whitney promised that our "dancing selves" would soon emerge, blending into the light of "blissful soul growth." He then gently asked Andrew about his childhood in Scotland.

Andrew swelled in the spotlight. "So good of you to inquire, Doctor. I had a hard-luck time growing up. My father was his regiment's sole survivor of the Normandy Invasion and came home shell-shocked."

Saving Private Ryan came to mind.

"Father forced me to leave school at fifteen to help run the family business."

Some business, I thought. A coal cart pulled by a nag named Dick.

"My older brother, Gordon, bullied and beat me," Andrew continued. "My parents were always out, leaving him in charge. No one ever truly cared for me until my Anna came along."

"Ah, I see," said the doctor. "Andrew, please look at your wife. Tell her how deeply your brother hurt you."

Andrew turned to me. "It was terrible, darling," he said in a trembling voice. "I shook at the verra thought of being alone with him."

Dr. Whitney's role-playing therapy was costing me hundreds of dollars. Excited about directing our little drama, he rocked faster and faster. Leaning forward, he said, "Now Anna, please repeat – mirror – the sad concerns of your husband."

Like a bad actress in a B movie, I took Andrew's stealing, cheating, beating hands in mine. "I feel your pain, dear. You were scared and alone. Your parents never protected you."

"Oh, darling," Andrew replied, blinking back tears, "you do understand. May I tell the doctor about the scary man who made me touch him in the cold alley?"

Wondering where this latest tale came from, I nodded, stroking the hands that had strangled Darby. "Sweetheart, you must tell Doctor Whitney everything that traumatized you into a lifetime of lies."

Andrew blubbered through the grotesque story, pausing halfway through to ask me, "How am I doing?"

I almost laughed. Dr. Quack had just earned $700. He looked at his watch and announced that with the time left, he would summarize the session. Leaning back in his rocker, he steepled his fingers as he delivered the summation. "We've made great headway today. If you read *Partnering* before our next session, you will experience an understanding you never dreamed existed. You must learn to communicate, to trust, to become better partners."

The lap dog by the woodstove stood and stretched, then yawned and curled up again.

"Anna," Dr. Whitney said, "you must leap across the great divide. You nurtured and praised Andrew like a good mother until you found out he had secrets. But we all have many facets to our personalities. To him, you have become a bad mother, analyzing and emasculating him. It is you who must integrate the two Andrews."

I didn't know what I was to Andrew at that point, but I was damn sure I wasn't his mother. I wanted to throw *Partnering* at Dr. Whitney, grab my check and run. Yet I knew the misguided psychiatrist was a perfect pawn. Andrew was smug, vindicated. He'd continue to believe that the annulment wouldn't change his life.

The good doctor continued. "And you, Andrew, must empathize with Anna's disappointment." After looking at his watch and penciling in another double session a week later, he stood and dismissed us. The $7 per minute fee didn't include a few paces to open his office door.

On the steps of the peeling gray house, I clutched the railing, fearing I'd collapse under the hypocrisy of it all.

Speechless, I chain-smoked during the long ride home, while Andrew scanned the radio stations.

Eventually, I turned the volume down. "So, I'd better learn to be more patient, right, Andrew?"

He patted my knee and suggested we enjoy the Indian summer sun and take Rumpus for a romp on Forest Beach when we got home.

JUST AS I stripped off my slacks to change into my bathing suit, he grabbed me. "I want you now," he growled, and swung me onto the bed.

I lay still, remembering that rape is about control. Detached, I watched him rip open his zipper, felt his cold penis enter me, and counted the seconds as he rutted to relief.

He rolled off, grinning. "Guess that doctor told you a thing or two, eh?"

"Do that again, Andrew, and I'll Bobbitt you."

He sneered. "You wouldn't know how. You never had a real man until I came along."

Ignoring him, I packed a canvas tote with towels and bottled water and we set off for Forest Beach with Rumpus. Andrew had morphed into yet another personality, ghostlike, unworldly and hollow. We walked down the long sandy path amid bayberry bushes, beach plums and golden grasses, still vibrant, offering a dramatic contrast to the sparkling blue water. I peeled off my sweatshirt and shorts and dove into the warm eddy of Nantucket Sound.

Rumpus paddled beside me for a few minutes, then turned and tried to swim back to shore. He couldn't make it. As he struggled and whimpered, I realized we'd been caught in a riptide. I couldn't stand; the tide was unusually high. My right shoulder seized and a sharp pain ran down my arm.

Andrew stood less than fifty feet away, watching.

"Help us, Andrew. We can't make it. The current is too strong."

A malicious gleam crossed his face.

Knowing I didn't have enough stamina to tread and float until the tide went out, I screamed. "Help us, damn you."

He continued to stare, still as a statue.

I grabbed Rumpus's collar with my right hand and cut madly into the current with my good arm. Using both feet as a rudder, I kicked for minutes and then finally touched the sandy bottom. I cradled Rumpus, carried him to shallow water, then dropped to all fours and crawled to dry land on my hands and knees.

"Why didn't you help us? You could've walked in, tossed the leash and pulled us out. Some 'real man' you are."

He shrugged. "You knew what you were doing. Grand ladies always do."

He sauntered away, singing a vaguely familiar tune, his sweet tenor carrying on the breeze. I recognized the old sea chantey, then remembered its last line. "Down among the dead men, let her lie."

Chapter 48

A sane woman would have run. I held my ground, keeping my emotions in check, navigating cautiously around Andrew's fluctuating moods and suspicions.

During autumn, locals traditionally throw impromptu gatherings to celebrate the end of tourist season, and our telephone rang steadily. I charged into the social swirl of oyster festivals, fiddle concerts and cranberry harvest fairs, dragging friends and neighbors back to my house for potluck suppers. Every occasion gave Andrew an opportunity to do what he did best: dress up and show off. When guests asked if we'd be wintering in Sanibel again, I nodded. "Oh yes, and you must visit."

Unbeknownst to Andrew, I'd confided in the Connecticut Carters. They offered to drive my mother up for her birthday weekend, to buffer the mounting tension. Andrew provisioned for her favorite meals, carved a pumpkin and bought her a dozen red roses.

And so it was in mid-October they all arrived in a rented minivan, complete with Mother's wheelchair, walker and medications. "Where's Andrew?" she cried, looking through me.

"Right here, my angel," he called, sprinting across the driveway to place the roses in her lap.

His standing roast was rare, the baked Alaska a flaming masterpiece, but my mother seemed confused. When I tucked her into bed that night, she asked if Andrew used drugs. I assured her he didn't.

"Well, there's something peculiar about a man who acts like he's acting. You drive me to the ocean tomorrow, Anna." She yawned and kissed me goodnight.

The next day, Andrew prepared lobster-mango salad for lunch and the Carters' son dropped in en route to Nantucket to finish one of many "McMansions" he'd helped build. Mark regaled us with tales of "the Island, where millionaires mow billionaires' lawns…"

Reaching for seconds, he added, "By the way, Andrew, Eric Clapton is building an eight million dollar house in Wellfleet and I'm doing the woodwork. Didn't you say you know him?"

Andrew jumped up from the table. "Indeed I do, Mark. I'll ring his mother right now, ask Erin to have him call me here."

He was on the phone for a few minutes. With tongue in cheek, I reminded my guests that Mrs. Clapton places flowers on Paula's grave every week.

The Carters chorused knowing "ahs." My mother said the story sounded fishy.

Andrew returned out of breath. "I had a spiffing good chat with Erin. Her 'boy with the guitar,' as she calls him, is heading for the Cape in a few weeks. Are you up to entertaining Eric, Anna?"

"Sure," I said. "Maybe we should drive to Wellfleet this afternoon, see where Eric plans to build."

No one took the bait. Mark left to catch the next ferry and his parents opted for a Sunday seal-watch. I cleared the table as Andrew launched into the tale yet again. "It was Paula, my late wife, who first met Mrs. Clapton…"

My mother interrupted. "Who are these people?"

I headed for the kitchen as he began his explanation. Running water drowned out his voice as I opened his address book and punched in the number for the rock star's mother. I reached Tiffany at Phone-A-Bet.

After seeing them off for an afternoon of seal-watching on Captain Dave's Boston Whaler, I tucked Mother in for a nap. As soon as she was settled, I opened Saturday's mail and found a notice from Cape Cod Bank and Trust. My checking account was overdrawn by $2,000. Andrew was getting sloppy. Or getting ready to run.

I called the bank manager at home; Teri told me she'd debited my cash reserve to cover the check and would begin an audit.

WE SAW THE Carters and Mother off after breakfast on Monday, waving from the driveway until they were out of sight. Andrew gave me a generous smile as we headed back inside and then scowled when I took the annulment papers from my desk drawer. "Is this really necessary, Anna? I gave your mother a wonderful weekend. Now you're breaking my heart."

I stroked his arm and reminded him that without the annulment, we'd have no money to live on. "Just write a few sentences on the nice stationery I gave you last Christmas. Then we'll take the forms to the bank and have your signature notarized."

"Notarized?" he cried. "You said it would be private."

"Heavens, Andrew, no one cares what you're signing. The notary simply verifies that you're doing it of your own free will, under oath."

I brought out the dove gray stationery with his name and my address printed in bold black at the top. I was pleased that frugality had prevented me from having it engraved. It would soon be obsolete.

I held my breath and looked over his shoulder as he picked up his fountain pen and meticulously copied the words from the complaint onto his own stationery. "I, Andrew Menzies Macdade, misrepresented myself to gain access to my wife's assets. I agree to the annulment…"

What a coup. I swept up the documents and rushed Andrew out the door to the bank.

Teri ushered us into her office, all business, as if we were closing a million-dollar deal. And we were. She watched as he signed, then blotted his dated signature and notarized it, graciously offering her assistance in the future.

Wearing a morose expression, Andrew refused my offer to drop him at the house. Once again, I adjusted the seat and the mirrors, wondering whose car he'd be driving next. I flew past Marta's driveway, honking twice, and sped to the Barnstable County Courthouse to officially file *Macdade v. Macdade*.

The marriage hadn't lasted a year. If all went according to plan, I'd be free of him by December 20, an early Christmas gift. I crossed off the days on a pocket calendar, like a convict awaiting parole.

Chapter 49

As November approached and the days grew noticeably shorter, I felt more and more like one of Job's withered leaves. Paper-thin and constantly nauseous, I wondered if I'd become allergic to Andrew's cooking or if he was adding a little something extra to his recipes. Some days I took a Dramamine and went to bed to sleep off the dizziness.

Always compassionate, Marta grounded me. And Morgan's phone calls sometimes brought comic relief. She vowed to "get the goods" on Andrew in Britain.

My son, James, inadvertently handed me a temporary reprieve when he called from Annapolis to announce the birth of his first child, a beautiful little girl. When Andrew came home hours later, I told him we were expected the next afternoon and we'd stay through the Thanksgiving weekend. It came as no surprise when he balked. "I won't go. Barging in so soon would be brash. It's not done in Scotland. I'll drive you to the airport and stay home with Rumpus."

Early the next morning, dressed in his navy blazer and gray slacks, he adopted a chauffeur's role, dropping me at the airport to catch the ten o'clock shuttle to Baltimore. "I won't sleep a wink or eat a morsel without you," he promised.

I smiled absentmindedly.

"What are you thinking?"

"Just listening to your beseeching lilt, Andrew," I said, then left him standing at the security gate.

FOUR DAYS LATER, I felt nothing but dread as the plane landed, wondering how much longer I could stand the sight of him. He kissed me, threw a bouquet of cloyingly sweet lilies in my arms, and reminded me of the next *save our marriage* appointment, two days hence.

Chapter 50

Paranoia and anxiety attacks became the norm. When I realized I had nothing left, no reserves to draw upon, I thought more and more about calling Rupert, telling him I'd take my chances in divorce court. But fate had other plans.

Just after we set up the Scrabble board that evening, my daughter and granddaughter pulled up in a rental car. "Surprise!" Sally shouted from the driveway. "Merry Christmas, Mom and Andrew!"

Emma climbed out of the passenger side, singing *Jingle Bells* and clutching her mewling tabby, Fluffy.

Thrilled beyond belief, I rushed outside to a flurry of hugs and kisses, then shepherded them into the kitchen with their duffle bags and Fluffy's crate. Andrew stood by the kitchen sink, his face near purple.

Emma giggled. "You look funny, Granddad Andrew. We're on the hols for fifteen whole days," she sang, lifting Fluffy up for him to pet.

"Away with that mangy thing," he sputtered, then glared at me. "Is this your doing, Anna?"

"No, Mr. Scrooge, but remember, 'tis the season of miracles."

He stormed off, leaving my girls astonished.

I felt nothing but relief. Sally and Emma had thwarted whatever plans he had for me. At least for now.

My daughter's soft brown eyes clouded with disappointment. "We thought we'd be welcome, Mom. Emma came home from Sanibel enthralled with her new grandfather. Do you want us to leave?"

"Never," I said, folding her into my arms. "I'm in trouble, Sally," I whispered. "He's after our money."

Andrew reappeared, pointing at the cat. "I won't feed it. And I won't empty its stinking litter box."

"You're not expected to. But you are expected to be civil, to show some of those Christian family values you're always blabbing about."

Rendered speechless, he returned to the living room to stoke the fire.

Emma was crestfallen. "Why has Granddad Andrew changed, Grammy?"

Taking a notepad and pencil from the counter, I wrote, *He's a pretend person, like Voldemort.*

Sally lifted a sympathetic eyebrow at me, hugged a pensive Emma, and suggested she take a hot shower while we make grilled cheese sandwiches. Emma went off reciting "Snape, Malfoy, Lestrange…"

A few minutes later, we heard Andrew close the bedroom door.

"Thank God we came, Mom. Are you okay?"

"No, but I will be. Promise you won't breathe a word about this to your brother. I've got the situation in hand."

ANDREW'S DEADLY SILENCE filled our bed that night. He lay on his back stiff as a board, staring at his copy of *Partnering*, but its pages never turned.

I reminded him that when his kids had visited I'd pulled out all the stops. "Now it's your turn to welcome my daughter and granddaughter."

"What choice do I have? It's your house."

He turned off the lamp and snuggled up to me. "Don't make me second-best, Anna. I couldn't live without you."

"You don't have to. We'll be fine. They're only here for a visit. In no time, we'll have our privacy again."

I gave him what I hoped was a convincing kiss good-night, spooned against his back as usual and lay still in the darkness for a long time before I fell asleep.

THE NEXT MORNING, Andrew left the house to see the Baron in Orleans, who'd asked him to cater a holiday cocktail party.

Sally and Emma were dumbfounded when I filled them in. "So the guy who hung out at *Scuzzy's* and *Fingers* has sticky fingers?" Sally said, stifling a laugh.

"I'll help you, Grammy," Emma said solemnly. "I'll spy on him." After a pause, she added, "I'm sure glad he's not my real grandfather."

I laid out the ground rules. "Be nice. We have little more than a week before the hearing and we don't want him to hire a lawyer. He's nervous, but he's holding on. Don't leave me alone with him any more than you have to. And don't leave him alone in the house. He'll steal whatever he can and sell it for quick cash."

"I wondered about him," said Sally. "He was always so perfect on the phone." She frowned. "He's a *sweetheart swindler*, just like on TV."

Sally and Emma's visit gave me the excuse I needed to postpone the next *save our marriage* appointment with the *sweetheart swindler* and Dr. Quack.

AFTER SERVICES THAT SUNDAY, members of the congregation greeted Sally and Emma warmly. Basking in the limelight, Andrew told everyone who'd listen that "nothing makes a Scotsman happier than being surrounded by his bonny lassies at Yuletide."

Chapter 51

The days passed, with occasional flare-ups between Sally and Andrew. She baited him with double-entendres and fiendishly worked her way under his skin, only to apologize moments later. Emma added comic relief as she swept through the house waggling her fingers behind *Fingers'* back. Like a Nancy Drew clone, she reported seeing him in *Yellow Umbrella Books* bragging about first editions, and flirting with the waitresses at Sandi's Diner, promising front row seats at the Melody Tent.

I wasn't surprised to discover the gold pocket watch chain he'd given me was missing. When I bellowed for help searching for it, Andrew nonchalantly looked up from his Kovel's Price Guide. "Oh, Anna, it's a piece of junk. Go look in one of your suit pockets."

"Junk? It was appraised for $3,000. If we don't find it by dark, I'm calling the police."

"They'd laugh at you. They haven't time to squander on misplaced trinkets. Who would have robbed you, anyway?"

"Maybe Ali Baba and the Forty Thieves," I suggested.

At sunset, Andrew rose from his chair with a condescending air and led me into our bedroom. "My dearest, you must stop this nonsense about the police. They're too busy to be bothered with such petty matters."

He opened my closet door, ran his hands over the hanging jackets, then moved into the bathroom and deftly plucked the missing watch chain from my cosmetics bag. "Here it is, darling, right where you left it," he said sympathetically. "You've worked yourself up over nothing. You should relax, take a wee bath."

I looked over his shoulder at Sally and she smirked. We'd emptied the bag on my bed an hour before; the chain wasn't in it.

CHRISTMAS WAS A BLINK AWAY and we all looked like hell. Dinners were deadly affairs of exaggerated manners and forced conversations. Long evenings before the crackling fire were lethal. Andrew guarded the remote, blasting sports programs filled with holiday commercials.

Carols pealed from the Congregational Church's carillon as we sipped mulled cider, strung cranberries, popped corn, and half-heartedly decorated the tree. When Emma practiced *Joy to the World* on her flute, Sally pecked out the melody on the piano, and Andrew seethed in silence on the couch. He refused to sing a note, even when we celebrated Emma's twelfth birthday.

I polished silver and monitored the thick atmosphere, poised to referee when needed. Our monogrammed stockings were hung and presents were stacked under the tree. December 20 was three days away.

Chapter 52

I had no reason to believe that night would be different from any other. Andrew and I brushed our teeth, climbed into bed and read our books. When he heaved his customary *that's it* sigh before snapping off the bedside lamp, I spooned my back into his stomach and muttered "nighty-night."

He didn't answer. Instead, he propped himself up on one elbow, lightly traced his fingers across my shoulders, then shifted his weight ever so slowly and encircled my neck with both of his hands. In the next few seconds of paralyzed silence, I knew my husband was capable of murder.

He didn't move or say a word.

This is it, I thought. *This is how I will die.*

Instinctively, I snuggled closer to him, gently took the hand that pressed against my throat and whispered, "We forgot to say our prayers."

Andrew withdrew his other hand from my neck. He cupped my breast as we recited the Lord's Prayer in chilling unison.

THE NEXT MORNING, feeling hung-over, I stumbled around the kitchen wondering what to do next. I was flabbergasted when Andrew asked Sally and Emma for their Christmas lists and then left to go shopping. Minutes later, Rupert called. I knew the news was bad as soon as I heard his voice.

"What's up?"

"I just discovered that Andrew has thirty days from the date of the annulment to petition for counsel. You'll have to keep up the charade until the end of January."

"I don't think I can. He's getting bolder, more menacing. Sally and Emma are a godsend but we're all ready to crack."

"It gets worse," Rupert said. "Mr. Bayley had planned to fly up, to press criminal charges against Andrew right after the hearing. He would have been arrested and you would have been rid of him."

"Mr. Bayley's not coming?"

"No, there's no point. Pennsylvania's five-year statute of limitations for theft has expired. We missed nabbing Andrew by four months."

I felt sick. "I was planning to drop him at the Salvation Army shelter after the hearing. Now you're telling me I have to keep him on another thirty days?"

"Unless you find a way to finesse him out of the house. If you try to force him, he may seek counsel. And at this point, a divorce would take even longer."

"We have less than forty-eight hours before the hearing, Rupert. You must think I'm a magician."

He chuckled. "A witch, maybe. Do what you can. I'll see you the day after tomorrow."

The next day, the 19th, Providence intervened again. Andrew received an early morning phone call from Baron von Mahler, who needed transport to Boston's Logan Airport at noon. Andrew affably agreed to chauffeur, then struggled with the logistics of returning the Baron's car to Orleans and finding a way back to Chatham. He looked across the room and asked, "Can you follow me to his house when I get back and drive me home?"

I agreed. Because I had a plan. My heart pounded all afternoon. Sally and Emma were on the alert.

After backing up the driveway in the Baron's white Suburban late that afternoon, Andrew walked into the kitchen and took me into his arms. "Tomorrow we'll be annulled, my love. Give me a last married smooch."

I kissed his lips and then braced his shoulders. "Andrew, something terrible has happened. I don't want the girls to hear. Let's sit in my car."

Wary but resigned, he followed. I sat in the driver's seat, turned on the ignition and blasted the heat.

"What's going on, Anna?"

"The jig is up. Rupert called this afternoon. You're about to be arrested. There's nothing I can do. Nothing at all."

"Why, Anna? What have you done?"

"It's not what I've done. It's what you did, years ago. Rupert grew suspicious and called Mr. Bayley behind my back."

"Why would he do that for a simple annulment?"

"Rupert has always been protective. He was outraged when he learned you'd made a fool of him."

"What? I like Rupert. I thought he liked me."

"You told an avid historian that you saw King George take tea at your grandfather's stables. Rupert discovered your grandfather died in 1937."

"So?"

"You were born in 1944, Einstein."

"Rupert called Mr. Bayley to check me out because I was born in 1944?"

"Even you, my dear, couldn't have witnessed an event seven years before your birth."

"What did the old tyrant say about me? I slaved for him, you know."

"He said you're a thief. He's flying up from Philadelphia tomorrow morning to charge you with stealing Mrs. Bayley's jewelry."

He smashed his fist into the dashboard. "Mrs. Bayley gave me that jewelry. She knew her husband was a tomcat. She didn't want some bimbo wearing it after she died."

"You told me your father bought it in France, from a Jewish refugee."

"Anna, you're my wife. Why are you doing this to me?"

I ignored his idiotic question and spoke calmly. "After the hearing, the police will send you back to Pennsylvania to serve time. Then you'll be deported."

"What am I gonna do?"

"Run, Andrew. As fast and far as you can. After 9/11, no one in this country is going to give an alien a break."

His eyes darted back and forth, then settled on the Suburban.

I grabbed his arm. "Take it. But before you go, I want the truth about Paula."

"Stop it, Anna. Let it go."

"Tell me who she was, and what happened to her, or I'll call the police right now."

He stared at me, then apparently decided I wasn't bluffing. "She worked at Beechwood Pharmaceuticals and lived in Sunningdale."

"Where in Sunningdale?"

"Greystone Manor, out on London Road. You're my true love," he sobbed. "She was just a fling."

"Did she really die skiing?"

"How many times do I have to tell you…"

"Where is she buried?"

"Dorset. Nowhere near Sunninghill. Her parents buried her in Dorset."

I almost laughed. "You mean Lady Margaret and Sir Robert?"

"Paula's parents were shopkeepers. I made up the rest. I've nothing more to say about it. I gotta get outa here. Where am I gonna go?"

"Maybe central Florida; it's full of folks on the move. Just go and go fast."

"What about my things?"

"You've got the Suburban. We'll help you pack."

"I don't have any money."

"I'll give you a few hundred. You'll find work. Try Ocala. It's horse country."

The girls were ready. We flew about the house, stuffing Andrew's worldly possessions into green garbage bags. In the cold December twilight, we tramped like pack mules, loading golf clubs, pictures, books and his fine new clothes, bundled up like rags.

Packed and ready to flee, Andrew had morphed into a disheveled fugitive. It dawned on me that he'd had narrow escapes before. He headed for the door but Sally stopped him. "Not so fast, Andrew," she said. "You broke my mother's heart. Do you have anything to say for yourself?"

He looked at his Rolex. I wondered which of his employers was missing a watch.

He shrugged at Emma, said "Sorry, kid," and then walked out the door. When I followed, he threw his wedding ring.

I caught it. "Surely you're not mad at me, Andrew. I tried to help, remember?"

"I could still drive you to Sanibel," he offered.

"I don't think so, Andrew. It shouldn't have come to this, but I wish you well. If you need money, call, but don't tell me where you are. The police will be crawling all over this place tomorrow."

EARLY THE NEXT MORNING, behind closed doors, the annulment was granted in less than three minutes. Looking down through weary, wise eyes, the judge wished me the best first day of the rest of my life.

Neither of us could have known that my best first day was a long way off. As events unfolded, I was forced to endure Andrew Macdade far longer than anyone could have foreseen.

Chapter 53

That night, Marta arrived at my kitchen door holding a can of pepper spray and a referee's whistle. "You and the girls are alone here," she said. "And sooner or later, Andrew will put two and two together and double back."

"He's on his way to Florida."

"Get real, Anna. If you don't call the police, I will."

"But Rupert says I have to pacify Andrew for another thirty days."

"When he calls, tell him what he wants to hear. But contact the police now. This isn't some cozy mystery, Anna. You've worried your friends long enough."

Suddenly, Emma flew through the living room and into the kitchen, screaming. "He's here. I heard a crash out by the shed, Grammy."

"Just raccoons," I said, but quickly punched in the number for the Chatham station as Marta bolted the doors and flipped on the outside spotlights. Two uniformed officers arrived within minutes, thrashing through the thickets wielding nightsticks and squawking radios. Another cruiser delivered a grim-faced detective who sat stiffly in the living room taking copious notes while I stumbled through the humiliating tale.

When I finished, he took a deep breath. "We've had Andrew Macdade in our sights for years," he said. "And we've kept an eye on you, Mrs. Wells, since the day he vandalized your neighbors' property. He has a history."

"A history?"

"Sheila Peters and her sons called more than once. Their reports are public records; you can read them at the station anytime."

I thanked him.

"We'll nail him one of these days. Tonight, keep all the windows and doors bolted. Tomorrow, change your locks. And ma'am…"

When I looked at him, he smiled gently. "Don't worry. We'll patrol your property and the neighborhood until further notice."

A CHRISTMAS CARD from Andrew – Madonna with Child - arrived on the 26th, just after Sally and Emma left for the airport. My heart sank when I saw the Hyannis postmark. "My darling Anna, Remember: To Live in the Hearts of those we Love is not to Die. Goodbye, my angel. Andrew XX"

Not knowing whether it was a suicide note or a death threat, I made a copy for my file, then delivered it to the Chatham police station.

His first telephone call, on New Year's Eve, was a sniveling monologue allegedly delivered from a "freezing, foul-smelling Hyannis marina." My caller ID said he was holed up in Baron von Mahler's Orleans home. I played along. Eventually, he said he had to go; the drunks prowling around the docks were making him nervous.

Two nights later he called again, "faint from hunger" and begging for money.

"Clearly things aren't working out for you, Andrew. Maybe it's time to go home, where your children and Archie will help." I offered to renew his passport and buy him a one-way ticket to Edinburgh.

He agreed to think it over, but only if I'd register him at my address and promise to keep his whereabouts a secret.

With two weeks to go in the critical thirty-day period, I suggested we meet the next day at the Hyannis mall's food court, promising to bring the renewal application and cash. "I'll need a copy of your birth certificate," I told him, "and of your green card."

HIS HOBO ACT was impressive. I almost didn't recognize the unshaven, shivering bum who sat waiting amid the lunch crowd.

"I'm sick. I've been sleeping in an unheated garage in Dennis," he rasped, blowing his nose. "Met the owner at the Food Pantry. She lets me in twice a week to shower and shave. Can't I come home? Please?"

"You know you can't. The police are watching." I gave him a strained smile and opened my pocketbook. "Where's your passport, Andrew?"

He rummaged through a dirty backpack as I laid the application form and a stack of twenties on the table. He handed over the expired passport along with copies of his birth certificate and green card, eying the money.

"Sign the form," I told him. "I'll fill it in and take care of the fee. After lunch, we'll pop into a camera shop to get your mug shot."

He sighed and shook his head, but he signed. "What'll I do without you, Anna? I miss our beautiful life."

"You'll manage. Take the money."

He did, of course.

"I'm gonna get help and make amends," he said through tears. "When I'm stronger, I'll send you a first-class ticket."

I coughed. "We'll see, Andrew. Right now, let's eat. How about a bowl of minestrone to warm you up? Why didn't you go to Florida?"

"I couldn't leave you, Anna. You're my best friend, the best I ever had." He confessed he'd started drinking again, then quickly added he'd joined AA and a new evangelical church to get help. "To make you proud of me," he sobbed.

And to con a whole new batch of vulnerable Christians, I thought.

After that meeting, he sent a few cutesy cards and called occasionally to inquire about the status of his new passport. When it arrived a couple of weeks later, I was surprised and disappointed; Interpol hadn't stepped in.

We rendezvoused at the same table in the mall's food court but this time Andrew was impeccably groomed in a black cashmere turtleneck and black trousers. Reeking of lime aftershave instead of gasoline, he placed a nosegay on the table. "Happy anniversary, darling. It's a month today since our annulment."

As if I didn't know. "Time flies," I said.

"Just think, if you hadn't brought me to my knees, I'd still be telling lies. I've got a new job, heartsweet. I owe it to you for teaching me right from wrong. And to the Baron. He arranged for me to manage a Pleasant Bay estate."

I was immediately suspicious.

"Two psychiatrists," he announced, looking satisfied. "They're tyrants but I've got a grand room with a view and all I can eat. Better than sleeping in a garage, eh?"

"Much better," I agreed. "Who are they?"

"Dr. Albert Selby is an eccentric, does nothing but write articles for JAMA. His wife, Dr. Louise Selby of Philadelphia's Main Line, is a verra stuffy lady. They pay me a paltry 25 quid a day and I'm on duty 24/7."

In my gloomiest tone, I asked, "Is this it, Andrew? Will I ever see you again?"

"I'm gonna work hard, go to church and live for the day I'll be worthy of you. Will you pray for your true-blue boy?"

"Twice a day, Andrew."

I meant it. I'd pray to see him exposed. And arrested.

He caressed my cheek and then dashed off. I walked away slowly, feeling sorry for the Selbys.

Chapter 54

Upon arriving home from the mall, I dumped out the cardboard boxes Andrew had left in the basement, searching for traces of Darby. One address book listed her in Traverse City, Michigan but the number had been disconnected. Remembering her mother's name was Roberta from the private detective's report, I got numbers for nine R. Hamiltons in that area code from directory assistance. I scored with number seven.

"That's Bobbie's daughter," a male voice boomed. "She married a great guy a few years back. I've got their number right here."

Pen in hand, I dialed. A man answered on the third ring.

"This is Anna Wells calling from Cape Cod," I said cautiously. "I'm trying to find Darby Hamilton."

"Darby is my wife." His tone was friendly. "May I tell her what this is about?"

"Sad to say, it's about Andrew Macdade, sir. Until a month ago, I was married to him."

"My condolences," said Darby's husband. "I'm glad you tracked us down. I'll get my wife."

Moments later, she was on the line. "Hello, Anna. Are you okay?"

It was the unmistakable voice of a friend. "I'm okay most of the time," I told her. "At least I think I am."

"That man is a monster. It's been years since the Philadelphia police took him away in handcuffs but I live in fear that he'll find me."

"I'm so sorry, Darby. Is it too upsetting? Would you rather not talk about him?"

"No," she said firmly. "I've prayed that someone like you would call. I'm ashamed of having married him. I need to talk."

"So do I, my friend." I sighed. "So do I."

And talk we did.

Andrew moved Darby and her girls to Philadelphia a month after they married, not to work for the Bayleys but to chauffeur "for some muckamuck." The job didn't last long. After lacing her drink with something that knocked her out cold for more than a day, he locked her children in their room with Cheerios and apple juice, then spent the weekend partying with the Irish housemaids, getting them all fired. "We were thrown out of our quarters," Darby said. "We stayed at a seedy motel until one of my girlfriends took us in, and he promptly hit on her."

"The man is pond scum."

"He was unemployed for three months before he landed the job with the Bayleys," she continued. "Months later, while unpacking back in Michigan, I found my friend's diamond ring mixed in with my own jewelry."

"Hiding in plain sight."

"He'll steal anything that's not bolted down."

I gave her a thumbnail sketch of his grief-stricken widower routine and of my odyssey through his briefcase.

"He put on the widower act with me, too, and he hid his marriage to Grace Jamieson until our application for a marriage license was rejected. When her name popped up in the system as his second wife, Andrew was caught in a bald-faced lie."

And yet the pattern continued, I thought. "He told me that Grace divorced him in England and then moved to Durban. Are you telling me that she was with him in Michigan when he met you?"

"Oh yes. When she discovered Andrew was seeing me, she flew back to Edinburgh. And still I married him as soon as his divorce was final. Was I stupid or what?"

"Welcome to the club, Darby."

She lowered her voice. "I also believed he was an under-cover CIA agent, about to retire from "the Company" and from flying for Mr. Taubman. Can you believe I typed his reignations?"

"Oh, I can believe it."

"My mother was onto him from the beginning but I wouldn't listen."

"We should all listen to our mothers. Even mine, approaching senility, saw through him."

"Mine hired a private detective and copied his address book."

Another address book. "Do you still have it?"

"I sure do. I've saved everything, hoping that someday someone would show up to make use of it."

"I'm particularly interested in Paula Barnett. Do you know anything about her?"

"He said she was a doctor. I suspect he had an affair with her in Sunninghill, while he was married to Grace."

"He was busy during that marriage," I noted.

"Don't I know it?" Darby replied. "After Grace left Michigan, he was desperate to marry me, but I refused until he introduced me to his kids and friends. He tried to wear me down but I was adamant: no trip, no wedding. Finally, he bought the tickets. On the flight over, he said we were in danger; he'd been betrayed by a CIA contact. By the time we landed, I was sorry I'd made him go. We spent the week skulking around like secret agents."

Another performance from Andrew Macdade: espionage.

"We stayed in London," Darby went on, "but visited Sunninghill one afternoon. He took me to *Duke's*, a pub near the Highclere, but when we got there, he said he didn't know anyone. He seemed to tune out, to make himself invisible. He kept glancing at a table of women, saying he could always spot a nurse because her fingernails are longer on one hand than on the other."

"Probably recognized someone he scammed," I said. "Did you meet his children?"

"Just once, on that trip. They joined us for lunch in London. I got funny vibes from both of them. Maybe they disapproved of the age difference between Andrew and me. I called them when he started beating me but they weren't interested."

"Neither had the common decency even to mention your name. And neither has ever heard of Paula. Did Andrew show you the photograph of her gravestone?"

"No, but after we left the pub he drove past an old cemetery and asked if I wanted to stop in and meet her."

That's a long way from Dorset, I thought.

"It seemed too sad and I told him no," Darby continued. "Then I wondered why he hadn't dropped me off somewhere for a cup of coffee and gone back to pay his respects. I was young and clueless."

"I'm old, Darby, and I believed every word he said. Did Andrew have nightmares about Paula?"

"Like you wouldn't believe. He'd jump out of bed screaming for her, slobbering all over the place. Scared the wits out of me. Every autumn before the anniversary of her death he'd melt down, drink more and pick more fights. Once, he disappeared for a couple of days, turned up hung-over, wouldn't say where he'd been."

"I found a few glamorous pictures of her but I never saw one of them together. Did you, Darby?"

"No. I only saw one snapshot of Paula, a small blond in ski clothes."

"The Paula I saw resembled Grace Kelly."

We paused, letting it all sink in. "Darby," I whispered, "do you think he's capable of murder?"

"Yes. He's an evil, jealous man who goes to church to fool everyone, including himself. Did he tell you the grizzly stories about husbands who get away with murdering unfaithful wives?"

"No. My God."

"One poor woman was found in the shower with a broken neck; another ended up in a ravine."

"What do you think happened to Paula?"

"Maybe she refused him sex and he lost it. If I refused him, he'd slash a red X through the date on a racing calendar he kept in the kitchen, then hurl obscenities at me all day."

Suddenly, she laughed. "Did you know he dyes his hair?"

I howled. "You mean even his hair is a lie?"

"I came home early one afternoon and caught him coloring his head and his bush. Had his penis wrapped in foil."

When we managed to catch our breath, Darby promised to copy the pages of Andrew's address book and send them along. Then she asked if I planned to search for Paula.

"The more I hear, the more determined I am to find out what happened to her."

"This is the first time I've spoken with anyone who gets it, Anna. Only someone who's lived through it can understand. I'll do anything to help you. I'm your friend for life."

"And I yours, Darby."

Inspired by her courage and warmth, I carefully composed a note to Andrew's fourth wife, Sheila Peters, and mailed it before I went to bed.

"Dear Sheila,

My marriage to Andrew Macdade was annulled in December. I suspect we have much to talk about. Please come for tea on Saturday at four.

Yours, Anna Wells."

Chapter 55

Sheila Peters's black cape billowed in the wind as she teetered up the icy brick walk in fur-trimmed boots, clutching a yellow hatbox to her chest. A real girly-girl, I thought. Her bobbed red hair, bright red lipstick and bronzed eye shadow gave her a dramatic, bohemian look.

"I've seen you at the post office," she called in a cultured voice. "Always thought you were beautiful, Mrs. Wells. Or is it still Mrs. Macdade?"

"Hardly." I ushered her in through the kitchen door, took the hatbox from her outstretched hands and placed it on a chair.

She chuckled between labored breaths, dropping her vintage Kelly bag to the floor. "Yes, he would've liked you, a tiny blond. Look at me; I got sick and fat after I married him."

"Tiny? I'm scrawny and wrinkled like a monkey. He takes a toll on a girl, doesn't he?"

We eyed each other like long lost sorority sisters. Seconds later, we erupted into raucous, uncontrolled laughter.

"Not every woman would take pity on her ex-husband's ex-wife," I said. "Conned or not, I'm more than sorry I ever encouraged him to leave you."

"I won't throw stones. You've suffered enough." She handed me her cashmere cape, fragrant with the scent of my favorite perfume.

"Caléche?" I asked.

I was surprised to hear that Andrew gave Sheila a bottle of the classic scent after their first date. "Told me it reminded him of Paula," she said. "Aromatherapy to calm his demons. I've worn it ever since."

I felt disconcerted, exposed, as I hung her cape in the kitchen closet. "No wonder he seemed so pleased each time I dabbed it behind my ears. Isn't it weird that he wanted his wives to wear the same perfume?"

"I'll tell you what's weird," she said. "The man has no odor anywhere, even down there. I called him *the alien*. And his penis was colder than my gynie's spectroscope."

I gave her a lame smile. "No need to compare notes on that disappointing subject."

"*C'est la vie,*" she sang, and then sighed. "I missed him for a long time, Anna."

Moved by the vulnerable look in her eyes, I felt ashamed. "I betrayed you, Sheila, and all my married sisters, but when I first met Andrew I assumed he wore a wedding band to honor Paula's memory. I thought I'd found that special someone who knows your heart, finishes your sentences and anticipates every whim."

Sheila nodded knowingly. Had we met under different circumstances, we could have become close friends. But we were back-to-back ex-wives, bound only by deceit and sadness.

"Although I haven't wanted to admit it," I said, "I still sometimes miss the man he pretended to be. It's loony to miss someone who wasn't real."

"He's real, all right. A real chameleon. Changes his stories and moods to suit the occasion. I confused his Prince Charming act with love, too, even though he made me miserable most of the time."

"Has anyone else ever so thoroughly convinced you that you were the love of his life?"

"Never. After he left, I felt sure he'd come back. You can imagine my shock when I saw him pull out of your driveway, in your car, a week after he told me he was leaving 'to catch the music in LA.'"

She laughed. "I told him the only stars he'd ever meet were on the sidewalk in front of Grauman's Chinese Theater and with luck he'd be hired to polish them."

It was my turn to laugh.

"I suppose you've heard about his phony hit record?" she asked.

"*Concrete and Clay*. I listened to it all the time, like a little groupie. My son was so impressed he played it at work, told his co-workers all about his famous stepfather."

"Well, I never believed it," Sheila said smugly. "But listen to this. A few months after he moved in with you, he showed up at my door one afternoon looking for photographs. I was at my worst, hating myself for loving him and hating him for leaving. When I said he was nothing but a gigolo, he purred, 'A temporary position, my dear, while I earn enough to make the trip.' Then he begged me not to ruin his chances. Swore you were nothing to him but a neurotic, spoiled employer."

"He described Mrs. Damato as neurotic and spoiled, too. Do you think they had an affair?"

Sheila shrugged. "Audrey's a lonely rich man's wife and Andrew can be quite sexy. He's yummy, Anna. Women fall for him like ninepins. But who cares? After months of therapy, I realized you did me a colossal favor."

I led her into the living room, where I'd lit a fire. "Gorgeous coral walls," she mused, looking around. "I collect seascapes and illustrated children's classics, too. I see Shakespeare and Homer. Bet there's a Danielle Steele squirreled away somewhere."

Sheila Peters didn't miss much.

"I'm a typical Libra."

"Andrew said you were a grand lady. Are you always so gracious, Anna?"

"Nothing gracious about an old fool stealing a cuckoo bird from another's nest." I pointed to the yellow wing chairs. "He was so devastated by Paula's death and your, um, affair, that I pitied him."

I poured our tea and nudged a tray of cheese, grapes and scones across the coffee table, closer to her.

"The romance is all true," she said, drawling through *all*. "It drove Andrew mad."

"Spoken like a femme fatale." I suddenly loathed the thought of Sheila and Andrew making love. I wished I hadn't seen his photos of her.

She buttered a pecan scone and glanced at the leather footstool next to the couch. "I've gone crazy looking for that thing."

I gasped. "It's yours? He told me Mrs. Damato's decorator asked him to take it to the dump."

"Some dump. See that?" She nodded at a wooden decoy on the mantel. "He gave it to me one Christmas. Then it disappeared."

Feeling drained already, I tossed another log on the fire and reached up for the antique bufflehead. "He gave it to me for my birthday. Take it, Sheila, please. It's yours."

"You keep it," she said. "It belongs on the Cape and I'm moving back to Philadelphia as soon as I sell the house. But if he gave you a pair of silver salad tongs, I'd like those back. They belonged to my grandmother."

"God help us all." I stood and went to the sideboard in the dining room, rummaged through the silver I'd inherited from my own grandmother and lifted the stolen tongs from the drawer. "These?"

She nodded. I handed them over and she tucked them into her bag.

"He told me they were his mother's," I said. "Along with a diamond brooch and my sapphire engagement ring. I recently learned that he stole the jewelry from Mrs. Bayley."

"He pawned those gaudy things off on me, too, but I gave them back when he left. Thought his daughter should have them. In case they really were heirlooms."

"Did you ever meet Drew and Andrina?"

"No. He said they were too grief-stricken over Paula's death to accept a stepmother. I remembered them every birthday and Christmas, but since I never heard from either of them, I assume Andrew tore off my labels and mailed the packages as his own."

"How cruel."

Sheila snorted. "He'd steal the gold from his grandmother's teeth. When I needed new tires, I discovered he'd taken my mad money from under my nightgowns. He accused my boys of stealing it."

"And stealing isn't the half of it. I called Darby, his third wife, a few days ago. She's still terrified of him."

Sheila stared at me as if I'd slapped her. "Third wife? I thought I was the second. How many are there?"

"Five, as far as I know. Who did you think was the first?"

"Paula," she said, looking dumbfounded. "The mother of his children who broke her neck skiing. The beautiful cancer surgeon he has nightmares about."

I shook my head. "His children have never heard of Paula. And my friends in the UK can't find any information about her."

Sheila frowned. "She haunted him. He wouldn't let me go to church with him because it was his one sacred hour a week to mourn her properly."

I handed her an enlarged photograph of Paula's gravestone.

"He kept the 3x5 taped to the mirror over his bureau," she said. Looking closely at the blow-up, she added, "Two different kinds of lettering. Do you think it's a fake?"

"I do."

She fingered the photo and recalled watching him slip out of bed and into the bathroom each night as the anniversary of Paula's death approached. "Every time, I'd find him crumpled in a heap on the floor, moaning her name. Then, a week or so after October 2nd, he'd seem like his old self again."

"I begged him to talk to our minister. Worried he'd drop dead from grief."

"I kind of hoped he would."

"Were you afraid of him, Sheila?"

"He never beat me, if that's what you mean. But he got rough with me once, before we married, and I told him we were finished. He was shattered. When I finally agreed to have dinner with him, I blacked out after a few sips of my whiskey sour; he must've slipped something into it. I woke up at home, in bed, and he fluttered over me for two days. Almost lost his job with the Bayleys."

"He doctored Darby's drink, too."

Sheila suddenly looked tired. "I was afraid of growing old alone. When he popped the question and fastened that fabulous bracelet on my wrist, I said 'yes.' My sons called him a creep from the beginning. They moved in – with their motorcycles and dorm furniture - about a week after we got here."

I laughed. "So I've heard. By Andrew's account, he slaved night and day while they lounged around drinking beer."

Sheila's eyes filled. "I'd been widowed and then divorced for years when he swept me off my feet. I was sixty when we married. He said we'd always be lovers." She blinked. "Today is our anniversary and I'm spending it with you."

Retrieving the tartan blanket Morgan and Ian had given us only months before, I draped it around Sheila's shoulders, telling her how I'd huddled beneath it on my wedding night. She wrapped herself in it and yawned.

"Maybe this is too much all at once," I said. "Should we save the rest for another time?"

"We've just begun piecing together his psychopathic life. Let's not stop."

Rumpus needed a walk. I left Sheila flipping through a garden magazine and returned twenty minutes later with a replenished tea tray and a half-baked plan to gather all five wives together.

She whinnied. "We'll need a month of Sundays to sort out his filthy lies. You must organize it."

"Maybe I will," I said, grinning.

"I've spent the worst three years of my life here in Chatham," she said. "Not long after we arrived, I got sick and my hair fell out. My boys think he was poisoning me."

"And I was nauseous for weeks before I got rid of him. Threw up a plate of curried chicken he made a few days before he left. Wonder what he used."

"Maybe one of the pesticides he sprayed on his damned dahlias." She laughed. "Did you get the 'ily' notes, too?"

"On the dresser every afternoon."

"Do you know he spied on me while he lived with you? Looked in my windows and even went through my trash, according to a neighbor. A week before our divorce was final, he came to my door to inform me that, should I 'meet with a sudden fatal accident,' he would inherit a third of my estate. The police said he hadn't broken any law."

Sheila glanced toward the windows. "I almost didn't come here today. I'm afraid he's watching."

I had felt him watching, too. Books moved, clothes missing, leftovers gone from the refrigerator; I'd convinced myself it was all in my head. But I didn't want to add to Sheila's fears. "You're a brave woman to risk coming," I told her. "What did you bring in your hatbox?"

"His missives," she answered, retrieving the yellow box from the kitchen. "Cards, letters, notebooks. Now I'll show you just how crazy he is."

The postcards Andrew had sent to Sheila after he moved in with me made my head spin.

Dear Sheila, You're my one and only Valentine. XX

Dearest, here come the dahlias again. XX

Dearest Sheila, Belated birthday wishes from Lake George. XX

Dear S. I enjoyed my little visit last week. XX

Darling, Now in Sanibel, modeling for Burberry

Won the Plantation Cup Open with a 230 yard hole in-one. Up to the Masters in Atlanta to meet Sandy Lyle. XX

"Sheila, this one is postmarked the day before our wedding. What was he doing?"

"Hedging his bets, like any good gambler," she said. "He knew you'd catch on sooner or later and kick him out."

"He's a fool, if you think about it."

She giggled. "Bungles every golden opportunity. Do you know he's a voyeur? He'd hide behind the living room drapes and watch our neighbor weed the garden in her bikini. And he's a sex addict. My life would've been even worse if I hadn't serviced him twice a day. That's why I was so shocked when he left."

"He told me a different story," I said dryly, then changed the subject. "Did he 'bequeath' the Admiral Macdade manse to you?"

"Oh, yes." She laughed. "And the Sunninghill house next to the Highclere Hotel, where he lived with Paula."

"In his dreams, Sheila."

"Before we left Philadelphia, I promised to stake him for a tea shop in Chatham, but our attorney smelled a rat, refused to release the funds from the family trust. That's why Andrew became a handyman." Sheila's eyes gleamed mischievously. "To supplement the money he made gambling and stealing."

We both laughed.

"I think he expected to skip off with a tidy sum when my mother died," Sheila continued. "Probably would have dumped me in the cemetery with her if you hadn't come along."

"If only you'd been with him in church that day."

She grinned. "Then he would have gotten my money, instead of setting his sights on yours."

We stared at each other in frozen silence as the clock struck six. "It's a lot to absorb," I said. "Are you okay, Sheila?"

"Splendid," she chirped. "But I must run. Before I go, tell me, who was the mother of his children and who are the other ex-wives?"

The file was hidden on the top bookshelf, behind a set of encyclopedias. Together we pulled down several volumes and I read the updated *Who's Who*. "Laura Sinclair is the mother of Andrew's children. She divorced him after twenty-three years in 1988. Grace Jamieson married him three months later, then divorced him on grounds of adultery in 1993. He married Darby Hamilton two months after that and she divorced him in 1997. Four months later, he married you. I won the prize in 2002."

"Where did Paula fit in?"

"Darby thinks he had an affair with her in Sunninghill, while he was married to Grace."

Sheila's eyes bugged. "Holy cow. I wonder if Grace knew."

I shrugged. "I've been reluctant to contact her. She works for Drew."

"You know what hurts most, Anna?"

I waited.

"When Andrew and I first came here, we took long romantic walks each evening and passed your lovely home every time. It was our favorite house in Chatham. He promised that someday we'd live in it, happily ever after."

"It's a painful coincidence, Sheila."

She shook her head and blew her nose. "No. He set you up. He got your name and somehow learned you attended the Methodist Church. We used to go to the UU services. Then suddenly he started going to the Methodist Church. Alone."

"And sitting in the front pew to be closer to God," I added, rolling my eyes.

"Well, if he wanted you to notice him, where would he sit?"

Chapter 56

Long after Sheila left, I was still reading the contents of her hatbox. In a letter sent from Assateaque Island during their courtship, Andrew described the same dream he ran on about on our way home from Sanibel, the visitation from Paula.

I knew the truth about her lay somewhere in Great Britain, but I wasn't ready to travel. I wasn't up to planning a trip or even packing a suitcase. I needed help.

I found it on my bookshelf the next evening. English-born Margot Arnold had been my anthropology professor years before at Cape Cod Community College. She was one of the Cape's most prolific mystery writers and I'd read almost everything she'd written. I knew she'd understand the modus operandi of a predator.

The directory listed her Hyannis number. I scribbled it on the cover of her most recent paperback, which I brought to bed and read that evening. It wasn't until the last chapter that a character's name jumped off the page: Paula Barnett.

What are the odds?

I summoned up the nerve to call her the next day. A week later, she and her three cats welcomed me to her bungalow.

It bulged at the seams with books and archeological artifacts from her digs in Turkey and East Africa.

Her eyes twinkled as she listened to my saga. She assured me that the Paula Barnett character in her book was entirely fictional. "You're not mad, my dear," she said. "Most women would have taken to their beds, but you're prepared to charge ahead like a Chief Inspector from Scotland Yard, to shed light on the fate of this mysterious Paula."

"Will you help?" I asked as a well-fed cat jumped onto my lap.

She smiled. "I'm between books. And this sinister story intrigues me, calls up a similar tale about a charming gentleman who married a feeble diabetic and fed her a steady diet of cream puffs. She died soon after they wed and he had her body cremated immediately. No one could prove he'd poisoned her. I know all about these hypocrites. You must be careful that Andrew doesn't kill you."

"He tried. He came close with Darby. I'm pretty sure he had it in for Sheila, too. And I fear he may have succeeded with Paula."

"Begin with Grace Jamieson," she advised. "She was with him in Sunninghill. But use caution. Perhaps a short letter of inquiry to her home address."

Throughout the evening, Margot fortified me, filled me with hope. "May I visit again?" I asked.

She nodded. "Shall we say Wednesdays at six from now on?"

Despite Margot's advice, the letter I sent to Grace the next day was attached to an updated file on Andrew. I introduced myself, suggested she might find her ex-husband's activities since their divorce interesting, and asked if she knew of Dr. Paula Barnett.

Andrew continued to send cards with messages that alternately boasted of grandiose schemes and lamented bitter hardship. I tended to mundane tasks around the house and lived for Wednesdays with Margot, a little dynamo of positive energy and wicked humor. She methodically elicited the details of Andrew's lies, drawing parallels with infamous unsolved mysteries. Eventually, I regained enough equilibrium to organize my thoughts and make preliminary arrangements for my trip to Great Britain.

Baron von Mahler phoned in late February, asking if I'd seen Andrew. I apprised him of all that had transpired in his absence and then reminded him that Andrew was working for the Selbys.

"The Selbys?"

"Andrew said they hired him about a month ago," I offered, "on your recommendation."

"I've never heard of them."

My stomach knotted.

"I got back to Orleans late last night, found a bag full of Andrew's clothes in the laundry room and a four-hundred dollar repair bill for the Suburban. It looks like he camped out here after he left your house, helping himself to my car."

I felt a twinge of guilt, recalling the night I urged Andrew to take it.

"Don't know how he had the gall to charge me for new tires and deluxe detailing," the Baron continued. "But never mind that. Are you all right, Anna? I'm sick about what's happened."

I thanked him for his concern, told him I was managing day-to-day and hung up wondering how Andrew had landed the plum position with the psychiatrists.

Faced with more deceit, I burrowed under an electric blanket, mindlessly flipped through the pages of *Cape Cod Women* magazine and then bolted upright. Dr. Louise Selby was staring at me.

The article described her practice and her affiliation with an Orleans church. She'd divorced Dr. Albert Selby a year ago and had come to Cape Cod to start over. Alone.

Somehow, Andrew had weaseled his way into her house. As a servant or a boyfriend? I knew one thing for sure: she was in harm's way.

I leapt out of bed, bundled up and set out to walk the five-mile loop around the village. Halfway, I paused on the wooden drawbridge, staring at the choppy gray waters of Mill Pond. The fishing vessel *Booby Hatch* plunged deep into the icy waves, straining to break free from her mooring. Her name was an apt descriptor for the shambles of my life.

Determined to sabotage whatever designs Andrew had on Dr. Selby, I braced against the howling wind and marched down Bridge Street. After passing the Coast Guard station, I headed toward the village, where locals make the most of near-empty pubs and shops during winter, catching up with friends and neighbors not seen during the hectic summer months.

When I stopped at Lynda's *Hair Company*, she waved a can of hair spray and gave me a hug. "We've heard about your Scotsman, Anna, and we're not surprised. He used to sail in here for his monthly trim, telling his tall tales. What a showboat. We worried he'd either break your heart or take your last dime."

He'd damn near done both.

Lynda laughed at my mortified expression. "You know me, Anna. Blunt. Like my cuts."

"Who's the man in black?" I asked, changing the subject. "Is he new?"

"Miguel. From Provincetown. Fills in twice a week until our regular manicurist gets back from St. Croix. Why don't you get your nails done? You'll like him. Want me to do your hair later?"

I passed on the hair but decided to have a manicure. Miguel took my hands in his and pronounced them pitiful. "The salon is buzzing about your Scotsman, Mrs. Wells," he said. "Where is he now?"

"With Dr. Louise Selby in Orleans, allegedly managing her estate."

Miguel dropped my hands and pressed his own to his cheeks. "Dr. Selby is my client. I give her a manicure every Sunday. I've met her perfect servant who worked for Queen Noor. We've got to do something, Mrs. Wells."

"My file on him gets fatter by the minute. But if she confronts him with it, she'll expose me. The proverbial messenger has been shot before, Miguel. And if I call or write, I'll undoubtedly reach her perfect servant."

"Mrs. Wells, you don't know her. She's the epitome of discretion."

I felt lightheaded. Dr. Selby and I now shared a mani-curist on this sandy spit. As uncanny as Portobello's own Kate Campbell showing up at the Chapel by the Sea.

An hour later, I drove back to the *Hair Company* and gave Miguel a copy of my file. He promised that Louise Selby would call on Sunday after she'd read it.

She didn't. But Andrew called on Sunday evening as I was drawing a bath. "Four policemen escorted me off the Selby estate like a common criminal. Why did you do this to me, Anna?"

"It's your own fault, Andrew. Not mine. Don't call here again," I shouted, then slammed the receiver into its cradle.

After my bath, while pouring a cup of tea, I noticed the message light blinking. Reluctantly, I pushed the red button and listened. "I don't know what you said or did, but I'm homeless again, thanks to you. Were you jealous?" He hung up sniggering.

I began to shake. Why hadn't Dr. Selby called the minute he was taken from her house? She must have known I'd be at risk. Her lack of concern was insulting, but I wondered why I'd expected better. She was a shrink, after all, a member of Dr. Whitney's club.

Chapter 57

Monday afternoon at three, my phone rang. "Mrs. Anna Wells of Chatham?" asked a breathless soprano. "This is Dr. Louise Selby. Is your line clear of recording devices?"

"This is Anna Wells," I said calmly, "and my phone is not bugged."

"I'm in great danger."

"Yes, Dr. Selby. I am, too. And Andrew Macdade's former employer, Baron von Mahler, has been victimized as well. You can see from my file…"

"Then I must see you and the Baron together. Please phone him immediately and arrange a meeting in the Snow Library parking lot at precisely eleven tomorrow. Call back to confirm – 'yes' or 'no' - don't say anything else."

I was tempted to remind her that she might have servants, but I wasn't one of them. Then she said, "Andrew Macdade threatened to kill me last night and he may have tapped my lines. I don't trust anyone at this point."

My judgment softened; the woman was terrified. I agreed to make the call.

When I reached Baron von Mahler at his Orleans number, he asked if the good doctor might feel safe meeting inside, given the freezing temperatures, rather than powwow in a car. I could hear a slight amusement in his voice and I loved him for it.

I called Dr. Selby to confirm and risked adding that the Baron would reserve a conference room. She'd meet there, she said, only if the door locked.

ON THE WAY to the library Tuesday morning I collected my mail. Andrew had written to blame me for his dismissal. "I was asked to leave in dramatic fashion. Why do you want to destroy me? I am trying to lead a Christian life and now, thanks to you, I am once again homeless. I might snap."

I read it twice and tucked it into my pocketbook.

At ten to eleven, I parked next to the Suburban. Wearing faded jeans, a red plaid flannel shirt and a sheepskin vest, the Baron crouched between our cars stealing furtive glances around the parking lot. "Mrs. Wells," he said when I joined him. "I'm Lars Mahler. Though I feel more like Inspector Clousseau at the moment."

I laughed as we headed for the library doors. "It seems a bit much."

Lacking the sand and salt that encrust most Cape Cod cars in winter, a shiny black Mercedes pulled into a corner space. The woman who emerged was six feet tall and slim as a wand, dressed in a black suit with matching pumps and attaché case. Her straight, jet-black hair and ashy white skin reminded me of Morticia Addams. She swept past me with an aloof nod, extending her hand to the Baron.

"Dr. Selby, I presume," he said, drawing me forward. "This is the brave Anna Wells."

Again, she nodded. The Baron led us to one of the library's private rooms. When the door was locked and we were seated at the table, Dr. Selby told a story that was every bit as unbelievable as most of Andrew's.

"I am a pilot and an advisor for the FAA."

She sounded like Eleanor Roosevelt, without the warmth.

"I'm a medical doctor, a psychiatrist, a nutritionist and a spiritualist. Nothing like this has ever happened before in my life. I'm sure Andrew Macdade has been stalking me for years, ever since he worked for the Bayleys. I knew them, of course, from the Main Line."

I piped up. "How did he get into your house without references, Dr. Selby?"

"He had impeccable references, I assure you," she answered without looking at me.

I found her hard to believe. "How can that be?"

She sat up straighter. "I am an international motivational speaker. This past Memorial Day weekend, I shared the podium with my friend, Queen Noor, at West Point Military Academy. When I mentioned I was looking for a live-in estate manager, the queen gave me Andrew Macdade's name. He was working for her in Manhattan but he'd wanted to leave the city since 9/11. She thought he'd do well on Cape Cod."

I was incredulous. "I assure you, Dr. Selby, Andrew was not in Manhattan over Memorial Day weekend. Neither was *your friend,* Queen Noor. She was delivering the commencement speech at Mount Holyoke College."

"And from there she traveled to West Point."

What a load of codswallop. Dr. Selby lied with the ease of Andrew Macdade. But she wasn't nearly as good at it.

"Andrew sent a letter of inquiry," she continued, "enclosing the queen's references. I interviewed him on January 15th and hired him on the spot. He moved into the servants' quarters in the west wing that day. And for six weeks, he was the perfect servant."

"I'd sure like to see those references," I said.

"He stole them, among other things, before the police escorted him from my property."

How convenient, I thought. "What did you do after you read my file?"

"I called the district attorney on his private line. Michael O'Keefe is a personal friend. He arranged for four state police officers to take Andrew away."

"Did you have any inkling that he was unstable? After all, you're a psychiatrist," I said.

"Not until last Friday. He was in the kitchen preparing for one of my dinner parties, flushed from sipping wine. When I told him my plans had changed and I'd be dining out, he shook me by my shoulders, kissed me violently and called me a selfish bitch. Then he threw me on the sofa and tried to mount me."

The Baron was staring intently at his folded hands.

"But you got away?" I said.

For the first time, she deigned to look at me. "As a trained psychiatrist, I know how to handle these cases. I talked to him."

"And?"

"And he collapsed on the floor. Secretions gushed from him; tears, saliva, foam, urine and sweat. This is what happens to people in severe trauma," she lectured.

"I've seen his night terrors," I told her, "but I never saw him wet his pants. Maybe he's going downhill. What did you do?"

"Do? I went out to dinner, of course."

Her tale was absurd. I glanced at the Baron, who was still studying his hands.

"You left him alone in your house after he attacked you? And then you returned? Why didn't you go to the police the minute you escaped?" I asked the delusional doctor.

"I knew he'd simmer down. I brought a friend home after dinner, just to be on the safe side."

"Had Andrew made sexual advances before Friday?"

She gazed off and half-smiled. "Well, maybe. On Valentine's Day, when he brought the breakfast tray into my bedroom, my toast was cut into little hearts. I told him that was inappropriate."

"What was inappropriate?"

"His cutting my toast into hearts."

"Dr. Selby, I find it strange that he was in your bedroom at all."

She stiffened and turned toward the Baron, placing her hand on his arm. "You were good to come," she said. "I'll call about drinks. I'm sure we have mutual friends, here and abroad, and far more interesting things to discuss than this unstable servant."

He gave her his business card, too polite to mention that she'd called the meeting to discuss the unstable servant.

I piped up again. "Had he calmed down when you got home on Friday night, Doctor?"

"Andrew? Why, he was on the living room sofa reading a book, meek as a lamb."

"Wasn't he out of line to be sitting in your living room?"

"Perhaps, but he mixed well with my friends. They thought I'd hit the jackpot. He was so charming."

"Until he tried to rape you," I muttered.

She glared at me. "When he saw the cruisers in the driveway, he threatened to run me over with the Jeep he bought from my son."

I thought it unlikely that Andrew had bought a Jeep, or any car, from her son or anyone else.

"After he was removed," she continued, "my housekeeper found a razor-sharp knife under the couch pillows. I have nightmares."

"So what's your clinical diagnosis, Doctor?"

"He's criminally insane. You and that Sheila Peters woman must petition the court for restraining orders immediately. I got mine yesterday."

It was just after noon when Dr. Selby headed for the door. Baron von Mahler and I followed. I had to give the doctor credit for one thing: she was right about the restraining orders.

A WEEK LATER, standing side by side in Orleans District Court, Sheila Peters and I were granted a year of protection from Andrew. As we turned to leave, he waved boldly from the rear of the courtroom. Sheila screamed.

Everyone turned, spectators and court officers alike, but in an instant Andrew had disappeared. When we faced the judge again, he'd gone pale, his eyes still fixed on the vacant back bench. "This case worries me," he said quietly. Then he rescinded the one-year restraining orders and signed new ones, granting each of us a lifetime of protection.

Chapter 58

Like an answer to a prayer, Grace Jamieson's e-mail arrived the next morning. She'd "read every page" of my file over "pots of tea," she said, and considering "Andrew's perverse personality" it all rang true. "He is capable of all the evil you've documented."

She went on to say that Drew had sacked her a week before and that she'd never heard of Paula Barnett but was anxious to help "unravel the mystery… Let me know when you're coming over. We'll go to Sunninghill together."

I replied at once. "Bless your willing heart."

I added her e-mail to my file, grateful for cyberspace. I hired an on-line detective that day, who matched Andrew's social security number to an alias, Andy Stevenson, to an outstanding warrant for driving while intoxicated in Michigan, and to a "writ of eviction" from West Palm Beach that linked him to a mob family.

Armed with that information, along with Darby's accounts of Andrew's violence, Mr. Bayley's narrative, a list of items missing from my home and a 5x7 of Paula's gravestone, I scheduled an appointment with the Chatham police. It was the first of many frustrating trips to the station. "Liberal legislation" tied their hands, they said, reminding me I had no proof of any crime. They encouraged me to continue fact-finding and to keep them informed. But each time I brought new information to the dispatcher, he treated me like a nuisance.

Weeks later, when Andrew posed as a grieving widower at a Brewster church, a sympathetic member invited him to join a private prayer group in her home and a small antique clock disappeared. I wrote to her minister, sent a copy of my file, and urged him to alert all of Cape Cod's clergy. When I followed up with a phone call, he refused to spread the word. "Churches are in business to redeem troubled souls, not to reject them," he said.

Pastor Gil also refused. When I approached him at a local gas station, he said, "It's time to move on, Anna," and quickly drove away.

Even my faithful friend Rupert lost his cool, telling me to be grateful that Andrew had been excised from my life and leave it at that.

But Andrew wasn't gone. He'd found a foothold on the Damatos' Chatham estate after they left for the winter. Claiming ownership, he posed as a bankrupt victim of Enron to explain its *For Sale* sign. I sent a file to Mr. Damato's office, urging him to protect his waterfront property, but never received a response.

A distraught woman called to ask how I knew her boyfriend after finding my number in his address book. When I warned her off, she called me bitter and hung up. That week, a spray of withered red roses landed on my doorstep. I knew it was a thinly veiled threat.

A Home Health Care representative called to ask why I'd written a letter of reference for Andrew Macdade. I told her I hadn't. "He must have forged it," she said, "on your stationery." She then reported that he'd stuck one of her clients with a $200 phone bill. The old man was too afraid to call the police.

Andrew strutted around town, alternately claiming to be Senator Kennedy's personal chef, the president of an Ascot recording studio searching for talent, a Berklee music professor, Rod Stewart's songwriter, or a Key West neighbor of Jimmy Buffett.

Determined to protect Chatham's residents, I *went public*, warning everyone to steer clear of him, even people I knew only superficially. Some were sympathetic, some were speechless and others were annoyed, reminding me that "shit happens." It was yesterday's news. I felt like Typhoid Mary.

But I knew I could still count on Morgan and Kate, my team of ex-wives and the rock-solid Marta. The more I organized my information, the clearer it became: it was time to rent my house for a month and cross the Atlantic.

Chapter 59

I arrived in Dublin at dawn on July 3. When the customs officer asked whether I was traveling on business or pleasure, I answered emphatically, "Both."

The Merrion Hotel was a perfect place to regroup, just steps from the National Gallery and a quick walk to St. Stephen's Square and Trinity College with its Book of Kells. The misty morning did nothing to dim the luster of the Georgian hotel's painted black doors or their ornate silver knockers.

Wearing a gray morning suit, the doorman swept me into the hushed lobby to reception. Fragrant early morning peat fires burned behind burnished brass fenders. The concierge greeted me by name and saw me to a private elevator that whisked me up to a quiet corner room.

Tears of relief filled my jaded eyes as I took in the creamy walls, heavy damask draperies and windows that opened to terraced gardens. The queen-sized bed was made up with crisp sheets, down-filled pillows and a linen duvet. Finally, a reprieve from Andrew and his madness.

After unpacking, I called the front desk, scheduled room service at one, a massage at four. The concierge arranged for a bus trip the next morning to Wexford, home of the best Irish stew, and tickets to the Abbey Theatre two nights hence.

I closed the drapes and sank into a deep, much-needed sleep until room service knocked.

Feeling somewhat refreshed after a pot of tea with fruit, cheese and biscuits, I donned my bathing suit, wrapped myself in the hotel's terrycloth robe and rode the elevator down to the spa and its Olympic-sized pool. An hour of swimming laps alongside a tall, pleasant woman, followed by Swedish massage, renewed me for an evening out.

It was still light at 7 p.m. when I ambled over to the Shelburne Hotel's café for a soup and salad supper. The sounds of the piano and muffled international voices moved me deeply. How alike we all are, I thought, and what a complicated, beautiful world we share.

Heading back to the Merrion, my steps quickened as the past eclipsed the present. I was lucky to be alive.

THE ABBEY WAS PACKED for *The Plough and the Stars,* a wrenching portrayal of Ireland's working-class revolt. When the audience gathered in the lobby at intermission, I stood off to one side sipping coffee from a paper cup. The tall woman I'd seen at the pool stood next to an even taller woman with a cane, who looked familiar. I made my way through the crowd to join them, an impulse I'd never act on at home.

"Is it really you, Janet Reno?" I smiled, extending my hand. "Anna Wells. We met at the Sanibel Community Center during your campaign for governor."

"Yes. And here we are," she drawled, her handshake firm, "a long way from Florida. I've been teaching a course at Trinity. My sister Maggie here gets me back and forth in one piece."

"Hello, Maggie," I said. "We saw each other at the hotel's spa the other day."

"Janet and I are going to miss that pool," she said. "We'll be sorry to leave tomorrow morning."

We chatted until the bell beckoned us back to our seats. By the time I reached mine, I'd devised an audacious plan.

UPON RETURNING TO THE MERRION that night, I asked the concierge to arrange for the hotel's secretarial service to copy my file. Then retreating to the privacy of my room, I smoked a cigarette, wrote a cover letter and packed for the next morning's flight across the Irish Sea to Prestwick Glasgow International Airport. At midnight, I handed a sealed envelope to a sleepy-eyed clerk and asked him to place it in Janet Reno's hotel letterbox. He did so while I watched.

Just a year before on Sanibel Island, Janet Reno had promised to make our country a safer place for women and children. She'd warmed the audience with her candor and entertained us with homespun tales. If she could drive a red truck, smoke a pipe and build a concrete house to withstand hurricanes, maybe the former United States Attorney General would get my file to the Department of Homeland Security.

Chapter 60

Morgan pulled up to Troon's Courtyard Condominiums, a granite, horseshoe-shaped complex with a glorious center garden. Once a castle's servants' quarters, it had been converted into luxury flats by a local developer. A neighbor's golden retriever bounded up just before we saw the welcoming committee: David wearing his signature Deerstalker hat, and Ken, whose golf bag had bent him like a crooked limb, along with Catherine and John.

"Hello, you old bird," John called, giving me a good-natured wave. "Got yourself into a mess, did you? Should've bought a flat here on your last visit, spared yourself a heap of trouble."

Catherine kissed my cheek and offered her sympathy. I was grateful to be back among some of the friendliest people I'd ever known.

Over an early lunch of BLTs, my favorite chocolate-ginger biscuits and many cups of tea, I filled Morgan and Ian in on my plan to meet Grace Jamieson the next week. I also told them I'd asked Janet Reno for help.

"Bet she'll sic the IRS on him," Ian said, "and they'll nail him for tax evasion, like Al Capone."

Morgan handed me the list she'd compiled of every Gordon Macdade in the Edinburgh area, sixteen in all. "With luck, one will prove to be Andrew's brother and he'll know something about Paula Barnett. You should make the calls, because of your accent. Scots love Americans."

She was right. Everyone was interested in my search for my long lost brother-in-law. Some offered advice. A few wanted to talk about their holidays in the States. One old gent invited me out for a pint. But no one was related to Andrew.

THREE DAYS LATER, Ian drove us to the Troon railway station. Morgan and I boarded the ten o'clock to Glasgow and transferred at Queen's Station to the Edinburgh-Waverly train. Kate Campbell met us at the taxi stand and whisked us off in her little red Opel, tearing into the heavy traffic like a kamikaze.

She lifted her tote and told me to dig out her notes. "I've made a few trips to the registry, Anna, but never had enough time to finish. The hours are limited and it's slow going. We'll scroll through the names on microfiche and then write out specific requests. If the clerks are busy, we'll slip into the archives ourselves; that would be best. With three of us working, we'll surely find Gordon. And maybe some trace of Paula."

We climbed the registry steps laden with umbrellas, notebooks and hope. When we paid the five-pound entry fees to a white-haired gentleman in a tweed jacket, he stamped our tickets, perked up when he heard my accent, and wished us luck.

I searched birth, marriage and death records looking for Paula Barnett and found nothing.

Morgan decided to flesh out the information she'd already unearthed about Andrew's parents, to find out more about the people who'd spawned such a devil.

Kate learned that Andrew's brother Gordon had been married and widowed twice. His last reported address was ten miles from her house.

It was late afternoon when we got to Friar's Mews. We knocked and waited, holding our breath, until a fey woman appeared at the next door. "Are you looking for Gordon Macdade?" she lilted. "I've been watching from behind the curtain. Gordon moved away. Would you like to talk to Peter and me?"

She ushered us into her lounge and perched on the edge of her chair, hands clasped in her lap. "He's such a gentleman, that Gordon. He and Jane were married just a year when she was stricken with cancer. He took such good care of the poor lassie. When she died, he moved to the Commodore Club on Marine Drive. He did the electrical work there, or maybe the plumbing."

"Do you know where he is now, Mrs. Clark?" I asked.

"Noooo, not exactly. He stopped by a few months ago and told us he might marry again. His son owns an escort agency in Edinburgh; perhaps you could call the agencies. And I think Gordon still goes to the Portobello Bowling Club on Friday nights, doesn't he, Peter?"

Peter wasn't sure, but thought it might be worth a try.

We thanked the Clarks for their help and I promised to send a postcard from Cape Cod to accompany the framed Niagara Falls card on their wall.

Mrs. Clark walked us to the door, patting our backs. "Lovely visit, wasn't it?" she whispered. "Better than the telly." She rolled her eyes heavenward as her husband turned on a soccer match.

We stopped at Rupee's for curry before the intrepid Kate flew toward home in her tiny missile. Morgan searched the phone book for Edinburgh's escort agencies: After Hours, Gilmour Girls, Playmates, Scruples, Executive Sauna… Between fits of laughter, she called out each name and number from the front seat and I dialed the cell phone in back. "Is Mr. Macdade there, please? I'm a distant relative," I repeated over and over. Each time, a smarmy male voice said Mr. Macdade was not available and invited me to "accept the services" of an on-duty escort.

It was almost nine when Kate parked the car and we crawled out with red eyes and aching sides. Her little brick house, its window boxes filled with whirligig flowers, suited her. She served a pot of strong black tea as I dialed one last number for the evening, the Portobello Bowling Club, and once again introduced myself.

"Jus' a minute. Quiet. It's an American lass calling for Gordon."

I could hardly understand him through the cacophony of male voices.

"Aye, Jimmy, America. Aye, Danny, for Gordon."

I gripped the receiver, hoping I was one step closer to Paula.

"This is Jerry," said a serious, formal voice. "Gordon and his wife just left. You missed them by a few minutes. You could come 'round tomorrow morning after ten, Miss, when our president will be here. Alistair will give you a tour of the club and see to it that you get Gordon's address and phone number. I'm sorry to say that information is locked up for the evening."

I thanked him profusely, gave the girls a high-five and hung up smiling. "A good day's work, ladies. Tomorrow we're off to the bowling club. What do we wear?"

Chapter 61

We decided on simple dresses. In a smoky paneled room with four television sets, each broadcasting a different sport, we found clusters of gentlemen in blazers, some hunched over pints, others playing dominoes. Alistair spotted us in the doorway, coasted across the polished floor and squired us around the room making introductions and pointing out portraits of the club's past presidents.

"Is Gordon among them?" I asked.

"Aye," he said, nodding toward a framed photo hanging nearby. "There's our Gordon."

I leaned closer to the portrait. There was no mistaking the family resemblance.

Alistair spun a few degrees and clicked his fingers at a round-faced man, telling him to fetch Gordon's information from the safe. "Now we'll step outside and show you the greens."

The grounds were impressive, meticulously groomed. We snapped pictures of the members standing in front of the black-and-white *Portobello Bowling Club* sign, declined a "wee dram" and gratefully accepted Gordon's address and phone number. We shook each man's hand warmly before leaving, charmed by their attention and generosity.

I called from Kate's cell phone as she sped toward Gordon's address in East Lothian. I explained my mission to the woman who answered and asked if Gordon might see me.

"Gordon, come quickly," she called. "A lady's come all the way from America to see you."

A hesitant Gordon came on the line. "Hello?"

I thanked him for taking my call. "I was married, briefly, to your brother," I said.

"You married Andrew?" He sounded flabbergasted. "How did you find me? Our number's not listed."

"Through the Portobello Bowling Club."

"You've been to the club? Did you meet Alistair and Jerry?"

"I did. They led me to you. It's a complicated story I have to tell, one best shared in person."

"I'm a wee bit deaf so I'll put my wife, April, back on to give directions. Can you come right along?"

I smiled and said yes. Speed demon Kate was already parked a block from their house. We waited a half-hour, letting them collect their thoughts as we collected ours.

"More joy." Kate laughed. "In less than twenty-four hours, we've found the key to Andrew's past."

We arrived to find Gordon and April waiting on the front steps alongside a blooming dahlia garden; the brothers shared more than a family resemblance. But Gordon was taller and slimmer and he didn't dye his hair.

Kate and Morgan held back while I climbed from the backseat and introduced myself and my friends to my new-found in-laws. They shook our hands and then Gordon turned to me. "I don't know how I can help, Mrs. Wells. I've had nothing to do with my brother since the day we buried our mother."

April intervened and ushered us into their bright and spacious home, where the dining room table was set for tea. Folding my hands on my lap, I told Gordon about the bizarre events of the last year and said I'd be grateful for any information he could offer about his brother.

Gordon looked at April. Almost imperceptibly, she nodded.

"Sorry to be crude, Mrs. Wells, but if my brother were on fire I wouldn't piss on him. He's a liar and a thief. We called him *Pudge*, a fat spoiled boy. At seventeen, he stole our father's earnings from a box under the bed and ran away to London for two years. Eventually, he was forgiven and came back claiming he was a rock-and-roll star with a number one hit; had a 45 record to prove it. When I peeled off its white label, I saw it was one of Cliff Richards' songs. No Macdade ever hit the big time. We're a family of coal miners."

Holding my gaze with his, he continued. "Andrew delivered coal until the day our mother died. He arrived late to her funeral and I soon discovered he'd hired a lorry to clean out her house. He stole everything, even my home movies."

"Unfortunately, he's still stealing," I said.

"He got away with wrongdoing his entire life."

"Your parents must have been devastated."

"Aye. Put them both in early graves."

"Do you know his best friend, Archie?"

"Ach, thick as thieves, they were. I blackballed Archie from the bowling club."

"And what about Andrew's family?"

"Laura handles herself okay, runs a dockside pub in Leith. Drew is a chip off the old block. My son sees him at the pubs, blethering on about his father outwitting the Feds. And Andrina is expecting again, I hear."

I handed him a picture of Paula Barnett's gravestone and told him Andrew had carried it with him for years. "I think he hurt her," I said.

April bit her lower lip and stroked Gordon's back. He stared at me, dropped the picture on the table and covered his face with his hands. "I'm ashamed of him, ashamed that a member of my family could harm so many people."

Suppressing the urge to offer useless words of comfort, I slipped the photograph into my handbag and quietly thanked Gordon for seeing me.

He smiled sadly. "You're always welcome in our house, Mrs. Wells," he said, rising from his chair. "But I hope never to see my brother again."

April stood and put her arms around his shaking shoulders as we said our somber good-byes.

WITH DIRECTIONS FROM GORDON, we sped toward Portobello's High Street and found the shabby walk-up flat of Andrew's boyhood. Laura's Admiral Macdade manse, the one he'd bequeathed to Sheila and me, was a small stone house. And the Royal Hotel was now a workingman's pub with seedy rooms to let by the hour.

Archie lived in a bungalow with an overgrown yard across from the public baths. I phoned and knocked but no one answered.

Chapter 62

Grace Jamieson and I boarded the early morning train in Edinburgh and settled down for the circuitous ride to Sunninghill. Elfin in size with big blue eyes, she squeezed my hand and swept strawberry-blond ringlets from her freckled face. "Here we are then, darling. Andrew's caused quite a fuss, hasn't he?"

"A fuss and then some."

She smiled knowingly. I stared out the window at the murky Firth of Forth, craning to see Portobello's distant shoreline, when a bolt of indignation shot through me. "You're so gentle, Grace," I said, turning toward her. "I don't know how he could have hurt you."

"I'm fifty now, Anna. Despite his ugly side, I was devastated to leave him behind in Michigan. My life was bleak for a long time until I joined the Duddingston Kirk and found the strength to start over."

"A continent away from him," I added. "Did Andrew ever try to win you back?"

She giggled. "Oh yes. And I actually considered giving that man a second chance. But then he wrote a love letter to Darby and put it in an envelope addressed to me."

I handed our tickets to the portly conductor, telling Grace how well-acquainted Andrew's American wives were with his purple prose. And with his cast of superstars, including Jethro Tull. "Claimed he's your half-brother."

Grace rolled her eyes. "Jethro Tull is a group. Andrew's gone soft as a wee grape."

I laughed. "Were you working for his son when Andrew and I met?"

"Yes. I'd been Drew's office administrator for more than a year before I heard your name. He lured me away from a competitor, made me an offer I couldn't refuse."

"Didn't his mother get her knickers in a twist?"

"Drew could have hired a tart so long as he made bags of money for Laura to rave about in that pub of hers."

Grace adjusted her seat and leaned closer, her excitement endearing. "Soon after Andrina returned from Sanibel, she and Laura burst into the office telling Drew that Dad was up to his old tricks, passing off hot rocks as his mum's. They all thought it was hilarious. From then on, I kept my eyes and ears wide open."

"It's so incestuous." I snorted, imagining Grace listening to Drew talk to his father and me by phone while his mother and sister flitted in and out of the office.

"And while Drew and Jill bragged about Andrew's rich widow when they returned from Chatham," Grace continued, "no one mentioned your marriage."

"Seems to be a pattern," I said.

She nodded. "The apple doesn't fall far from the tree. Andrew gambled away thousands we'd saved to buy a B&B

years ago, leaving me financially desperate. Thanks to Drew, I'm in the same straits now."

"Why did he fire you?"

She shrugged. "Maybe his father told him you'd discovered my existence and they assumed you'd contact me. The truth is, Anna, if Drew hadn't sacked me, I would've clammed up to keep my job. I wouldn't be sitting here with you today."

We released the tray table and spread out the photographs that had buttressed Andrew's myths. His yacht, the *Hey Paula*, was a hired Thames launch. His prized red Jaguar belonged to the Highclere; he used it to chauffeur guests. The Queen Mum's chef, Eddie, was an East End fence. The distant speck of Paula boarding a plane for the Himalayas was Grace, en route to Edinburgh to visit her sick mother.

Grace was taken aback. "I knew he lied but I didn't realize he'd pilfered pictures from our album for backup. He gins up a new cockamamie story for each new audience. Wouldn't you like to know what tales he's telling about you?"

I thought of the pictures of my house I'd found in his briefcase.

Grace had met him at a wedding a few weeks after he left Laura. Two days later, she found him waiting on the front steps of the Royal Hotel looking for work and a bed. Taking pity, she set up a cot in the laundry room and got him a job tending bar.

Impressed when business increased, she noted the respectful attention he paid to customers and quickly fell for him. They became engaged two months later and somehow, Andrew managed to post their wedding banns while his divorce pended.

A few days after the banns were posted, Andrew's mistress of seventeen years showed up at the hotel, accusing him of stealing racks of gowns from her bridal boutique. Andrew told Grace she was nothing more than an older woman he'd tried to help get back on her feet and Grace believed him. Convinced she was saving him from a deranged stalker, she drained her bank accounts and paid the woman off.

Unbeknownst to Grace, Andrew later sent the mistress to Spain on holiday, promising to join her when his "business crisis" was over. When she returned and discovered he'd married Grace in her absence, she vandalized their car, smashing the windshield and slashing the tires. Grace then took drastic measures to protect Andrew. She answered an advertisement in *The Scotsman* and off they went to manage the Highclere Hotel in Sunninghill, England.

"A man who succeeds at getting one woman out of the country so he can marry another is one slick SOB."

"Not slick enough, at times. He was so sure of getting the position in Jordan, he gave our notice before he left. When he wasn't hired, we took menial jobs at the Epsom Hotel. Overnight, well-paid respectable managers became housekeepers. I tried to sell my diamond engagement ring only to learn it was paste."

"Darby's diamond was paste, too. How did Andrew get his lowly foot in a royal door?"

"I knew the manager of Buckhurst, King Hussein's English residence, from the gym. Walter arranged the Amman interview, then felt obliged to refer us to an elite London agency that placed domestics in the States, where Andrew was determined to go once Jordan wasn't an option. We finally left for Michigan on our second wedding anniversary and went into service for the Arnolds."

"Not Mighty Al Taubman," I noted.

"No. The Taubmans were the Arnolds' neighbors."

I groaned. "How did we all fall in love with such a sleaze?"

She shrugged. "I was naïve. I never pegged him for a womanizer. He doted on me, held my hand constantly, even in the car. We went to church together; he was always home on time from the races; showered me with roses and trinkets. He insisted on wearing silk pocket squares to match my outfits so people would know we were together. I thought he adored me until the flight to Michigan."

"What happened on the flight?"

"He turned. His sunny personality changed. The year was a disaster. He drank on the job and kept irregular hours. He got sacked a month before our contract was up when Mrs. Arnold caught him bringing a woman to our garage flat while I was out shopping."

"Was he physically abusive?"

She hesitated. "Mrs. Arnold tried to help me once after she saw my bruised face. He must have overheard. In a drunken fit, he socked me in the stomach, threatening to drop me out the window on my wee head if I ever grassed on him again."

We were quiet for a few minutes, and then I passed her the picture of the woman in white lace. "Darby thinks Andrew and Paula had an affair while he was married to you. Maybe she threatened to tell you."

"If Paula had come to me, I'd have divorced him. The Michigan contract would have been canceled because the Arnolds wanted a married couple."

"Early on, he showed me a sad four-stanza poem he'd written for their unborn child, Skye."

"If I'd found out she was pregnant, it would've killed me; I couldn't have children."

I pulled Darby's copy of Andrew's address book from my purse and Grace eagerly flipped through the pages. "I know some of these names," she said, "but most are probably long gone from the village."

"Under 'P' he's written Paula's address, Greystone Manor on London Road in a place called Sunningdale."

"Less than two kilometers from Sunninghill," Grace explained.

"And see how carefully he penned the verse *To Live in the Hearts of those we Love is not to Die.*"

She frowned. "He's diabolical. Let's go to the cemetery first, then see what we can find out in the village. I can't wait to see the Highclere again. What was that story he told about hiding Paula's possessions?"

"He said he tore down a wall in a third-floor bedroom, hid her jewelry, books and clothes under the eaves, and then re-plastered to safeguard them until he returned from Jordan. The story was so heart-wrenching, I shared it with my minister."

She snickered. "How embarrassing. What was his reaction?"

"He mumbled something about most men's minds being full of dark closets, then dismissed me. Now I see what an absurd lie it was but at the time, I hoped to relieve Andrew's grief and guilt."

"Guilt?"

"He said if he'd been on the slopes that day, she'd be alive."

Grace hooted. "What malarkey. He's seen too many Alfred Hitchcock movies."

Chapter 63

The Highclere's current manager was outside watering the garden when we arrived. Yards of tangerine chiffon billowed in the breeze as the voluptuous South African rushed to greet us. I'd written ahead, telling her I was searching for information about someone who'd lived in the village years ago.

Firing questions, Lynne shepherded us through to reception, armed us with street maps and local tips and gave us a pair of keys to room #9. "You know the way, Miss Jamieson," she said, laughing.

Grace reminisced about her Highclere days as we dragged our luggage up to the second floor. Our room was small, decorated with Laura Ashley floral wallpaper, ruffled curtains and matching twin bedspreads. I swept the curtains aside and threw open the windows. "Does it feel weird to be here, Grace?"

She nodded. "Wouldn't Andrew be creeped out if he knew I'd returned after all these years with you, Anna."

After unpacking, we headed out, pausing on the landing outside our room to take in the narrow circular stairway leading to the third floor. We agreed we'd look around once the rooms were vacant.

The afternoon sun cast long shadows as we hurried up Kings Road, crossed the busy intersection to the Sunninghill Parish Church and passed through the cemetery's wooden gate. Patches of lichen covered most of the listing tombstones and carpets of moss hid crumbled slabs. We separated, searching for the headstone with the now familiar words, *To Live in the Hearts of those we Love is not to Die.* An hour later, I feared we were on a wild goose chase.

Then I screamed.

Grace ran to me and clutched my hand. We stared at the headstone, ran our hands over the engraved words. It was a match except that Paula Barnett's name wasn't on it. Edrich Dempsey's was. He'd died on September 20, 1989, twelve days before Paula.

Grace pointed at the nearest stone and smirked. "It's not the Clapton boy, now is it?"

"Another pathetic fabrication," I said. "No wonder he swore Paula was buried in Dorset. He didn't want me anywhere near this place."

"He knew if you saw this stone you'd know he buried Paula right here, just as he said."

"Here? In another person's grave?"

"Where else?"

I slid to the ground, unable to stomach the idea.

"Anna, can't you just see him staggering around with a body in the dark? Shoveling like a madman? Weeping for Jesus to save him?"

I stared up at her.

"But what can we do?" she asked. "The authorities will laugh at us. We can't even prove Paula existed."

I shook my head. "We won't contact the authorities. Not yet. Let's go back to the hotel and call the vicar."

Chapter 64

Grace and I huddled in the morning rain under a centuries-old oak tree in the Parish Church courtyard. At precisely eleven, the vicar strode toward us gripping a black bumbershoot. A gold cross glinted on the lapel of his black double-breasted blazer as he called out a clipped hello.

I extended my hand, introduced myself and Grace, and explained that I'd come a long way to solve a mystery that seemed to end in his cemetery. "I've brought a few photographs, Vicar. Might we step inside your church for a few minutes to look at them?"

He glanced at his wristwatch and reluctantly agreed.

Just inside the door of the dank Romanesque church, on a baize-covered Jacobean table, I unwrapped an enlarged photo of Paula's gravestone. I explained its history and filled the vicar in on our discovery of the day before.

At first, he didn't seem to comprehend the sacrilege that had besmirched his church's graveyard. But when we coaxed him back outside to look at Edrich Dempsey's headstone, fury erupted in his eyes. "Mrs. Wells, this is preposterous."

I handed him two more photographs, one of Andrew and one of the woman in white.

"I don't recognize either of them." He looked at his watch again. "I'm due at the Ladies Guild Annual Luncheon at noon. May I take these photographs with me? Nothing that goes on in the village gets by my little old ladies. Nothing."

We exchanged telephone numbers with a stunned vicar whose cool impatience had transformed into genuine concern. He cast a worried glance our way as he rushed off, clutching the photographs of Andrew, Paula and Edrich Dempsey's desecrated gravestone.

"DIDN'T I TELL YOU we'd unravel it all here?" Grace said, patting my back. "The rain's let up, so let's have a walk around the village and pop into the shops.

I followed, my head spinning.

Keith at Elcock Betting remembered Andrew well, said he was a gasbag who had twice tried to pass himself off as the winner of the two-year-old Norfolk Stakes. For good measure, we placed a nominal bet on Colin Montgomery to win the British Open before we left.

Grace was a few steps ahead of me. "Let's duck in here," she said, "the demon's favorite restaurant." The owner of the Jade greeted her with a smile and a bow. My gaze landed on a mural of Japanese Koi, swimming upstream toward a waterfall.

I nudged her. "Andrew bought a framed print of a similar mural and hung it in the bathroom, telling me he had hand-dug a pond for Paula's Koi."

She studied me. "I must admit, Anna, I doubted you at first. It all seemed too fantastic. But the more I read your file, the more the pieces fit together. And now I think it's time to visit the ironmonger."

"Why?"

"Andrew was there several times a week. Something at the Highclere always needed patching."

Within minutes, the owners produced an invoice he'd signed on October 2, 1989 for miscellaneous items that included plastic bags, rope, and cement.

Grace stared at the date on the invoice, shaking her head. "We were at the Epsom by then," she said. "Andrew had no authority to purchase anything."

She was quiet for a moment, then added, "He was arrogant to charge all this to the Highclere. And stupid to put his signature on this particular bill."

Chapter 65

Lynne met us at the door with a message from the vicar. Mrs. Polly Cook, who'd attended the Ladies Guild Luncheon, had recognized the photograph of Andrew. She planned to drop by the hotel at three. We'd gotten back just in time.

The aristocratic octogenarian sprinted up the walk in a floral frock, waving the photos like banners. "I know him," she trumpeted. "He lodged with me for a month, eleven years ago."

We settled comfortably in the hotel's conservatory and Lynne served ginger beer and sherry as Mrs. Cook shared her remarkable story.

"Our meeting is extraordinary." She held up the photograph of what we now knew was Edrich Dempsey's gravestone. "Mrs. Wells, you didn't realize this epitaph is forged?"

I forced a smile. "I was suspicious. But I wasn't sure until I enlarged the 3x5."

"You American girls are so naïve," she chided. "But I fell for Andrew Macdade too, and at my age I should've known better. He stole the engagement ring my dear Edmund gave me fifty years ago."

She coughed and pressed her handkerchief to her lips. "I've wept for that ring. It's wrong to mourn an object but I have. Andrew Macdade also stole my grandmother's Victorian diamond necklace and a ten-shilling note my mother used for a bookmark after they went out of circulation. I didn't realize he was stealing from me until he was gone."

"Mrs. Cook, how did he get into your house?" Grace asked.

"After my Edmund died, I occasionally took on lodgers to augment his pension. One evening, Andrew called from the Dukes Head Pub, told me he was recently widowed and wanted to buy a small hotel in the Windsor or Maidenhead area. Said he needed a room for a month. Normally I would have agreed at once but he sounded a little too glib. I told him he'd have to pass muster with my son."

Mrs. Cook sipped her sherry and leaned forward. "I love a good thriller," she said in her Surrey drawl, "especially when the crook gets his comeuppance."

Grace and I were spellbound.

"My son met Andrew the next morning," Mrs. Cook continued, "and said he seemed pleasant enough, thought his company might give me a lift. He moved in that afternoon and made himself indispensable. It was almost impossible to find a joiner and he repaired everything that needed mending. He was charming, I tell you, a perfect gentleman. But he liked his drink and sometimes bragged in a way that made me think he was a bit unstable. Then again, what man wouldn't be half-witted after losing his wife in such a tragic accident?"

"He spoke of Paula?" I said.

"Oh yes. Paula was the love of his life, a doctor at the Heatherwood Hospital. He was devastated by her death. Although he did seem interested in a woman from Phoenix, Arizona. Rang her every day. Left me with a three-hundred pound bill."

"Eleven years ago," I said, "he was engaged to his third wife, Darby, who lived in Michigan. I don't suppose you still have that bill?"

She shook her head. "I didn't keep anything that would remind me of him."

"Did he socialize?"

She nodded. "He'd wash the dinner dishes, pour me a glass of port and leave the house after eight. Didn't return until late. He said he wanted to marry the Phoenix woman but her father didn't like him."

"Hedging his bets again," I said, and told them about the postcards he'd sent to Sheila after moving in with me.

At about four o'clock, Mrs. Cook stood, smoothed her dress and promptly sat down again. She had another story.

"After I reported my diamonds stolen, I received a phone call from Sir John Terry. Unbeknownst to me, Andrew had managed his estate in the next village. Sir John said that while he was away on his honeymoon, Andrew stole all the wedding presents and emptied his wardrobe of cashmere jackets from Harrods."

"Mrs. Cook, Andrew gave me an old cashmere jacket he said he bought on sale at Harrods. I remember wondering why he bought such a small size."

"Sir John is a slight man and the Andrew I knew was chubby."

Steals for the thrill of it, I thought.

"Sir John and I drove together to the Thames Valley Police Station in Ascot," she continued. "The officers found Andrew that night in a room over a Chinese laundry with bundles of money in a bureau drawer, including a ten-shilling note. They brought charges against him but the case failed. We had no proof," she huffed. "I'd never recorded the note's serial number."

Mrs. Cook wasn't through. "Two weeks after that, I came home to find a Baccarat crystal vase on my kitchen table with a syrupy thank-you note from Andrew. I called Sir John; the vase was one of the wedding gifts. But again, we couldn't prove it; the police did nothing. I was terrified, realizing he'd made a key to my house. I think he slipped in to gloat, to prove how smart he was. I had the locks changed. For eleven years, I've wondered if he ever got caught."

AFTER OUR VISIT with Mrs. Cook, Grace packed, preparing to take the morning train back to Edinburgh and her new job managing the National Gallery's gift shop. When she finished, we set out for the Dukes Head in companionable silence. I felt more than a twinge of regret over her imminent departure.

We heard the muffled roar of laughter and music as we approached. "Good. It's busy," Grace said, chuckling as the heavy door swung open.

The bartender dashed toward us at once, wrapped his beefy arms around Grace and winked at me over her shoulder. "'Ello, Luv. Andrew sent us a postcard, said you'd drowned in some godforsaken lake in the States."

She pulled away from him, making a face. "Remember when he said he won the pool and bought the house drinks all night, then stuck you with the tab?"

She put her head close to his. "Jackson, this is Anna Wells. She's trying to track down an old friend. Is the Heatherwood crowd here?"

"They've been drinking at Stirrups lately. But Dr. Owen still comes in." Jackson pointed. "He's having supper and a pint over in the corner."

We crossed the noisy room and smiled at the distinguished-looking man reading a newspaper between bites of steak and kidney pie. His owlish eyes lit up with curiosity as he gallantly stood to pull out two chairs at his table. He listened attentively as Grace explained our search "for a prominent cancer surgeon who was once linked to this man." She showed him a flattering photograph of Andrew.

Dr. Owen grabbed it. "Good God. It's Andy Stevenson. I haven't seen him in years. He used to come into Stirrups to meet his girlfriend, Paula, after his overseas flights."

I nearly fell off my chair. "You knew Andy Stevenson and Paula?"

Dr. Owen nodded. "He was a British Airways pilot. Came in loaded down with duty-free whiskey and perfume. Owned a leg or two in Cheltenham, I think." The doctor chuckled. "Gave us damn good racing tips. Where is he these days?"

I was stunned. Here at last was someone who'd known Paula.

Grace recovered first. She gave Dr. Owen a rundown on the true character of Andy Stevenson, aka Macdade, and his string of ravaged wives, present company included.

I showed him the photo of the lady in white. "Is this Paula Barnett?"

"No," he said. "That's Andy's girlfriend, Paula Tamm. She was here years ago, a guest of Dr. Agnes Barnett."

"*Agnes* Barnett?"

He nodded. "A psychiatrist, an open-hearted spinster who befriended Paula, encouraged her to come to Sunningdale, take a break from London."

"Where does Dr. Barnett live?" I asked.

"She used to live at Greystone Manor out on London Road, back when it was a handsome place. Housed the Heatherwood staff and the Royal Holloway College academics. But Agnes passed on some years ago."

"Dr. Owen, was Paula Tamm also a physician?"

"No." He smiled softly. "She modeled, I think. She was what you'd call a free spirit, a delicate Slavic beauty. She was also somewhat naïve, not nearly as worldly as Andy. The age difference worried Agnes."

"Age difference? It was only three years."

Dr. Owen shook his head. "At least twenty."

I turned to Grace. She didn't look surprised.

"When Paula up and left without a word," Dr. Owen continued, "Agnes was terribly upset. She badgered the authorities for a long time but they never seemed to take her seriously."

"Would you be willing to post these photos on the hospital's message board, with a request for anyone who recognizes them to call me at the Highclere?"

"I'd be glad to," he said, "but you realize it's a long shot."

Dr. Owen paused, glanced from Grace to me and then confided, "Agnes's sister, Joan Miller, had a flat in the village. If she's still alive, she might know more."

Chapter 66

Mrs. Miller was listed in the directory. She answered on the first ring the next morning, agreed to see me at ten-thirty and gave me directions to her Queens Terrace flat, "the one with the glossy yellow door."

After peering from behind a frilly white curtain, she threw open the yellow door, waved me in and sprinted up the stairs. "I'm ninety-three and still drive," she announced proudly, "but not at night."

I puffed along after her.

Seated across from me in a Chippendale side chair, Joan Miller recited a long-winded history of Sunninghill's halcyon days "before the likes of those Beatles and Fergie discovered it."

I did my best to hide my impatience, folded my hands and listened politely, knowing she was sizing me up.

Suddenly she smiled and asked if I drove in the dark.

"With difficulty," I replied.

She tsk-tsked and asked if I'd like a slice of lemon cake and a cup of Nescafé.

I'd passed inspection.

"My sister, Agnes, was fond of that settee you're sitting on, Mrs. Wells. I inherited it along with her books, papers and paintings, after she died at only seventy-one."

"I'm so sorry," I whispered.

"She never married. After Oxford, she worked at the Heatherwood Hospital and at the London Clinic. That's where she met Paula Tamm."

And where she became the source of Andrew's many medical stories, I thought. "Was Dr. Barnett a recipient of the Order of the British Empire?"

"No, dear, but a few of her male colleagues were."

The glint in Mrs. Miller's sharp little eyes said Dr. Barnett should have been among them. Before I could ask, she told me that her sister had invited Paula to spend the summer in 1989, thinking the country air would do her good. "The girl was high-strung and much too thin. When my husband died in August of that year, she was still there. The months that followed are somewhat blurred but I do remember that Agnes went on holiday in early autumn. When she returned, Paula Tamm had vanished."

"No note?"

She shook her head. "But Agnes received an odd postcard that winter from somewhere in the States addressed to Paula. She took it to the police."

Mrs. Miller frowned. She seemed distracted. I feared I'd stayed too long, tired her out, when suddenly she sprung from her chair. "I almost forgot," she cried. "I've kept a photograph tucked in the family Bible all these years."

I crossed the room and hovered over her shoulder as she carefully removed a 3x5 Polaroid from an envelope engraved with Dr. Barnett's Greystone Manor address. Standing with Agnes in the picture was the woman I knew as Paula Barnett.

Icy needles ran down my spine as I traced her face and plum colored suit. The Celtic cross she wore, inlaid with bloodstone, carnelian, jasper and banded agate, matched the one Andrew grudgingly gave me on our wedding day, right down to the square stone missing from its center. I stared at the cross, physical evidence that linked Andrew to Paula, and felt faint.

Mrs. Miller watched me study the photograph and suggested I take it with me. "I always hoped someone would look into that girl's disappearance. It haunted my poor sister 'til the day her heart stopped."

I hugged her tiny frame and promised to call, with or without new information. We parted silently.

I hurried back to the Highclere and asked Lynne for my jewelry. She opened the wall safe and handed over my doeskin pouch without question. I climbed the flight of stairs to my room and bolted the door, eager to place the cross next to the picture. Paula was wearing my wedding present. The room spun and I put my head between my knees. When I finally stretched out on the bed, I slipped into a deep sleep.

THE TELEPHONE JOLTED me awake. Mrs. Doris Wisby, retired from Heatherwood Hospital, had chanced upon Dr. Owen's notice on the message board. "Mrs. Wells," she said, "I was an obstetrics nurse. Paula Tamm was a patient during the late '80s. What is your interest in her?"

Mrs. Wisby listened in silence for the next few minutes, and then continued. "I worried about that girl. She had no husband, no next of kin, not even a telephone number. I had lunch with a friend today at Heatherwood's canteen and she's as intrigued as I am. She works in the records department and retrieved Paula's file. Since I'm retired and she's about to be, we bent the rules and copied it. Did you know Paula was pregnant?"

"I thought she might have been," I said, and shared my suspicions about Paula's demise. "Her medical records, along with the pendant I'm holding and the photograph of her wearing it, should make the police sit up and take notice."

Mrs. Wisby agreed to meet me in Ascot with the file the next morning at ten, but declined to go with me into the station. "You're best on your own. The officers will find me if they need me."

I hung up, slipped the heavy cross on a gold chain around my neck and marched with cold anger to the Sunninghill Parish Church Cemetery.

Grace had known the truth as soon as she saw this spot. And I could no longer deny it. For a long time, I stared at what I now knew was Paula Tamm's grave.

Chapter 67

Perhaps Mrs. Wisby and I recognized each other because we were the only two women in sight who looked determined. She was plain-faced, with short curly white hair, wearing a loose pantsuit that matched her tan handbag and brogans. Her dark eyes were troubled as we settled on a bench across from the Thames Valley Police Station.

"Did you know Dr. Agnes Barnett?" I asked.

"Everyone knew who she was but I never met her. Psychiatrists and obstetrics nurses rarely cross paths. Paula's only visit was to confirm her pregnancy. She was nervous but in good health, as you'll see from the obstetrician's report."

I opened the file and read the intake record. Dr. Owen was right. Paula Tamm was only twenty-two.

"Where is the obstetrician?"

"Dead. Both he and Dr. Barnett are long gone. The only reason I remember Paula, Mrs. Wells, is because she was so beautiful and so wretchedly alone. It was plain to me she was carrying a love child. When she didn't keep her follow-up appointment, I suspected she'd had an abortion."

"I don't think Andrew Macdade gave her the chance. My file, these medical records and Mrs. Miller's photograph should go a long way toward proving it."

"Tell the police just what you told me," she said, her tone encouraging.

I thanked her and stood, gathering courage, and made my way across the street.

"Mrs. Wells," she called. "They'll listen, dear. I'm sure of it."

DETECTIVE INSPECTOR REGINALD GRANT closed the door quietly and nodded in my direction. Over six feet tall, he had a ruddy, angular face and the lean frame of an athlete. His wary hazel eyes fell at once on the thick manila folder on the table. I introduced myself and launched into a breathless explanation for my visit. I went on for some time, dismantling the copy of my file as I spoke.

He never interrupted, never dropped a hint as to what he was thinking. He listened, examining each piece of evidence I produced in silence. When my monologue concluded, I handed him the pendant and the snapshot of Paula Tamm with Dr. Agnes Barnett.

He stood, walked slowly across the room and stared out the window toward the bench I'd shared with Mrs. Wisby. "Are any of his relatives sympathetic to your quest?"

I told him that he'd get nothing from Drew or Andrina, but that Andrew's brother was forthcoming and that Grace Jamieson had been a tremendous help.

"You've put a great deal of time and effort into this matter, Mrs. Wells," he said. "And you've presented your case well. Would you care to elaborate?"

I sure did. "I believe Andrew Macdade killed Paula Tamm, Inspector. And that he dumped her body in Edrich Dempsey's grave."

He looked at me with guarded interest. "Ms. Tamm was living at Greystone Manor with Dr. Barnett when she disappeared?"

"Yes. The doctor reported her missing."

"I see. Where is Andrew Macdade now?"

"On Cape Cod. In Chatham, Massachusetts, posing as a widowed professor of music, among other things."

"And the Chatham police have a file on him?"

I nodded. "And the Orleans police and the Dennis police. They all say their hands are tied."

"Mrs. Wells, I need to read your file carefully, give it some thought and conduct my own investigation. How long will you be in England?"

"I was scheduled to leave in three days but I'd like to stay on."

"I'm glad to hear that," he said, and then smiled for the first time. "I'll call you soon. Thank you for coming in. I know it wasn't easy."

I shook his hand, thinking him a master of understatement.

Chapter 68

After leaving the Thames Valley Police Station, I stopped at a florist's and bought a bouquet of day lilies for Lynne. Her help had been immeasurable. At the height of the summer season, she'd offered me an executive suite with an office, complete with desk, telephone and computer.

There'd been no time for e-mail since I'd arrived. I needed to touch base with Morgan, Kate, my fellow ex-wives and Marta, who'd been terrified that Andrew would get wind of my trip to Britain and follow me over to shut me up – permanently. Dubbing them my "sister sleuths," I brought them all up-to-date and told them I'd turned the case over to a competent detective inspector.

Marta responded within minutes. She'd gone to a benefit at the Cape Cod Museum of Art the previous Saturday night and had seen Andrew working the room with his new fiancée, "a well-preserved seventy-something with a diamond choker and a Nantucket Basket twice the size of yours. And like you, she trotted him about like a prized pig. LOL."

True to form, Marta was spot-on.

"I overheard him whining about being tagged by the IRS because he hasn't filed in years," she continued, "but then he saw me and clammed up. Janet Reno is behind that development; I'll wager a lobster dinner on it."

A day later, Grace reported that she'd met Gordon for the first time ever, for dinner in Portobello. He suggested that one way to lure Andrew back to Scotland would be to tell him that their aunt, Uncle Napie's widow, had died and left everything to the two brothers. Gordon offered to have his solicitor send a letter to that effect. A short, cold letter, so as not to arouse suspicion.

"The aunt and uncle owned a tiny newspaper shop on the Royal Mile at the entrance to Dunbar's Close," she wrote. "The land alone is worth a fortune since the old town has been gentrified."

"Brilliant," I answered, then pored once more over my file, grateful that a copy was in the capable hands of Detective Inspector Reginald Grant.

Chapter 69

Five full days passed before Inspector Grant called and asked to meet with me at the Highclere after lunch. Lynne ushered him out to the shady garden where I was waiting and brought a tray of iced lemonade. He seemed energized, less guarded, and I welcomed his enthusiastic handshake.

"Mrs. Wells, I'm hooked. I found Dr. Barnett's missing persons report on Paula Tamm, confirmed the validity of the obstetrics records and paid a visit to Greystone Manor. It was built in the early 1900s by one of Thomas Holloway's descendants, the man who founded the college and patented 'pink pills for pale people.'"

The inspector smiled. "At some point, the place was converted into flats that were snapped up by professionals like Dr. Barnett. But it's run-down now. I combed the place yesterday with two of my men."

"Did you find anyone who remembered Paula?"

"No, but we found a moldering tapestry bag stashed in the cellar, buried in a shallow ditch, crudely patched over with cement. The bag held books, bits of tarnished costume jewelry, a broken bottle of perfume and clothes, including a plum colored suit."

I gasped.

"And Mrs. Wells, it *is* an old Armani."

My eyes filled. "What now, Inspector?"

"I have a warrant. Tomorrow at dawn, Edrich Dempsey's remains will be exhumed. If we're correct, we'll find he has company. But even if our fears are confirmed, extradition will take a long time."

I told him about Grace's chat with Gordon, about his plan to bait Andrew. The inspector nodded, approving the scheme.

"When you reviewed the missing persons file," I asked, "did you find a postcard?"

"Yes, addressed to Paula Tamm in care of Dr. Barnett."

"And the message?"

He studied me for a moment. "Apparently the sender was enjoying Disneyworld en route to sail the Florida Keys with Jimmy Buffett. But it was postmarked Traverse City, Michigan."

"Vintage Andrew," I muttered.

After scanning my timeline, he asked, "Why do you suppose Andrew risked returning to Sunninghill in 1992, Mrs. Wells?"

"Because his third wife wouldn't marry him unless they made the trip. Somehow, he got away with it. But he's more cautious now, Inspector. Gordon's solicitor's letter will have to ring true. Andrew Macdade may be delusional but he isn't stupid."

IT WAS STILL HOT AND MUGGY when I finished a late supper at the Jade Restaurant that night. Outside, I bought sprigs of rosemary and a yellow rose from a street vendor. For Paula.

Chapter 70

The last remnants of daylight drained from the sky as I followed the now familiar route to Edrich Dempsey's grave in the Sunninghill Parish Church Cemetery. With apologies to Edrich, I laid my offering to Paula at the base of the headstone. In a matter of hours, their remains would be wrested from the earth. And maybe – just maybe – the living would offer some small measure of justice to Paula Tamm. I bowed my head, fingering the Celtic cross she'd once worn, and prayed for both of them.

The wind picked up as darkness settled. I jumped when a small branch snapped on a nearby tree, and then again when a squirrel scurried across the path. It was time to go back to the hotel.

I leaned forward, ran my hands over the epitaph one last time – loving words never intended for Paula – and then froze. The sound behind me wasn't a snapping branch. It wasn't a squirrel. It was a footstep. And the wind delivered the unmistakable scent of Royal Lime.

"Here you are, my little one," he said.

My heart stopped.

"That foreigner on the desk at the Highclere told me she didn't know where you'd gone."

My mouth went dry.

"But I knew I'd find you here. I know everything about you, Anna Wells. Everything."

The snapping noise I heard next was one I couldn't identify. I turned slowly, not wanting to spook him. He'd pulled on a pair of latex gloves, the kind surgeons wear. And murderers who plan ahead.

"Paula is in this grave, isn't she?"

He shrugged. "I told you that all along. She came on to me at the pub while Grace was in Auld Reike, looking after her ailing mum. Stirrups, it was. And me, a married man wearing a wedding ring."

Keep him talking, I thought. Buy time.

"What did you do?"

"I'm only human. Took her to the Highclere and gave her what she wanted, then told her to get lost. She refused, kept coming back for more."

My mind was racing. He stood between me and the only gate. I'd never get past him. Even if I did, I wouldn't be able to outrun him.

He stepped closer. I backed up against Edrich Dempsey's headstone and broke into a cold sweat.

"She was expendable," he said, his face no more than two inches from mine. Through eyes of steel, he delivered a clinical account of the hours leading up to Paula's death. He'd taken her to lunch at the Jade, promised to marry her and to send for her and their unborn child, Skye, after he got settled in Jordan.

Paula didn't fall for it. She'd learned that morning at the beauty salon that Andrew was headed to Michigan with

Grace. "Threatened to tell my wife," he said. "How could I allow that?"

Paula didn't meet her end on an Alpine slope. She died in the passenger seat of the Highclere's red Jaguar.

"I told you she got what she deserved. And you're just like her. Another scorned woman out to ruin me."

He held up his gloved hands, staring at his palms as if he expected a nurse to appear with a scalpel. "I had chances to shut you up before," he said, licking his lips. "This time, heartsweet, I'll do the job properly."

He stared for a moment at the Celtic cross I was wearing. And then he lunged.

When I ducked, he rammed Edrich Dempsey's headstone shoulder first and dropped to the ground, catching me by the ankle. He crawled on top of me, pinning my arms with his knees, pressing his gloved thumbs into my throat.

The night sky seemed to grow light, and then lighter still. I remembered the stories I'd read about people who come face-to-face with death. In the end, they say, the light is pure white.

Chapter 71

Detective Inspector Reginald Grant was in my face, almost too close to recognize, his features distorted. "Mrs. Wells," he shouted, "can you hear me?"

I could, but I couldn't speak.

Uniformed officers were swarming all over the place, search lights illuminating the cemetery's landscape. Edrich Dempsey's gravestone had toppled backward. The yellow rose was undisturbed.

I was on a stretcher, suspended in mid-air with an EMT on each end. Inspector Grant was at my side. "It's over," he announced. "Lynne reached me at home after Macdade showed up at the hotel. We've got him."

Andrew stood six feet away, hands cuffed behind his back, babbling. "This is an outrage. She had a knife…"

The inspector issued orders and two officers led Andrew, still spluttering, toward the gate. "I'm to be married in September to a verra grand lady. My children are professionals. I'm an upstanding Christian…"

The EMTs followed a short distance behind Andrew and his escorts, carrying me to a waiting ambulance, and Inspector Grant walked alongside. "We'll nail Macdade for aggravated assault and battery. I assume you'll testify."

This time, I found my voice. "Oh, I'll testify," I assured him. "And that's not all..."

The medics paused outside the ambulance's double-doors and Inspector Grant looked down at me.

"I know exactly what happened to Paula Tamm," I said. "Andrew told me everything."

ANDREW MENZIES MACDADE was convicted of aggravated assault and battery after a two-day trial in mid-November. He was sentenced to twenty-four months in HM Prison Wormwood Scrubs, with credit for time served. "The Scrubs," Inspector Grant said, would teach Macdade a few things about life among *the yobs*.

The inspector and his team used the time to try to build a murder case against him, but in the end they failed. Andrew steadfastly denied every word he said to me in the Sunninghill Parish Church Cemetery, and the detritus retrieved from Edrich Dempsey's grave was so decomposed as to be worthless for forensic testing. Prosecutors refused to pursue a homicide conviction based solely on the testimony of the defendant's ex-wife. In hindsight, I understand. Paula Tamm's only advocates, after all, were the late Dr. Agnes Barnett and me.

Inspector Grant called on a hot day this past July, to tell me that Andrew Macdade had just been released. I appreciated the warning, and the effort he made to assure me that Andrew would not threaten me again. My restraining order remained in effect, he reminded me, and Macdade wasn't likely to risk a return to prison.

I thanked the inspector for all he'd done, for me and for Paula. I wished him well, returned the receiver to its cradle and went outside to dig up dozens of bulbs. Dahlias.

Inspector Grant meant well, but I knew he was wrong. Thanks to me, Andrew had a valid passport. And he wouldn't wait long to make use of it.

I went through the motions for the rest of that summer, taking beach walks, painting with Marta on Mondays and visiting Margot Arnold each Wednesday. Both believed Andrew was a coward. Both predicted he'd live out his life lodging with elderly landladies, scamming London's disenfranchised, and sinking deeper and deeper into fantasy.

Fall brought the usual array of local fairs and festivals. I surrounded myself with friends, volunteered at Cape Cod Community College's resource center and made plans to finish graduate school. The months passed with no sign of Andrew and I decided Marta and Margot were probably right. I began to breathe more easily.

On a crisp sunny morning in early December, I headed to Route 6A to start Christmas shopping. Sally and Emma were coming to Chatham for the holidays again, and so were James and Jessica, with two-year-old Lucinda Wells. It was time to renew old traditions and begin new ones.

By mid-afternoon, I'd filled the station wagon's backseat with packages and decided it was time for a bite at the new Cabbages and Kings Tea Room. The lunch rush was over and the dining room was almost empty. I settled at a table for two by a window and studied the menu. A printed message from the Teamaster invited guests to savor exotic blends, watercress sandwiches and scones with Devon cream in an atmosphere of old world charm. The Teamaster, "straight from Edinburgh's five-star Royal Hotel," had signed the message in script. *Andrei Menzies.*

My heart pounded. The menu trembled in my hands.

Andrew Macdade's smile expanded as he neared my table, as if he'd been expecting me. Towel draped over his arm, he filled my cup and bowed.

"Everyone loves a Scottish servant, heartsweet. Eh?"